About the Author

Maximilian Hawker works in frontline children's social care in Croydon, where he lives with his wife and two children. He has had poetry and short stories – occasionally nominated for awards – appear in publications run by Dog Horn Publishing, Kingston University Press, Arachne Press and Rebel Poetry, among others. He holds an MA by Research in English Literature from Kingston University, where he also studied at undergraduate level, and has previously worked in editing and education.

@MaxHawker

www.maximilianhawker.com

Praise for Breaking The Foals

'Original and beautifully written'
Theo van den Hout, Professor of Hittite and Anatolian Languages at the University of Chicago

'Combining evocative poetic imagery with the skills of a master story-teller, Maximilian Hawker presents an absorbing tale of ancient Troy. Through drawing on the city's traditions and on the history, politics, and culture of the era in which it flourished, Hawker has given us a highly imaginative version of what happened to Troy, its rulers, and their subjects. Throughout, Troy's king Priam lurks as a harsh though increasingly enfeebled despot, but the main focus of the story is on the crown prince Hektor and his fraught relationship with his bastard son. The significance of the novel's title becomes clear from its opening pages which set the scene for a tale which builds momentum increasingly and unfalteringly until it reaches its gripping finale.'
Professor Trevor R. Bryce, Classicist

BREAKING THE FOALS

BREAKING THE FOALS

MAXIMILIAN HAWKER

This edition first published in 2018

Unbound

6th Floor Mutual House, 70 Conduit Street, London W1S 2GF

www.unbound.com

ISBN (eBook): 978-1911586739

ISBN (Paperback): 978-1911586722

Design by Mecob

Cover image:

© Shutterstock.com

Printed in Great Britain by Clays Ltd, St Ives Plc

MIX
Paper from
responsible sources
FSC® C018072

To my wife, Johanna, and our daughters, Freya and Eleanor. May the sun always shine on your paths.

Dear Reader,

The book you are holding came about in a rather different way to most others. It was funded directly by readers through a new website: Unbound.

Unbound is the creation of three writers. We started the company because we believed there had to be a better deal for both writers and readers. On the Unbound website, authors share the ideas for the books they want to write directly with readers. If enough of you support the book by pledging for it in advance, we produce a beautifully bound special subscribers' edition and distribute a regular edition and e-book wherever books are sold, in shops and online.

This new way of publishing is actually a very old idea (Samuel Johnson funded his dictionary this way). We're just using the internet to build each writer a network of patrons. Here, at the back of this book, you'll find the names of all the people who made it happen.

Publishing in this way means readers are no longer just passive consumers of the books they buy, and authors are free to write the books they really want. They get a much fairer return too – half the profits their books generate, rather than a tiny percentage of the cover price.

If you're not yet a subscriber, we hope that you'll want to join our publishing revolution and have your name listed in one of our books in the future. To get you started, here is a £5 discount on your first pledge. Just visit unbound.com, make your pledge and type WILUSA18 in the promo code box when you check out.

Thank you for your support,

Dan, Justin and John
Founders, Unbound

Honoured Pantheon

Nazia Ali
Tim Atkinson
Jacqui Banton
Nathalie Barrett
Kelly Best
Oyinlola Fatunke
Daniel Gretton-Doidge
Tamara Hanley
Johari Ismail
Marcia Lindsay
Sandy Natarajan
Rebecca Smith
Rebecca Toennessen
Maggie Vine
Derek Wilson

Character List

Human

Hektor – *tuhkanti* of Wilusa, son of Priam and Parta

Hapi – bastard son of Hektor

Priam – *labarna* of Wilusa, deputy of the sun god on Earth

Parta – *tawananna* of Wilusa, joined to Priam

Ura – market trader and owner of Wilusa's foremost *arzana*

Washa – miracle worker and physician

Masturi – *labarna* of Seha, deputy of the sun god on Earth

Massanauzzi – *tawananna* of Seha, joined to Masturi

Luha – daughter of Masturi and Massanauzzi

Kaluti – half-sister of Hektor, daughter of Priam

Hawi – chief priest of the sun god's temple

Xiuri – landowner in the Bones of the Dead God

Equine

Kummi – Hektor's mare

Aras – Hapi's foal

Divine

Appaliunas – sun god, stallion that gallops the sky

Dead God – stallion god under the Mountain

Parraspeszi – protector god of Wilusa

Kaskalkur – goddess of the Under-Spring

Arma – moon god, stallion that gallops the stars

Tarhun – god of storms

Ishtar – hermaphrodite: god of war/goddess of love

Nash – goddess of purity

Istustaya/ Papaya – the Fates

Pirwa – nature god, stallion that gallops the Earth.

Earth Mother – original goddess born out of darkness

Ubelleris – the giant beneath the Earth

Kurunta – tutelary stag god

Tablet One

Hektor jumps from the saddle to inspect his horse's vagina; as he feared, a pair of twitching legs protrude. The mare grunts and wobbles forward onto her knees, collapsing in exhaustion.

'Gods, Kummi. Couldn't you have waited?' he huffs, slapping a hand down on the animal's swollen belly. 'We were almost there.' His eyes flick to the load slung over the horse's back: dusty leathers, a bronze sword, two severed heads, Father's baked clay tablets, and, below all that, the pouch of herbal medicine, rolling across the animal's flank, undelivered.

Hektor fixes hands to hips and squints beyond the turquoise musculature of pine trees under which he stands enjoying the respite from an Aegean sun, already skull-chiselling in its intensity. Here and there, across fields, farmers are busy about their work and livestock practise uniform stupidity. Further off, barely visible, bands of tradesmen writhe across the plains, more energetic than anything else in these rural parts and the beat of song, music and, more worrying still, *laughter* is present somewhere beyond the cicadas' rhythm of lazy emptiness.

Hektor snorts, turns back to Kummi and faces up to the inevitability of what he must do. The mare holds his eyes, blinks slowly, lays her head down, rolls onto one side and swishes her tail. The emerging foal's legs flex in a honeycomb of blood, sweet stink and elastic white. A moon early, but such is the lack of propriety of expectant mothers.

Hektor thuds to his knees. *I know this is not quite the same as when a woman gives birth*, he thinks, reflecting on his instruction regarding the nature of horses and, most pertinently, foaling.

Consequently, he decides to put all thought of common girls in alleyways with their labour screams out of mind. *Recently, one of Father's wives laboured a full day before her brat shot out. A day!*

But he knows foals are different. 'The little horses, they are eager for the light of Appaliunas, so they come quickly.' That's what Father once told him. 'Let the animal spill and do not force. Our patience must bow before the foal's *impatience*.'

Hektor's attention sneaks away to the pouch of medicine; he bites his lip against an impulse to run – *such a small dose, but no less than my boy needs*. Today, patience could be death. To gently ease the foal free; that could work.

Gently, Hektor acknowledges, grimly, glancing again at the severed heads of yesterday's bandit attackers, *will be a challenge for me*.

He looks back over the plains. On a haze-hidden hillside reclines the whitewashed city of Wilusa, which the Ahhiyawans, to the west, call Troy. Home. His eyes flash, yet again, to where he expects to see the medicine riding atop the horse's sweaty flank, quickly rising and falling with the speed of the animal's lungs. Where is it? Perhaps some demon has snatched it, taken it away to barter with a mother for her baby's breath? But no, there it is – present.

Somewhere much nearer: the possibility of a branch snap and murmur of voices. Maybe farmers close by, though he cannot yet see anyone. Probably nothing. A man in his position is always in danger when travelling alone; *Father hates that I do it*.

'*Dek*, Kummi. Get a move on, old girl.'

Hektor will not be riding her the rest of the way home – this he knows, yet there is grievance in his heart. *She's been the closest thing to a friend I've had since childhood*, so he cannot leave her.

Brittle thighs, thick with jellied blood, are now apparent. He snorts, wraps tender-yet-firm fists around the foal's legs. The limbs slither in his palms at first, but quickly enough he makes a grip and awkwardly eases the foal, twisting his forearms with the mare's contractions.

Gods! The damn thing's like an eel. Hektor holds his hands up, shakes them, hisses in disgust. He needs to dry off, but refuses to get Kummi's fluids all over his tunic or kilt. He wishes he had a servant with him to dry his hands on their clothes.

He looks about… Eyes lock on to the severed heads. He reaches over and grabs the one with the longest hair, wipes his hands thoroughly. Then he turns back to the foal and grips again.

Perhaps a rustle in the surrounding undergrowth but Hektor's snorts block out all other sound. His focus: the job at hand.

'What in the Under-Spring are you doing to that horse? Show your face, stranger.'

Hektor jumps, turns, looks up into the face of a man on horseback. Behind him is a crowd of men at various stages of ageing and dressing – farmers and other country workers, yes, by the look of the adzes and sickles they carry.

'Get out of here, Xiuri. Haven't you got some shekels need collecting?' Hektor barks.

'*Tuhkanti*? Forgive me.' Xiuri exaggerates a bow, smirking – always the contest with him between an attempt at sarcasm and the fear of overstepping the mark. 'I took you for some common bandit or horse thief. Now I see you're a *hasawa*.'

Hasawa: healer, diviner, midwife.

Behind Xiuri: cautious laughter.

Hektor turns back to the foaling. 'You're a landowner, Xiuri, leader of a rural community. Had the gods intended you for comedy they would have made you a midget, a cripple or a chained, travelling ape. As it happens, you are none of these, though your intelligence suggests otherwise. Why are you not attending your lands? Were you summoned to Wilusa by the *labarna*?... Come on, Kummi! Push!'

Xiuri's momentary silence fosters something, cuts bird song in trees. 'As it happens, I was,' he positively spits. 'I needed more farmhands, but I have only been granted these *gardeners*' – his arm sweeps over the men behind him – 'and told to make do. The *labarna* hasn't got a c— Does not *appreciate* what life is like for anyone with less than two hundred silver to their name, but what do you expect from the most powerful man in the region? Still, I can go home content that he has his own little crisis.'

The group of men cheer, sing, laugh – not cautious. Hektor recognises that distinct note of enjoyment he had heard earlier, lurking deep in the distance. He takes a firmer grip on the emerging midriff of the foal. Kummi swishes her tail, lifts her head, bares her teeth in what looks for all the world like an obscene grin. *Maybe it is.*

Maybe the politics of vegetable taxation and agitated administrators amuses horses.

'What are you talking about, Xiuri?'

'Tell him about it, lads. Tell him about the *miracle*.'

'The what?'

Xiuri chuckles. 'You mean, you haven't heard?'

It has been a quarter-moon since Hektor was last in Wilusa. 'Clearly... Good girl, Kummi! Almost there.'

'A glorious coming!' – a wavering voice.

Another voice – 'That's right. He has come to us! Your father's time is coming, Hek— I mean, *tuhkanti*, sir.'

Hektor turns briefly to the eager-yet-cautious faces behind him, looks up at Xiuri. 'What rubbish is this?'

'Like I said, it's the miracle, *tuhkanti*.' The landowner's voice is heavy with mockery, the tilt of his open mouth: poorly weighted scales. 'You heard these lads. A voice, bellowing out from the Temple of Appaliunas. Rumour has it that it's the mad, drunken physician, Washa. But they say He just... appeared. You should see Him – it's quite something. The crowd is growing.'

Hektor clamps his teeth together; *I am not in the mood for miracles*, as though the appearance of miracles is subject to his private whim.

'You mean, there is a – what? – a man yelling from the temple?' He can imagine what the *labarna*'s reaction would be, rubs his concern out like so much piss in the sand. 'What is he saying?'

'He says He is the god Himself. He says He has come to impart a divine message to the people.'

Hektor is as gods-fearing as the next man, and although he might otherwise be tempted to regard this story dubiously, he cannot help but take it seriously. *The commoners have been uneasy for some time...*

Hektor growls, turns back to Kummi. With a final push – and a fiercer pull on his part – the foal comes flooding out, actually quite like one of those common girls in the alleys giving birth with averted eyes. *Perhaps we are not so different from horses after all.*

'There we go. I can't imagine why women should make such a din,' Hektor mutters, loud enough for no one but himself to hear.

Kummi whinnies, revolves her head to see what all the fuss is about. The foal is bound in heat and stringy tissue, which Hektor tears through, scraping the blood and mucus from its mouth. It shivers, leans towards him. He harrumphs, folds his arms, realises too late that he now has birth fluids on his sleeves.

'Well, *tuhkanti*? Shouldn't you be getting back before this gets out of hand?'

Hektor sighs. His eyes flick: the medicine once more, mixing now in Kummi's bell-decorated mane. Bells are usually laced into horse hair during battle, the noise encouraging enemies to consider stepping backwards instead of forwards. *A madman in the temple claiming possession? Now there is twice the urgency to get home.*

'I cannot leave Kummi. I must stay with her. It's the compassionate thing to do.'

After a deadly pause, Xiuri jumps down from his own horse. Hektor turns to face him; the landowner's face has darkened.

'*Compassionate?* Don't you dare say that. There is no compassion, warmth or love in either you or your father, *tuhkanti*. To suggest otherwise would be an injustice to the pair of you.'

Hektor hangs his head, nods absently, then suddenly leaps up, marches around to Kummi's head.

'Xiuri. If I am as you say, then trusting me with this' – he gestures towards the shivering foal, looking up, perplexed – 'is out of the question. I might snap its neck or eat its face or something.'

Hektor *yank, yank, yanks* his equipment out from under the mare, grabs the medicine and stows it in his belt. *If the commoners can have their miracle, why not I?* He lifts up his sword, points it – at the landowner.

'You can wait here with my horse... horses, until stable-hands are sent out.'

'How dare you... You—'

Hektor pushes past Xiuri and heaves himself up onto the administrator's horse, throwing his equipment over its back. The animal grows more concave under the *tuhkanti's* superior weight. 'If any harm comes to either of my horses,' he booms, 'I will cut off your balls and mount them on a spike over the upper town walls. As you say, I have no compassion.'

A final glance at Kummi – she looks content – and the stuttering landowner – he does not – then Hektor whacks the appropriated horse and clatters towards Wilusa.

Hektor looks up, finds the details of the city increasingly discernible: the wooden palisade around the filthy lower town; the creamy stone walls crowning the bluff on which the upper town is sprawled; and the acropolis, in which the *labarna* and the extended royal family live with all the serenity it is possible for them to enjoy given that the head of this particular family has nine wives and thirty-three known concubines. And somewhere out of sight, beyond the care of everyone else's mind but his own: a tiny bed chamber where he last saw his son, Hapi.

I'm coming, son – hold fast.

His journey had commenced six days ago, when he ventured out to the rural community in the north-east – the Bones of the Dead God, as it was commonly called, for the colossal skeleton on the hillside at the centre of its situation – and been greeted coldly by various landowners, including Xiuri's brothers and colleagues. His task had been routine: force a new deal to ensure receipt of agricultural produce throughout the new harvest. Farmland, in these parts, is vulnerable to raids by opportunists, and the landowners had demanded increased security following a string of incidents in which pomegranates, apricots and wine had gone missing.

The thievery had gone unnoticed at first, so the landowners explained, but quickly enough, farmers in fruit orchards reported cases of missing flora. The *tuhkanti* had assumed boars, or even monkeys, were responsible, until a human figure was sighted one night during his visit frantically piling up a basket. The stranger was chased off, but persisted with his larceny over successive nights, each time evading capture. The thief's slipperiness aggravated Hektor, who prides himself on a well-honed ability to frustrate criminals. Among other duties, the *tuhkanti* oversees provincial security, so is responsible for dealing with illegal activity throughout the region. He had not managed to arrest the troublemaker, as the thievery stopped on the fifth night of his seven-day visit. However, he stubbornly imagines he will find the trespasser one day, *though in a region with a population of some ten or twelve thousand this will be a challenge...* After using the virtue of his political position, and a few crude threats, he had managed to broker a deal that he imagines will please his father.

But what of that? What of Hapi?

Hapi had been talking when Hektor left Wilusa, though bedridden and surrounded by healer-priests fond of down-turning their mouths and shaking their heads with an air of resignation. The demon Distraction had toyed with him mercilessly in his absence from Wilusa; Hapi's depleted little body ever present in his thoughts, and his impatience to return home had certainly sharpened his tongue in negotiations. And sharpened his temper when two bandits attacked him on his way back to Wilusa, leading to Kummi being adorned with their heads – ready for public display at a later time.

In the saddle, Hektor shifts uncomfortably. The horse is smaller than Kummi and seems to be attempting, at intervals, to throw him from its back. His testicles keep slipping under him and he curses himself for having such wayward genitalia.

Passing mule-drawn carts, tittering commoners – *and they do look happy; this is not good* – his horse *dup, dup, dups* across the bridge spanning a defensive ditch and arrives at one of Wilusa's postern gates, cut out of the wooden palisade that encloses the lower town – a heaving of mud-brick homes, market stalls, filthy roads and raucous peasants. Hektor makes several prayers at the man-sized, stone baetyl, a statuette carved in the likeness of the divine protector of travellers – *who did not see fit to let me finish my journey atop my own horse* – underneath the town walls.

'*Tuhkanti*, where is *your* horse? Are you alright?' a guard captain asks, jumping down from the embankment behind the palisade, his purple kilt swinging about his thighs in the coastal breeze.

'Yes, I'm fine,' Hektor grunts, vaulting gratefully out of the saddle and landing in the dirt with a *thunk*. 'Quick, tell me what's happening at the Temple of Appaliunas,' he demands, grabbing his possessions and chucking the severed heads to another guard, gesturing to a couple of spikes on the parapet as he does so.

'You heard then. Yes, well, I don't know much. Only whisperings and the conversation of traders leaving. Can it be true – a miracle?'

'No.'

'*Tuhkanti*, the *labarna* has commanded that you attend him upon your return.'

'Is he looking for me because of what is happening at the temple?'

'No, *tuhkanti*. He has visitors, and… well, visitors that, as *I* understand it, were not due to arrive yet. Perhaps the *labarna* made some error in…'

The guard's voice trails off; he averts his eyes as Hektor narrows his. Even after the passing of eight harvests there is still awkwardness, as though his father's condition is a cause for regional embarrassment. It probably is.

Hektor sighs, comprehends the guard's discomfort. He scratches at his head, trying to ward off another of his countless headaches; he can feel the little demons already settling inside his skull. *Visitors? Father dictated to our record keepers that the Sehans were not due for another half-moon for discussions of my joining ceremony. Can he have made a mistake? Is it them so early?* He clutches at the pouch containing the medicine, annoyed at this fresh distraction.

'I need you to do something for me.'

'Yes, *tuhkanti*.'

'Have one of your men run over to the stables and tell the hands to fetch my horses.'

'Hors… *es*? Yes, of course.' The guard puffs out his chest. Holds it. Breathes, focuses. 'Where shall the stable-hands go?'

'To the east of here, about three miles, there's a cluster of pines along the river. There'll be an angry landowner and a group of farmers. The farmers will still be singing if the stable-hands are quick; if not, the landowner, Xiuri, will have probably strangled them. The hands cannot miss this.'

With a furrowed brow, the guard *hmphs*, grabs a few other guards, runs off towards the upper town.

Hektor hands the reins of Xiuri's horse over to another guard and jogs in through the gate towards a small marketplace.

'Ah! Ha-ha!' An enormous, wrinkled woman lunges, with surprising speed, straight into Hektor, wrapping his face in seal-flipper hands. 'Ah! You look well! Hair – no, not greasy. Eyes – could be whiter. Healthy skin though? Definitely!'

'Must you be so indecent?' The *tuhkanti*'s cheeks burn as people stare.

The woman pulls away, exaggerating an expression of offence on a face quite remarkably ugly. 'Oh! Still so stuck being proper, eh? Not even a, "Hello, Ura, how are you today? I'm so happy to see you, the sun shines a little brighter now", what? They teach you so much chilliness up in that big house of yours, I think.'

Hektor relents. Despite his posture and gravity, he is still the little boy Ura nursed and cared for in the absence of his preoccupied mother, as he navigated childhood. Until the day she was made to leave the acropolis, of course. Still, she survives in the lower town, now a popular figure among the people, so Hektor has witnessed, *and despite her presumption and indiscretions she is my true friend.*

Ura smiles, walks back towards a stall. 'Don't be worrying. I know how it is for you. Must be hard living so carefully, eh? But then, who doesn't have it tough?'

The *tuhkanti* lags, hands behind his back, still gripping the pouch of medicine.

Ura shakes her head. 'Not a good day today though... You think to fool everyone with that face, but Ura always reads you. Yes. Yes.'

Hektor never discovered from where exactly Ura had originally come, but he always imagines it to have been an exotic and wild place to give rise to such an accent as she wields. Having travelled so much, Hektor finds that language varies even from village to village, carrying the unique flavour of every tongue that chisels it, language being, among other things, a material as fit for sculpture as bronze and marble.

'No. Not a good day. Look, Ura, I need—'

'I haven't seen you in several moons; you away all that time?' She points her forefinger at the postern gate and then returns to sorting through boxes filled with fruit, picking out rotten apples and pears or flicking away inquisitive insects.

'No, I have not even been away a quarter-moon. The rest of the time I have been busy in the upper town. I regret that I haven't been able to see you, but there are many demands of me. Now, Ura, I really must—'

Ura stifles a laugh. 'One day you will wake up and think, "To the underworld with duty, I'm going to enjoy myself for once!"... Did you ever consider that you have a duty to life itself, to enjoy it while it lasts, eh? You owe a debt to whatever power created you, and the best way to repay that debt is by enjoying the gift in what little ways you can.'

Hektor huffs. 'I believe you make your own value of how that debt must be repaid. The sun god saw fit to give me this position and my debt is to uphold myself so as not to betray His trust—'

'Oh yes! That reminds me. You won't have heard about the priest in Appaliunas's temple, if you've been away—'

'Actually, I was informed about him on the way home. I encountered some men, all of whom were singing and dancing at the expense of a day's work, no doubt – something you would commend. Now, I really must—'

'You'd think so, eh? But I am wanting to see you happier. So, naturally, anything that distresses you I am firmly against. Would you like me to contact some people who will make these men... disappear?' She winks, nudges him in the ribs.

Hektor glances up towards the upper town, bites his lip. 'Ura, I am not in the mood for jokes. And they did not... *distress* me, they simply...'

'Yes, yes, I know!' Ura chuckles. 'Anyway, what exactly did they tell you?'

Hektor snorts. 'Simple gossip. Poor attempts to make a mockery of me, no wager. Right, I had better—'

'I doubt it was anything that sinister. Besides, there is a lot of gossiping about what is happening in the temple. We "commoners" aren't allowed in, of course, so can you be blaming us for letting our imaginations carry us away, eh? Nonetheless, I have learned to tell lies from fact... and I have my contacts...'

Despite his urgency, Hektor cannot restrain his curiosity. 'What? Is there anything I should know before I see my fa— see the *labarna*?'

'Well, this intruder is being treated better than a prize winning bull, but then what do you expect if he's got a god inside him, eh? All I'm hearing is that he might be mad Washa the physician.' Ura picks up a sorted box of apples (having discarded a number), and puts them on the floor to one side, then picks her nose liberally.

'Hmm, I see. Well, I must be about my business.' *I must see to Hapi. Be firmer with her, Hektor.*

'Going so soon? *Dek.* Careful as you leave, don't fall over the crates.'

Hektor turns, his attention suddenly hooked. Accumulated are five large crates, all filled with an assortment of pomegranates and apricots, and pots filled with wine. His jaw stiffens.

'Ura, why are there such a large number of these? And...' – *oh no* – 'why do the boxes have Sehan markings on them?'

'Uh? Yes, I am needing to put those boxes in a separate pile – they're specifically for the sun god's temple. That's the only other thing I am knowing about this intruder, or god, or Washa, or whatever you want him to be – he seems to have a craving for pomegranates, apricots and wine. Funny tastes, no?'

The *tuhkanti*'s eyes widen with predatory delight. 'And the markings?'

'Yes, those were some gifts, specially requested by the Sehan *labarna*; his servants paid much money at market for them – I'm a bit late in processing them, unfortunately. He brings many presents with him also. He is quite curious about this... this intruder. Wanted to see him. The temple officials were very particular that pomegranates, apricots and wine are the only acceptable offerings that should be made. Very odd, if you ask me.'

'So, it is *definitely* the Sehans here? *Now?*'

'Complete with royal staff, oh yes. They were here already for some reason, before this man was possessed. But now that Sehan *labarna* – Masturi – decides to see him too. He is wanting to witness the miracle.'

Tablet Two

Outside the sun god's temple, a perimeter wall divides the earthly from the divine. The building itself swallows the Asian sun by day, its oiled stone apparently luminescent by night, lending credence to its use as a navigational marker for travellers approaching the city and for ships sailing into the local harbour. Hanging from the temple walls, animal skulls of countless sacrifices hint at osseous intelligence. Complex symbols emit a cerulean glow, oil fused with blue woad extract. At all times of day and in all seasons, this temple is revered as hallowed ground – it being the house of a god.

Hang on just a little longer, Hapi, the *tuhkanti* thinks, breathing a prayer. It takes all his will not to rush now to the boy's bedside, but the prospect of Masturi, the Sehan *labarna,* being entertained in the temple by a madman faking divine possession is of State importance – *no, Heavenly importance.* To ignore this transgression at such a critical moment would be to spit on the sanctity of Appaliunas Himself. He wonders whether he should allow a guard to bear the medicine to his son's attending priests, but decides he can only trust himself with such a task, *and to describe the instruction of the priest under the Mountain who gave me this medicine in the first place.*

The large crowd outside the temple chants various songs he has never heard before, all heads focus up towards the side of the building where a shadowy figure steps away from a balcony.

Hektor marches purposefully towards the perimeter of the temple and steps over it.

'*Tuhkanti.*' A guard runs up to him, draws his breath sharply. 'You know it is for—'

'Forbidden?' Hektor looks at the perimeter wall he has just passed and sniffs his tunic. 'I know it's forbidden… without washing and the necessary rites. I am sure Appaliunas will forgive this.'

'I cannot follow, sir, if you intend to go after the intruder. I am unwashed.'

Hektor nods. 'Go then. Bring twenty extra men here to disperse the crowd. I will *not* allow the number of commoners to increase.'

Breaking in upon the temple's interior, the *tuhkanti* is hit with a few shocked glances and intakes of breath. The cloistered world around him: as bluntly removed from the outside as a murderer's violence is removed from his pity.

He thinks to bless himself, offer an apology to the sun god, but resists the compulsion, strides along a wide corridor at a speed belying his lack of composure.

He reaches the main hall. A hole in the ceiling swallows sunlight and even, as he has heard priests cogitate on their visits to the acropolis, acts as a peephole for other members of the thousand-strong pantheon to gaze in.

In the communal murmur there is an excitement quite alien to the sombre atmosphere. Outside, the crowd: *hurrah, chant, hurrah, chant.*

Bah! I will put an end to this, Hektor swears.

'*Tuhkanti?* ... *Tuhkanti!*' hisses an elderly man, hobbling across the room. *Clack, cleck, cluck,* goes his walking stick. This is Hawi, chief priest of the temple. He blesses himself several times. 'For the love of Appaliunas, what are you doing in here? It is—'

'Forbidden in an uncleansed state, I know. I'm confident the sun god will understand my urgency.'

'I would have spoken to you from the window,' Hawi huffs, his fleshy brows raised in what Hektor guesses to be irritation, or possibly the pain of under-active bowels. 'Hmm, be it on your head then, *tuhkanti.* Now that you're here you can make yourself useful and get over to the throne room.'

'Why?'

'I presume you'll want to arrest the bastard who's desecrated the temple, see him, speak to him. Yes? Well, anyway, he's in there and he's sat his big hairy arse right on Appaliunas's throne. Arrogant shit.'

The passages uncoil before Hektor, visible only by the light of wall-mounted sconces. Occasionally, a hooded priest scurries past, dipping his head to Hawi.

'How did this happen, Hawi? In all my years, I've never had to deal with something quite like it.'

'Nor I, *tuhkanti*. Nor I.' Hawi does not elaborate.

'... Yes, but you are the chief priest here. How could *you* let this happen?'

'Oh! Don't lay this on me.' The old priest coughs, pointing one gnarled finger. 'Would you stop walking so damn fast?'

'No. Keep up or fall behind.'

Clack, cleck, cluck. Clackcleckcluck. Claclecluck. Hawi's panting is terrible; his coughing too.

'Perhaps if you weren't undoing your wits on opium every day you wouldn't be struggling for breath; and maybe you'd have anticipated this.'

'Don't you take that tone with me you... you... you...'

Hektor huffs. The pair walk in silence for a time, the *tuhkanti* finally slowing a little to compensate for the old priest.

'Well... did no one think to stop this man? How did he even get in?'

'I don't know, *tuhkanti*.' Hawi sighs; his head shakes. 'I've spoken with priests, the guards, I even tried to divine an answer in the entrails of a foal. Nothing. This man wasn't seen. Maybe it *is* magic.'

Hektor shakes his head, *because what can I do but bemoan the intelligence of both priests and guards?* 'Magic indeed! Who believes that?'

'Oh, a number of my flock. This man's sudden appearance, the way he's speaking, the *things* he's saying. Dear gods! Some of my flock believe we have to seriously evaluate the possibility that... What I mean to say is that if this is the real thing, then to arrest him would be blasphemy of the highest order.'

'Look, Hawi, this is a criminal – nothing more.'

The *tuhkanti* clutches at his head.

'Don't take that tone with me, young man! I feel just as you.'

'Hmm... And I have heard he has... unusual desires, requests. Requests that have reached Sehan ears, indeed. Explain.'

'He has a tongue for apricots and pomegranates, if that is what you mean by "unusual". And it was some of my juniors who spoke to the Sehans – understand that they shall be punished.

Outside the temple, these fruits are practically sacred. I even hear they are being worshipped in some squares of the lower town. Blasphemy! And still some of my priests play along with it. But, *tuhkanti*, you must hurry. The *labarna*, he... He is entertaining the Sehan guests, the Sehan *labarna* himself—'

'I know. You think I wouldn't know that?'

'—And the Sehan *labarna* is intrigued by the "miracle". He's on his way here.'

'What? Masturi is? ... Then I must act fast.'

They finally reach a heavy set of doors.

'Is this it? The *adyton*?' Hektor demands.

'Yes, *tuhkanti*.' Hawi gives him a look caught somewhere between warning and discomfort. 'I'll go and drag him out, yes?'

'Something you should have done already. But no.'

'*Tuhkanti*... No, no, this is too much. *Tuhkanti*, stop!'

Hektor sets his jaw, shoulders into the doors, pushing them past the threshold, creak by groan by creak – he shakes off the talons of the chief priest with deft slaps.

Inside, the walls are skinned with reliefs of men, women, beasts of legend, many incarnations of the sun god – white stallion, stillborn foal, horse-headed man. *Better to hedge one's bets when it comes to divinity*, he supposes. Precision makes way for loyalty. There is a slight haze from burning opium. *Clack, cleck, cluck*, Hawi's stick rattles, drawing the attention of a crowd of priests in the chamber, some of whom are kneeling, harnessed to prayers.

What are they doing in here? Are these the fools who have been taken in by this man? Hektor thinks to himself.

At the back of the room, beside a huge throne, is an equine statuette of Appaliunas: marble, stone, layered with gold filigree, bells, ribbons. Precision in decoration. Beside the throne, hands clenching hard on one of the chair's arms, as though superhuman effort might tear it down, is the intruder.

Hektor groans, the headache reinstating its presence. He reasons that the pain must be Appaliunas punishing him for his failure to protect the temple's sanctity.

He turns to the various priests, demands they leave. Soon, the last priest closes the doors.

'You have created quite a scene throughout Wilusa – especially among the commoners. What do you have to say for yourself?' the *tuhkanti* says in a bold voice, careful to ensure his words are inflated with sufficient authority.

The silence drags, time like sand kicked across rocks. Then, from the intruder: 'Not much.'

'You have attracted a huge crowd outside, I tell you.'

'Oh?'

'And there are shrines in your honour. *Shrines!*'

'Right…'

Hektor fixes hands to hips – not for the first time that day.

'Hmph. There are even priests in this temple who are taken in by your act.'

'Act? Wha' act? D'you thin' I have any clue wha' I'm doin'? Wha' do I care? It's all gone! In the lower town, y'know wha' they call me?' He contrives an attempt to stand, but fails in his efforts. 'They call me the *experimental* physician. Yes. Because I do things tha' shock, provoke. Things they've never seen before. But these things save… They all brough' their afflictions to me. An' I *cured* 'em.'

The voice is among the most bizarre the *tuhkanti* has ever heard. The intruder's words wobble as he speaks, as air might through a woodwind instrument. The vowels are ox-cart wheels clumsily catching stones along a road. Hektor can't decide whether this man is broken by wine, or simply foreign.

'Then you *are* this old Washa she mentioned.'

'She?… Yeah. An' it's all my fault.' He starts crying. 'I burned it all down – my surgery, I burned it down. And then I was drun'. An' I was outsi' the city—'

The *tuhkanti* leans in closer, a smirk of judicial pride across his mouth. 'Aha! To the Bones of the Dead God. Wine, apricots and pomegranates – unique tastes, if taken in one sitting. I have only ever come across one other person with such a preference, but, unfortunately, he… temporarily evaded capture after raiding the rural communities for gods only know how long. But here you are, mine now.'

'Ah. However' – the intruder taps his head – 'I may b'pissed, bu' I'm no' stupid. Eve' if presen' circumstances may sugges' otherwise. We both know you're in a predicamen'. I'm expectin' some distinguished company righ' 'bout now – oh yes, I know tha' Sehan *labarna* is on his way here – company who I wager you'd rather no' see disappointed or angered.' Hektor flinches. 'We're a' a stalemate.'

The doors open. Hawi *clack, cleck, clucks* in. '*Tuhkanti*, he's here! He's on his way up! What can I do?'

Indeed, from outside Hektor can hear the cries of the crowd, the musical pomp that accompanies a *labarna*.

'Le' him in t'see the god!'

'Shut it, you! Hawi – the cleansing should delay him. Take your time with it.'

'But *tuhkanti*, he is a *labarna* and doesn't need to be cleansed under the laws of gods and m—'

'Then do whatever you can. Say there's a fire, a flood, a plague, *rats*. Anything. Just don't let him in!'

Hawi nods several times in quick succession, trundles away.

Hektor stares with renewed horror at Washa. 'The penalty for what you've… Bah! You are damned enough for what you've done already!'

'The' compoundin' it should ma' little difference.' Washa swigs from a cup, tries to sit up but fails.

'This is not a game, you fool. Your actions could have serious consequences. If any of the Sehans find out you're a fraud then they will be *humiliated*, as will the *labarna*. They will think we did it deliberately. Our reputation would be mud in their eyes – if it isn't already. We need a strong allegiance with Seha.' *Despite what Father thinks…*

'The' the last thing you woul' wan' is to tell these people the truth.'

'What? Yes. No! Lying will not help. I won't let you do this. You steal, impersonate a priest, claim to be a god and now you will entertain foreign officials?'

'I did no'—'

Voices at the doors. Hektor twists his head around and crouches beside Washa, gripping his arm and wrenching him up onto his feet, but the intruder's balance is non-existent and he falls onto the throne, eyes squinting in the sudden assault of sunlight.

'I'm arresting you. Trying to arrest you... Damn it, Hawi – couldn't you hold them off? Now, *you*, get up, quickly, before they come in. Quickly!'

The doors open. Hektor removes his hands from around the intruder's arms, swears, recoils.

'I'm afrai' my arres' will have t'be postponed,' the intruder whispers.

Hektor growls, turns, strides towards the group of men entering the room, remembering only at the last to effect a welcoming smile. Despite the musky heat staining his skin, a chill clips his cheeks, forehead and chest.

If I say nothing, this criminal will be at liberty to pronounce any number of decrees with the authority of a god. From a political point of view this is clearly perilous. But on the other hand, he might say nothing of consequence and no one need be any the wiser. I would then be free to deal with him as I see fit... Or perhaps I could claim that this man is using a form of black magic to dupe others into believing he is a god. The *tuhkanti* doesn't approve of lying though, in the general sense. Besides, the Sehan dignitaries would still be humiliated, and, furthermore, might abandon trade with Wilusa on the grounds of the city – and the region at large – being a 'black' land, cursed by the gods when even the high-priest, the *labarna*, could be attacked, not for the first time, by supernatural malevolence.

Hektor greets the spidery Sehan *labarna*, Masturi, who responds in kind, though stiffly and with something of annoyance on his face.

'*Tuhkanti*, your father was somewhat confused at my appearance in Wilusa. It's almost as if... *one* of us was mistaken as to when my visit would be.'

Hektor blushes under the statement. 'I can only imagine... Were discussions propitious, nonetheless?'

Masturi's crooked lip twists in a mockery of a smile. 'Your father is not interested in my Luha joining with you. I must say that I am greatly saddened by his decision, but...' – the mockery of a smile becomes an actual smile – 'we discussed plenty besides.' Masturi takes a step towards the throne and looks upon the intruder. 'He was also rather dismissive of the *miracle*. However, we, in Seha, have more veneration when a god deigns to present Himself.'

With these words, the Sehans fall upon the floor with submissive greetings for the 'god', as they seem to consider him, who now pulls himself up into an unsteady posture. Hektor watches. *Dek, if he says one thing I disapprove of...*, the *tuhkanti* will take control of the situation. *Yes, that sounds reasonable.*

'My Sun! Divine judge of Earth and Heaven! Being in Your presence is a miracle, both terrifying and humbling. We have offered many gifts, but ask only for this moment with You.'

Hektor clutches his neck as he listens to Masturi.

Washa lowers his head, raises it. The Sehan entourage gasps and bows all the more, apparently grateful for even this minute affectation.

'Since coming to Wilusa a short while ago, before You descended to us, I was speaking at length with the *labarna*, and we have tried to work out two joinings – only one of which we can agree upon: the joining between myself and his beautiful, young daughter. Now that trouble in the region seems more commonplace, we try to provide some stability. But the possession of a woman by a man is – how do you say? – a *holy* act... May I ask if such an arrangement would have Your blessing?'

Hektor notes Washa looking at him for a moment. *Don't you even think about it*, the *tuhkanti*'s eyes say.

'A joinin' soun's like a won'erful idea. Y'have my blessing.'

Masturi throws his arms up and turns to embrace an equally energised administrator behind him. The two share a few muffled words. Hektor knows his father would never have journeyed to the temple as it is in the lower town, *such is his fear of what the commoners might do; not that he'd extend that fear to Masturi's safety, and not that Masturi seems to have expressed any concerns himself. At* last, the Sehan *labarna* turns back to speak again, while keeping a single hand outstretched towards Washa.

'Your blessing is most welcome.' Masturi turns briefly towards Hektor, his eyes filled with something that looks like distaste. 'It is a shame that Priam is not wishing for his boy to marry my daughter though. I was – how to say? – *confident* an agreement could be reached. But Priam… He denies me this pleasure of Hektor as a son-in-law.'

There is a momentary silence, and Hektor senses a malevolence on Masturi's part. Soon, the Sehan *labarna*'s face falls back upon Washa, smile apparent.

'Never mind. Let us move on. With Your all-consuming light and all-seeing eyes, my Sun, You will of course know that Priam – and indeed Hektor here – suffers terribly, as his young grandson, Hapi, approaches death. May I also ask, on his behalf, that You guide the boy through the darkness to the meadow of his ancestors, when the time comes?'

Hektor feels his stomach drop, tastes the vomit in his throat, feels a prickliness behind his eyes. He pictures his boy there in bed – all sweat, curling brown hair, dark eyes and horse-leg skinny. *Has he deteriorated so severely?*

Finally, Washa nods respectfully, and informs the group that, as a young, clear-sighted soul, Hapi would find his way easily enough when the time came.

The Sehan dignitaries now take a moment to pray quietly, seemingly basking in the radiance of Washa's otherworldly presence. The intruder blesses them all, including a distant Hektor.

'And so I will take my leave, *tuhkanti*.' Masturi's voice draws Hektor back to the present. 'I look forward to receiving the girl I have been promised. *Soon.* I will also pray that this miracle serves to bring light into the life of your father, who I love as a brother.' Again, the unpleasant smile.

Hektor politely sweeps the Sehans out, then flings the doors shut and glares at Washa, who is busy making sounds of contentment, perhaps pleased with how his first official meeting has concluded.

Hawi enters the room and looks from Washa to Hektor. 'So…?'

'Do not let this man' – Hektor raises a finger – 'leave this room. I will be back for him.'

Outside the temple, daylight is seeping away over the Aegean horizon. Hektor is already on his way back up the hill when a messenger reaches him, tells him to come quickly to Hapi – that a father must be present for the death of his son.

Tablet Three

The acropolis is pleasingly cool after the smithy heat of dusk; *it's also welcome not to have dust continually blown in my eyes.* There are stones in his sandals, but he accepts their unwelcome presence, such as is becoming of a man in his position. *After all, a* tuhkanti *does not lean against columns battering the grit from his footwear – that is behaviour for Hapi.*

Hapi. His quarters are near the back of the building where the staff live, away from the throne room, dining hall, kitchen, royal quarters and myriad other rooms – *the shame of his existence out of sight and mind, as Mother would say.* The various servants and public and religious officials fade into the gaudy colours and frescoes of the chambers as he strides through wide, shadowy passages.

When he reaches Hapi's quarters he stares at the door for several moments, steadying his breath, lifting the pouch of medicine up to ward off any dark presence that might await beyond. He whispers incantations he has overheard the deserving mumble in similar situations to persuade any demons not to contaminate them. *I suppose I'm afraid to enter,* though he does, of course.

The room is: … *soundless*: windows covered by the rugs so expertly woven by the women of Wilusa; the women knit enough each harvest to lay a carpet over the sea and make all lands one. At the heart of the scene: Hapi upon his bed, intertwined with blankets, so much so that he seems to have fused with them. He has not seen more than nine harvests, yet his face is colourless, minimalist – the antithesis of childhood. His eyes and teeth are clenched; one slender hand rubs back and forth across his belly. Servants take turns to daub his forehead with a wet cloth. At the foot of the bed, several priests mutter hymns, burning sweet-smelling resin to create an atmosphere more inviting to any deity who might wish to help the child. In a corner, the *hasawa* slouches upon a stool, the healer's face slack with failure, remnants of poultices around her ankles.

'What in the Under-Spring has happened?!' Hektor detonates. He does not lower his voice; *Hapi seems deeply unconscious, after all.*

A priest jumps, turns. 'He is deteriorating rapidly. He has not spoken in two days. He refuses food and it's all we can do to get him to drink any water. I must be honest: the evil in his body works its magic very well, and will shortly swallow him entirely…'

For Hektor, these words are eviscerating. When he left Wilusa, Hapi was not *this* bad – the priests had told him so, told him where to get the medicine to reduce his fever.

This happens to other people, not me.

'I can't accept that,' he manages. Something is happening in his eyes; his breath is short, his balance unsteady.

'Please, Hektor.' The priest takes the *tuhkanti*'s head with one of his grey claws. 'I know this isn't easy, or what you expected. You must… You must compose yourself, yes, and try to absorb what I'm telling you. Understand? Your son has a day at most. Hours, more likely. We have performed every ritual we thought might appease the spirit, but it's all been useless. The time you have left together is prec—'

'No, no, no. I'm not accepting that. I have it, look, I have the medicine – yes, the medicine you told me to get.' He hands the medicine over, shakily, pricking the attention of the other priests and the *hasawa*.

The priest rubs his eyes. 'And you received this from the priest—'

'Who lives at the foot of Mount Parraspeszi. Yes. He said that it needs to be placed on the afflicted area. Then you need to—'

'Propitiate the demon, yes. Here.'

Hektor is shaking; the priest notices, smiles – perhaps reassuringly. *What is reassurance now?*

'We will try, Hektor, but… This will possibly conciliate the demon within your son. How's that then? I beg you sit over there.' Indicates a chair. Can he even sit? 'We'll begin at once.'

Fine, yes, he stalks over to the chair, sits in the corner, next to several of Hapi's toys: soldiers, chariots, Kuressar the cloth-cat. 'He's called that because he's spare cloth, *tati*,' Hapi once told him. Kuressar should be tucked under his arm, like always, but the priests say he needs his space.

just half a moon ago... He had been, what, running around the lawns, had he not? Angering the gardeners. Climbing trees. Asking about the different types of bird that make their nests in eucalyptus trees. *And they are made as different as we, yet they all remain – their places in this world allocated.* Imitating the geckos that wobbled defiantly along the walls until the *tuhkanti* could not help but laugh, *careful not to let the boy see me, of course.* And Hektor reciting for him his oral history and the stories of Gilgamesh – *when pushed; that damned hero* – as Hapi lay in bed, ready for sleep: the Mesopotamian king's adventures with his friend Enkidu, Enkidu's death, Gilgamesh's quest for the secret of immortality – *Hapi loved it all.*

And then the pain had started. What did he miss? Only light at first, catching in his belly. But it had spread, the sweat had come on. The day Hapi collapsed had been the most frightening experience of— Yes, an experience that drained the blood right out of his head. Hapi had been walking downhill, the sun's heat uninterrupted by any cloud line. He had dropped so awkwardly, so suddenly, as though the gods had been holding him up with thread, which they had severed. Puppets, toys are discarded every day, every which way, lost forever and only later half-recalled as an adult when the fickle loyalties to childhood companions are grieved over. And here he is, Hapi, unvisited by anyone save his father – too much danger of contamination for anyone else to dare. Other priests had thought this sickness a sign from Appaliunas, the fiery stallion, that Hapi should start to grow up and leave his playfulness – his foalhood – behind, or worse yet that He had finally indicated His offence at the boy's birth. Royal blood mixed with— *No, enough of that.*

The priests are rubbing the medicine into Hapi's belly: a green pulp, like marrow stew, smelling familiarly of the kitchen. The priest at the foot of Mount Parraspeszi is said to be a specialist in the demons that find their way into children, or so the acropolis priests had claimed.

'What is it?' Hektor asks, absently.

'The medicine?' replies the *hasawa*, who seems to have become quite interested and involved in proceedings. 'A mixture of the four mountain herbs favoured by the spring goddess, Kaskalkur. We ask

Her to bar Hapi from entry into the Under-Spring, where the demon wants to take him. We ask that She send Hapi back. Don't worry. This will work; don't mind this foolish priest. The gods will not be calling Hapi yet.'

Hektor notices the priests glance at each other.

'How can you be so sure?' *Yes, I want to believe her; what parent wouldn't?*

'Hapi is a child of the second moon.'

Hektor shakes his head. *A child born under the second moon will be healthy of heart,* it is said. The *tuhkanti* was born under the first moon and regarded warily for it. *A child of the first moon will demolish his house.*

The priests light sooty tapers of burning stink from a wall-mounted sconce, shaking their heads still, the smoke trailing around the dim room like jellyfish stingers. The *hasawa* stands at the end of the bed, the priests either side. Hapi is eclipsed by robe, smoke, fidgeting limbs. The *hasawa* raises her arms, yet her voice reaches higher, and a warble snaps from the back of her throat – the sound of tomcats squaring up. Her movements are wild, spasmodic, and there is an energy in her pleading to the spring goddess that the *tuhkanti* finds, well, *awkward* to watch.

He is not sure how long the ceremony, ritual, healing – *whatever you'd care to name it* – lasts, but he must have fallen asleep at some point, despite the noise. The rugs are raised from the windows: outside, the sky is dark. *How long have I been asleep?* The priests have gone; only the *hasawa* remains, sat back in her chair again. Hektor looks at his boy, the red light drinking him.

'Is it done? Is he okay now?' the *tuhkanti* demands, jerking up and away from the last tethers of sleep. *Go away Sleep, this one is awake now.*

The *hasawa*: dead-eyed. 'The goddess has heard us… but it seems She does not answer.'

'What do you mean, "She does not answer"?' he spits. *Did she lie to me?*

He steps over to the bed, *thunks* to knees. Hapi sweats profusely –

bruised tree rings around his eyes, staining amber skin. Something is very wrong.

'I mean, that our offering is not accepted. No, no. Kaskalkur stands at the Under-Spring even now and does not block Hapi's way. She must be angered, or something. I don't know. I… I don't know.'

'You said… Wait, wait, you said you could save him.'

'It is never in my hands; always in Hers. I petition, that is all.'

'Is there nothing…' But what is the point? The *hasawa*'s eyes have dropped, perhaps out of respect for the pain in his voice, perhaps from a sense of discomfort or shame. He turns back to Hapi, and takes one of the boy's hands. Such a little hand, and hot.

The *hasawa* slinks back into her chair, shadows unravelling her features.

Hektor looks around the rest of the chamber, checking that no demon is curled up in any corner, and leans in close. 'Hapi… I don't know if you can hear me, but… your death. I do not wish it.' He huffs angrily, shakes his head. 'I want you to live. I'm the *tuhkanti*, the closest thing to the *labarna* himself – the gods can't do this to me.' He chokes, clearing his throat. 'And… And I co-command you not to die, yes. It is not Kaskalkur's turn to have you. I cannot ride into the Under-Spring, no, no, to bring you back. Kummi cannot carry me there, no – she's finally foaled. You would love to have seen that, I know… Please. You are needed here. Come back.' The first tear warms his wrist. He chokes again, closes both eyes tight, gripping any further tears. *Get a hold of yourself.* He only reopens them once he has regained a little composure.

But this cannot be the end, no; he is not a man to accept such dictates. There must be a way. *He can't die, for gods' sake! He's Hapi; it's not like Hapi to die.* And in this moment, it hits him. A way. A perverse way. *No, I couldn't – but…* If this is Hapi's time then he has nothing to lose in this one possibility.

He finds the *hasawa*. 'You. Stay with him until I get back.'

'Wh-where are you going?'

He makes to leave, but pauses, moves over to his son's toys, clamps a hand around Kuressar the cloth-cat and tucks it under one of Hapi's arms.

'I make my own miracles.'

Forty minutes later, under starlight, Hektor returns to the upper town and to his son's chambers. The *hasawa*'s snores are loud, obnoxious, interlaced with the occasional phlegm-rooted cough, brought about, no doubt, by years of opium inhalation. Hapi remains as he was, breathing steadily inconsistent, Kuressar the cloth-cat taut in his pale hand. Not dead.

'Get in, quick. Watch your head,' Hektor hisses, pushing the prisoner into the chambers. A bucket of cold water, coupled with the nip of the upper town's wind and several vicious slaps, has served to sober Washa sufficiently – *I hope, but what other choice have I?* – for the task ahead. 'Are you sure you need her to tell you my boy's symptoms?'

'I'll nee' her for a lot more besides.'

The *tuhkanti* sighs, nods, walks over to the *hasawa* – jabs her with one finger.

'Wah! What? What? Ah, you! It's you. What is it? Is he okay?'

'I told you to watch him and here I find you asleep. What if his condition had changed?'

'Has it?' She looks around him towards Hapi, suddenly alert.

'It doesn't appear so.'

The *hasawa*'s shoulders drop; she notices the prisoner. 'What is that?'

'A physician, of sorts,' Washa replies, before Hektor can. 'Someone who uses medicine and surgery to help people. You might have heard of such.'

'Where did he come from?'

'Never mind that,' Hektor cuts across. 'Just do as he says.'

'What?'

'You heard me! Whatever he needs, you help him.'

The prisoner motions for the *tuhkanti* to step back, so Hektor walks over to the chair he was sat in earlier and collapses. *I could sleep, really I could.*

Hawi had gratefully relinquished Washa into Hektor's custody, and it had been a simple matter of smuggling him through the streets and into the upper town, jumping from shadow to shadow in the dying light. Hektor was relieved to find the temple intruder sobered rapidly in the salty bite of Wilusa's wind, and he was quite lucid by the time they reached the acropolis.

Washa breathes in heavily, turns to the *hasawa*. 'Tell me his initial symptoms and what you've done to help.'

The *hasawa* glances momentarily to Hektor, returns her gaze to the prisoner. 'The boy has been complaining of a stabbing in his gut for a little while now.' She makes a stabbing motion. 'It was only a half-moon ago that he started to suffer severe pains, a fever and loss of appetite. He vomited a few times and his faeces was watery. We examined his vomit and his faeces and urine too... Is this bothering you?'

Washa clutches his head, releases it. 'No, no. Please, carry on.'

'Right. Well, we examined the different fluids but couldn't find anything out of place. The spirit in the boy is cunning,' the *hasawa* rasps, 'and in its maliciousness leaped into the right side of his belly a few days ago. Since then, he has been clutching his side and whimpering at intervals. I applied these ground-up herbs' – she motions to the medicine that the *tuhkanti* had returned from the country with – 'to both his belly and his forehead and propitiated Kaskalkur, but it has had no effect.'

'Anything else you've given him?'

'We used castor plant seeds and opium to ease the discomfort, but the demon inside him is stubborn and remains tightly wrapped beyond the reach of our prayers.'

Washa preserves the silence. Somewhere in the distance a dog barks and cicadas celebrate the starlight in verse.

'You say you found nothing untoward in his faeces or urine?'

'That's right.'

'Did you evacuate his bowels at any point?'

'Yes, we did that many times to try and flush the demon out,' the *hasawa* huffs, clearly irritated. 'But it's still up there. Look, what do you think you're going to do that *I* didn't? Huh?'

'Hmm,' he continues, ignoring the *hasawa*'s professional indignation. 'And the boy seems to suffer pain in the right side of his belly...

May I?' He indicates to Hektor that he wishes to examine Hapi. The *tuhkanti* nods, folds his arms.

Washa massages his impressive moustache, looking Hapi up and down, and there is something close to sympathy or distress passing over his face. He *hmms*, pulls the covers back to reveal a belly pooled in a mucilage of sweat, and gently pushes Hapi's hand away as it seeks to comfort the area. Below the navel, to the right, the flesh is bulbous, as though inflated from beneath the surface with a gust of wind. Hektor raises a hand to his mouth. The prisoner flicks away the mulched herbs that had been applied earlier, the *hasawa* complains in his ear. He fingers the swollen area, jumps as the boy spasms with an accompanying cry. Hektor makes to stand, but stops himself.

'No, no. I see.'

'Can you do anything for him?'

'Yes, yes. I have seen this type of "demon" before.'

'How is it to be exorcised?' the *hasawa* asks.

'Surgically.'

The *hasawa* gasps at this suggestion.

'I need several instruments to do it. Get me a lancet – two would be better – one big, one small. I'll also need a knife with a very fine blade; a bowl of hot, salty water; some more cloth – we don't have enough here; a needle, with plenty of thread; a very small piece of metal, purified through scalding; forceps; and a lot of opium.'

The *hasawa* files off without complaint, her sense of medical duty apparently reinstated.

'Do you know what's wrong with him?'

'Yes. It's a condition I've seen a few times before.'

It hits the *tuhkanti* there and then: the risk he has taken in bringing this man here. But what does it matter? *Kaskalkur has no claim on my boy today. Perhaps life is not a procession of incidences driven by logic; perhaps it is more the messy stitching together of decisions we pretend to have thought out.*

The *hasawa* returns a short while later – over her shoulder: the surgical implements in a small potato sack; in each of her hands: the bowl of water and purified metal.

Washa sets the equipment along the bedside, washes away the

remnants of the poultice on Hapi's belly, burns opium, leaves it by the boy's head. As Hapi murmurs, the prisoner steadies his breathing and tells the *hasawa* to stay close by in case she is needed.

And now Hektor observes, in horrified fascination, as the lancet's incision opens Hapi like a temple being forced to surrender its secrets. But the opium is not enough and the boy's torso snaps up, accompanied by an ungodly howl of pain, Hapi's neck muscles clenched, his eyes wrinkled and teary. Hektor, Washa and the *hasawa*, as one, jump at the sudden din.

'Hold him down! Hold him *down*!' Washa barks at the *tuhkanti*, who leaps forward and forces Hapi down into the bed by the shoulders. He turns from Hapi's agonised face, finding it too much to bear, and watches Washa working awkwardly away, fighting against the child's wriggling.

At first, skin gives way in a mess of blood, then the elastic white of muscle, until, finally, a small hole is completed. Hapi screams all the while. Hektor thinks to ask Washa what he is doing, but exercises restraint, remembering that he is desperate. Washa tells the *hasawa* to use the forceps to keep the incision open. The idea suggests itself to the *tuhkanti*, absurdly, that what he is witnessing is a sight forbidden to mortal eyes. Naturally, the body is a wondrous design of the gods, so he was taught, and to peer inside its muddled construction is to look into the nest of Creation itself.

'Can you see the demon yet? Is it there?' the *hasawa* gasps, quite transfixed by such an otherworldly form of healing.

'Not yet.'

Hektor feels a little queasy as the prisoner inserts a crimson finger into Hapi's belly and begins to extract something that looks very much like a chunk of uncooked chicken. Hapi retches, gives one final cry, passes out. Hektor himself gags, moves cautiously back from the now relaxed body of his son. He has seen blood, yes, hot guts before, yes, but this is not the same.

Washa draws the growth until he seems to have pulled out an amount he finds satisfactory. His fingers slip through the meat with awkward sweeps, a sound of slithering wetness punctuating the quiet. 'Yes, there it is. Good, it's just as I suspected.'

The *tuhkanti* cranes his neck to see that Washa is holding out a swell of flesh. In an apparent show of spiritual and medical curiosity, the *hasawa* leans in and gags, just as he did. 'Is that the demon there?' she manages, after swallowing.

'Yes, that's him; fresh from the mouth of Kaskalkur. You see how he has attached himself to the boy's intestines? That's why the child's sick. The demon hooks its mouth onto the healthy body and sucks all the spirit out for itself. See?' His voice: sarcasm, tiredness.

The *hasawa* murmurs: awe-struck approval, pretence – Hektor would call it – of understanding.

'How will you convince it to leave? Should we make an offering? Or should we try and speak to it, encourage it to go?'

'No, that won't work. It's tricky and it realises we want it gone. It won't leave its food behind; it would be like trying to snatch a starving baby from its mother's breast. The only way to safely remove it is to sever the connection it has with the boy ourselves. Get the larger lancet ready for me, the needle too. And thread – I'll need all that shortly. Thankfully, the boy's condition isn't as critical as it might have been, so I'm confident I can safely remove the demon. However, this is the tricky bit. One wrong move and I might not be able to stop the bleeding. Both of you, keep quiet for me. And still. If you move, it puts me off.'

So, the *tuhkanti* leans back, *thuncks* his head against the wall, the pain knocking away his own tiredness. Up on the ceiling of Hapi's chambers is a fresco of horses running across the sun-smacked Wilusan plains sprawling beyond the city. He closes his eyes, just for a moment, remembering how he showed his son the right way to brush a horse. *No, run with the hair. Kummi likes it on her fat belly.* Hapi has been looking forward to the birth of Kummi's foal, arguing with the *tuhkanti* on a name: Hektor wants something martial; Hapi wants to call it Aras – 'friend'. *Well, he can call it 'friend' if it means he comes back to me. I wonder how Kummi is doing. I hope the stable-hands reached her okay.*

Once he has cut away at the growth and chucked it on a side-table, Washa cleans the 'site of entry', as he refers to the wound, with the warm, salty water and lets the flesh close naturally, as a jaw might clamp together after a particularly satisfying yawn; he takes the threaded needle and clumsily punctures the skin around the wound, tugging it through the flesh and back out again. All the while, the opening continues to bleed, red bubbles popping as the crooked sewing tightens the wound. A short while later, Washa knots the end of the thread, cuts what is spare and stands to wash his hands and arms.

Hektor also stands and moves across to his son, who looks achingly fragile. He strokes the boy's hair.

'Is that it?' the *hasawa* asks.

'Yes,' Washa confirms.

'Praise the gods! And the demon? What's to be done with it? We'll have to burn that side-table as it's been contaminated by the creature,' the *hasawa* suggests, indicating a thumb of flesh sitting unhandsomely on the furniture.

'Here.' Washa picks it up and lobs the growth at the *hasawa* who leaps back with a yelp. 'Why didn't you catch it? You can keep it if you want. But it's touched the floor now. Does that mean we have to burn down the whole acropolis?'

Hektor shakes his head, tears away from the momentary weight-lessness of relief, lifts his hand from Hapi, clenching it into a fist. The *hasawa* is watching him, as is Washa – though there is a voice in the look he gives the *tuhkanti*.

'Who is this man, Hektor?' the *hasawa* rasps.

'I want you to go now,' he tells her. He would very much like to yell at her, beat her, damn her for nearly killing his son. Deep down, he knows she will not keep her mouth shut, and will have to be dealt with. For now, she must slip away to bed and do nothing more. 'Thank you for your efforts today. You must be very tired and I beg you go and get some rest. Please.'

'Well... if you're sure?'

'Quite sure, quite sure.'

She waddles towards the door with a restrained nod. 'I suppose I do deserve a little sleep now. I have toiled for hours for your son and—'

'And been instrumental in restoring him. If you weren't at hand to fetch those items for the pr— for this man here, then gods only know what tragedy might have befallen us.'

Hektor sweeps her out, closes the door with a creak and a click, turns upon Washa.

'Is that it? Will my boy live?'

'I've done what is in my power to do,' Washa responds, drying his hands. There is a bitter smell in the room, like that of a chamber of armaments after a battle. 'Now is the difficult part: the waiting. The next few days will be telling. In my experience, if he's still with us – you – then, then I believe he'll be okay.'

Hektor exhales brutally, nods his head, sweeps a hand through sweat-infused ringlets of hair.

Washa averts his eyes. '*Tuhkanti*, our deal. What you told me on the way up here…'

'Stands. You will remain imprisoned for the next few days. No harm will come to you, I'll see to it. If Kaskalkur refuses my boy then you have bought your life; if he dies, then the gods will not call it unjust for me to kill you.'

After calling for two guards to collect Washa and escort him to the prison, Hektor absently picks up Kuressar the cloth-cat, collapses into the chair, smiles once at the toy, and is asleep before his head bumps once more against the wall.

Tablet Four

Hektor awakens the following morning to the sound of birds twittering in the eucalyptus outside Hapi's quarters. He glances across at his son, chest gently rising and dropping. He grunts as though in acknowledgement of something and closes his eyes.

A hesitant cough: Hektor is not alone. 'I'm sorry to intrude, *tuhkanti.*'

Hektor jumps, looks across at the door. 'Yes? Yes? Well? Well?'

'My Sun demands to see you in the throne room right away, *tuhkanti.* He has been... waiting for you.' Ever since the incident all those years ago, Hektor has refrained from addressing the *labarna* as 'Father', as it is customary for Priam to be referred to as 'my Sun', the address linking him closely to the sun god.

For a man in my father's position the appearance and circumstance of divinity is crucial

Hektor flicks his head to an angle, sighs. '*Dek.* Go back and tell him I will be there momentarily.'

It is only a short journey from Hapi's quarters to the throne room, and Hektor manages to shake off some of his tiredness by stabbing fingers into his eyes and rubbing at them. He rounds a corner, hears familiar voices, steps behind a nearby pillar so he is not seen, finds the image of a cackling half-man/half-goat beside his cheek. *He looks happier every time I see him...*

'... which is why we offer the gods the first of our harvest. Wouldn't you give a friend the first of a meal you'd prepared? Out of respect.'

'Yes,' a young girl begins, looking off over an old man's shoulder – the old man is Hawi, the chief priest of the sun god's temple. 'But I don't think my friends would like to eat the food I prepare. I'm not very good.'

'Hmm,' Hawi says, scratching his head. 'I don't think the priest-

esses or I believe that – not for a second. Your friends – the gods even
– would be lucky to have some of your bread or carrot soup—'

'It's not carrot, Hawi!' the girl says, smiling. 'You see?'

'Oh, not carrot? Well, it's… still the nicest carrot dish I've ever
had.'

The girl appears affronted, shakes her head.

'Go on, Kaluti, off you go now,' Hawi eventually says. The girl –
Kaluti, apparently – nods, skips off past the *tuhkanti*, whistling a hymn:
'The Spring that Refused to End'.

'Hi, big brother!' she yells over her shoulder at Hektor as she
rounds the corner.

'Err, yes, hello,' the *tuhkanti* calls after her, clearing his throat. *I
really must try to remember the faces of my sisters.*

'She is a… fine girl,' Hawi manages, *clack, cleck, clucking* over on
his stick to the *tuhkanti*. 'I hear she is to be given to Masturi; he has
always had his eye on her. Then again, that Sehan has his eye on any
girl who's barely started to grow tits.'

Hektor sweeps his head up, a trained warmth casting over
momentary distaste.

'How is he? Uh-hmm. Your boy…'

'He is… alive.'

Hawi maintains the same cool expression. 'There doesn't come a
point at which we will stop breaking ourselves to save our children,
wouldn't you say?'

'I would agree.'

Hawi tilts his head to one side: inquisitive, assertive, avian. 'Yes, of
course you would.'

From inside the throne room comes a deep, stuttering voice, muffled by the closed doors. 'M'boy! Is that you?'

Hektor looks at Hawi, who retains his inquisitive expression.

Hektor nods briefly, throws open the throne room doors.

'Ah! M'boy, m'boy. Come closer. Yes, yes. We want your ear, you
can look Us in the face.' Priam pauses for breath between slurs, his
speech a catastrophe.

Even after all these years, the *tuhkanti* still finds it disconcerting
whenever the *labarna* uses dual-referential pronouns. But he is both

Priam and deputy to the sun god, so speaks with the authority of himself as *labarna* and Appaliunas as deity. *We, Us,* in perfect harmony. *Though it is a quirk of his, and Masturi feels no need to do likewise.*

Hektor steps forward. The throne room is colossal, the ceiling supported by several thick, red columns, four of which square the ashy traces of a hearth fire that would normally billow up into an open skylight when lit.

'We looked for your presence. Yes. But you were absent' – Hektor begins a protest – 'No, no. Nothing more for it. We must talk. Sehans. Possessed men. It is all so much, m'boy.'

There will be no enquiry as to how Hapi is doing, as neither of his parents have ever looked favourably on the boy, given the circumstances of his birth.

Up a small set of steps is a platform on which the throne itself is positioned. Priam – *the 'half-labarna', as I have heard commoners refer to him* – sits atop the throne. A goat-skin rug, tamed by bronze fastenings, entirely covers the left side of his body. Hektor does not often see what is underneath, but he knows that the *labarna's* left leg is withered and twisted, his arm scrunched up like the featherless wing of a runt chick, such as cats often snatch in the acropolis gardens when their mothers toss them from nests. His left eye hangs, unseeing, though his right darts about from inside a caldera of kohl, the cosmetic reserved for the richest in these lands, though Hektor refuses to wear the substance himself. His white hair is as fine as any mare's and laced with as many bells and rings. Lengthy gold earrings nip distended lobes, the flesh eroded with all the harvests spent chipping out new holes to adorn him with more finery. His right arm, especially muscular to compensate for the loss of ability in his left, claws a donkey-headed sceptre – the symbol of his *labarna*ship – cast in gold, unyielding, heavy. He is not smiling. He cannot smile. And he leaves the lowing for his various personnel who are always swarming, like worker ants about their queen. Beside him, as always, is his wife and Hektor's mother, the *tawananna*, Parta.

'You must not exert yourself,' Parta pleads, clinging to her husband's good arm.

Priam holds his sceptre up, closes his eyes. 'Wo-woman. Leave Us be.'

Parta *hmphs*, but withdraws obediently.

Silence.

The silence is awkward, so, 'My Sun, my mission to the Bones of the Dead God was a success and I have ensur—'

'Never mind that, never mind thát, m'boy! What's this nonsense your mother is so concerned about – this possessed man?'

Hektor looks up at his mother who, indeed, is the very fresco of worry. Her eyes widen; she nods slightly as though to say: *go on then!*

'My Sun, it was nothing more than a madman – a commoner – who broke into the temple and had too much to drink.' Hektor thinks of Washa in his cell; *I may still need him for Hapi.* 'And... he has since vanished.'

'Indeed. Y-You are responsible for the security of Our city – Our lands. Hmm? How could this happen?'

Parta leans forward. 'The commoners have rallied about this – this *miracle*, is what they call it.'

Priam's face is grim.

Hektor runs a hand through his hair. 'My Sun, I have spoken at length with Hawi and I am certain it will not happen again. As to the commoners, I assure you: this is a temporary excitement.'

Priam inclines his head slowly, seems to consider Hektor's words, then, 'Hmm. We are disappointed, but you have Our faith. If you are sure the commoners will cease their braying...'

'My Sun,' Parta interrupts. 'Do you understand how serious this is? A man claimed to be Appaliunas, the god Himself, and the common-ers are more than just *excited*, as the *tuhkanti* suggests. You *know* they have been uneasy for some time – think what this could—'

Priam moans, as though in pain, drops his sceptre. It lands with a clatter that echoes about the throne room. Hektor starts forward, but Parta holds up a hand, helping Priam pick it up, though he *tuts* and says he is fine. Hektor makes brief eye contact with his mother; her eyes hold a weight of such magnitude that he looks away. She pats down her husband's robes until he has managed to fend her off.

'So, do you see, my Sun?' Parta continues, not to be deterred. 'And

that *vile* Masturi visited him as well – he did that deliberately, know=
ing how it might inflame the situation and make you look.'

Priam holds his sceptre up again, eyes closed.

'If the *tuhkanti* says it is temporary We trust to him, as Our right
hand – or perhaps Our *left* hand.' He tries to chuckle, his one good
eye fixing upon the goat-skin rug concealing his shrivelled arm.

Hektor reddens, glances again at his mother.

'And as for Masturi…' Priam continues. 'Mmm. Predictable. Predictable. He would sell his sceptre if it meant undermining Us.'

Parta sighs. 'Yes, well Masturi's presence here was… unforeseen.'

Priam *tuts*, closes his eyes, shakes his head. 'Woman. We have told
you. It is recorded to tablet. The arrangement was to meet in a half-
moon. *Half-moon.*'

Parta raises her eyebrows, looks towards the ceiling. 'Yes, my Sun.'

Hektor reflects on what Masturi disclosed in the temple about the
timing of his arrival. *I should have anticipated Father's mistake.*

Hektor clears his throat. 'And… how were negotiations, my Sun?'

'Mmm?' Priam looks up at Hektor, narrows his eyes as though see-
ing his son for the first time that day. 'Ah! Just as surely shit smells, so
Masturi is Masturi. We know his designs. He knows *We* are the power
in this region. He will not give up on having you for a son-in-law' –
Priam leans forward, eyes narrow – 'But We need you, *tuhkanti*, and
We will not relinquish you.'

Hektor nods, *because the last thing I want is to be joined with that
man's blood.*

'Mmm. Masturi. Predictable. Predictable. We offered a daughter
though. One to his liking. He accepted her for an *esertu* wife. Kal-
something. He shall have her in due course. Throw a child a toy and
he will play. Keeps him out of trouble.'

Hektor thinks of the girl who called him 'big brother' outside the
throne room. Then he pictures Masturi. *What rot we men conceal…*
But he cannot shift a sense of foreboding. This is not the first time
Masturi's approaches have been refused, his offers snubbed. Though
Wilusa is the regional power, Masturi's Sehan territory is large, its
people many. *How much longer can this fragile brotherhood between he
and Father last? And though the commoners will surely settle, it would be*

*good to shore up their faith. And what better way to do that than with the-
atre?*

'My Sun, I have a proposal.'

'Mmm.' Priam stirs, his one good eye locking on to him afresh
from within its inky whirlpool. 'And what is that, m'boy?'

'The commoners have been momentarily dazzled by the "miracle",
as they see it. We need a miracle of our own.'

'I thought this was a "temporary excitement",' Parta remarks,
coldly.

'I am sure it is. But why not erase all memory of it with something
better.' Hektor braves a rare smile. 'In just a short time, it will be the
Parraspeszi festival, and we will make our pilgrimage to the Mountain. On this occasion, allow the commoners to follow the pilgrims;
let them come to the Mountain also, and there is where it will happen.'

Priam's jaw moves up and down, grazing on his own thoughts.
'Mmm. Well, m'boy?'

'You will speak to them as their *labarna* and as the representative
of the god on Earth. Remind them of the power invested in you. Let
them see that you are not the cruel figure they whisper about. Let
them see that you still… that you still function. Rumour is a demon.
Do this and you supplant any notion they have of what happened
in the lower town being a divine act. The commoners only saw this
madman from afar, on a balcony; let them be close to you though.'

Priam lowers his face, sighs. 'You ask much, m'boy. To *see* is to
know.'

'How many commoners see you at Gate, when you entertain their
appeals to the law?'

'Precious few!' Parta snaps. 'My Sun is not to be gawped at by the
likes of them.'

Hektor clears his throat. 'So again I say that Rumour is a demon: it
runs about too quick to be caught, biting at people's ears.'

Parta makes to retort, but Priam holds his sceptre high. 'Mmm.
Perhaps Rumour has prowled Our lands too long. Let them see then
Our sceptre. Let them hear Our decree. Until then, We leave you

to your duties. Ensure the defence of Wilusa. Keep the commoners docile.'

Hektor visits Hapi in the days that now pass, but duties take precedence and he is unable to spend as much time with his son as he might. Having a servant inform him of his progress provides some solace. Hapi remains dangerously unwell for the 36 hours following Hektor's meeting with his father, but slowly finds energy and appetite. On the fifth day, he is still bedridden, though manages, as Hektor hears, to hold a conversation with the many acropolis children who are sensitive to his condition. They apologise for the *tuhkanti*'s frequent failure to materialise at his bedside, explaining that Hektor is occupied with various issues in the lower town – something to do with pomegranates and apricots, they believe. Unfortunately for the *tuhkanti*, Hapi is fully informed about the 'miracle' of the priest who was possessed by Appaliunas and recalled to Heaven on the day of Hektor's return, and his own operation. The children, it seems, are all agreed that the coming of the sun god is a clear sign that Hapi is meant to recover, and go on to lead a life befitting the heroic protagonists of ages past.

The servants tell Hektor that Hapi is also subject to artistic accounts of the demon that was removed from his belly. At first, he is simply told how it spat and snarled as it was cut out. However, these accounts quickly develop into fables in which the demon is endowed with limbs, a tail and a constipated expression. Upon being removed from Hapi, it allegedly grew wings and flew to the pinnacle of Mount Parraspeszi where it now preys upon small, unfortunate animals living in the forest below. How this story reaches such an extreme, Hektor does not know, so he can only wonder at the imbecility of imagination. The truth of the matter is that the demon was taken to the sun god's temple, where it was stored in a room believed by the priests to be protected with spiritual power. Regrettably, a stray dog slipped into this room and carried the demon off to enjoy, no doubt, as a delicious snack. Though this theft was witnessed by several priests, it quickly falls into common belief that the demon took it upon itself to burrow through the ground back to the Under-Spring, into the arms of its mistress, Kaskalkur.

On the 10th day after Hapi's surgery, Hektor is busy dictating yields of wool to be recorded by a scribe on the tablet record when his boy actually *summons* him to his bed chambers. The room is brighter than the *tuhkanti* remembers, lacks the smell of rot, urine, faeces, vomit and, worse still, the opium and gods only know what herbs the priests and *hasawa* had seen fit to char.

'*Tati*! Where have you been? Didn't they tell you I was awake before now? It's been one, two, three, four, five... six, seven, eight, nine – no, eight whole days.'

'It's been 10 days, actually. I've been here as much as I could, though you slept, but my duties and the work of the region do not stop for— What are you doing? Hapi, I demand you get back into bed.'

Hapi is chuckling, prowling on the top of his bed, hands out-stretched like claws towards his father. 'Rrr,' he growls, intimidat-ingly.

'Hapi. This can't be good for you. You will not be childish. I for-bid it.' He points one finger out, driving home his point with all the authority he can muster.

'Yaaarrrghh!' Hapi yells, leaping like a mountain cat into the *tuhkanti*'s grip. 'I love you, and I missed you! I wanted your stories but you weren't here.'

Hektor's face burns, but he allows Hapi to tie his arms behind his head. 'Yes, and I am happy also that you are well again.' He is unsure what to do with his own hands and decides that a pat on the boy's back should suffice in demonstrating the depth of his feelings; he does not want to get carried away, after all.

'Oww. My belly hurts now.'

'Serves you right. Come on, back to bed.' He gently relinquishes Hapi, motions him beneath the one thin sheet. He folds his arms, lifts his chin a little. 'So, you wanted me for something?'

'I did. Kummi had her baby! When I was poorly, in my head, I was in the stables – that's where I feel safe. It's warm in there. And quiet. If anything ever happened to me, *that's* where I'd go... What's her baby like?'

Hektor clears his throat. 'You called me away from recording wool yields for this? Could it not have waited?'

'Waited?' Hapi sounds genuinely nonplussed.

Hektor shakes his head. 'I am the *tuhkanti*. You cannot just call me away from my duties.'

'Why not? Duties are boring.'

'No. Duties are fulfilling and stimulating.'

'What's "stimulating"?' Hapi chews through the word's constituent parts.

Hektor cannot help but growl. 'Never mind.' Yes, his duties have necessarily meant that he has seen much of Kummi, the mare and her foal having been safely returned, though the stable lad had been quite vocal as to how angry Xiuri the landowner had been. Something about making the *tuhkanti* pay compensation for time wasted. *But it was not time wasted, so he will get nothing.* In the last 10 days, Hektor has noticed Xiuri in Wilusa more often than he should be – once or twice in the lower town even. Though he imagines he should wonder more at this curiosity, he is preoccupied. 'The foal – not *baby* – is well, as is Kummi. And, yes, you can call the foal Aras if you must.' Hapi cheers; Hektor grimaces. 'You will see them both when you are better.'

'But I want to see them now.'

'No. You have endured a lot and are lucky not to be dead.'

'If I was dead I'd haunt you and throw cups at you whenever you were trying to get to sleep.'

'I'm glad you're not dead then.'

A moment of silence. Outside, the wind teases trees.

'... Everyone says what happened to me. About the demon. What was the demon like, *tati*? Tell me.'

Hektor sighs once more. *No point trying to get out of this one. He is too bloody-minded.* 'Dek. I suppose – now that I'm here.' He sits down in the chair beside Hapi's toys and looks up at the horse imagery on the ceiling. 'Well, the demon had horns and a... a tortoise beak... and a...' This is not like the tales of heroes that Hapi enjoys; they are easy to recite because he has learned them so well. *What am I meant to say?* 'And feathers.'

'Feathers? No, no, no. It had wings and a tail and teeth that did this' – he gnashes his teeth, quite viciously – 'and then it flew away. You've got it all wrong, *tati*.'

'How would you know? You weren't conscious when it was removed. You are the one who is wrong!'

'No, I'm not!'

'Yes, you are!'

'Really? So what did happen then? Kuressar' – he waves his cloth-cat at Hektor – 'told me that you brought a man here who saved me – a *magic* man.'

The *tuhkanti*'s extremities ice over. *Marvellous. He cannot have been sufficiently drugged to not notice. Composure, Hektor, composure.* True to his word, Hektor had released Washa once it was apparent his son would survive. 'You will leave this city and make a life for yourself elsewhere. I don't want to ever see your face again,' he had commanded. To appease the sun god, Appaliunas, he had, however, been forced to execute a substitute prisoner to restore the balance of the universe, as is customary. After all, Washa had upset the gods on a cosmological scale with his actions in the temple, and They would surely demand blood in recompense. At the end, he had held a degree of respect for Washa; the man was a skilled healer, yet an ignorant commoner, nonetheless – a contradiction with which the *tuhkanti* had struggled to come to terms.

'Another story, hmm?' His voice catches and becomes that of an 11-year-old boy until he coughs. *Idiot, Hektor, idiot. Now he's looking at me suspiciously.* 'What does it matter how you were saved? You were saved.'

Hapi seems to accept this, but... 'Can I have a real story? *Please*.'

Hektor reflects on the last time he told a story. *Hmm, he would be expecting the next instalment of my oral history*, but Hektor had not been enjoying any success with his poetry. *It is difficult maintaining the poetic voice for Hapi when the boy asks the who/what/why/when of everything I put into verse*, which forces the *tuhkanti* to go off on a dry, prosaic tangent, quite out of keeping with the oral tradition. Strangely, he enjoys these tangents, yet they are not customary and so he must affect disdain.

'Wilusa is a city, Hapi,' he begins, deciding to combat all this fantasy by giving the boy insight into his own approach to the uniform facts and measurable angles of life, 'and therefore cannot be conflated with the airy fantasies of children and the imaginative. Its walls are as thick as a man is long, built of solid granite blocks shunted together through workers' sweat and an engineer's mathematics. They were not willed into place by gods, nor were they stacked by one-eyed giants. The watchtowers are not painted with molten gold; they are daubed with oils which the sun catches for the eyes of domestic sailors farming sardines, mullet and bream off the coast. The gates are not impenetrable; Wilusa has fallen to foreign opportunists and traitorous neighbours. And I'm afraid the tree by the spring does not have a face and is certainly not celestial; the roots have bulged and gnarled with life to give the appearance of an old man – and you and the other children must stop throwing taunts at it and running away. You think I don't notice?

'Wilusa is a city like any other. Its people are real; they are not the static motifs of pots and frescoes. We trade in horses and our tablet records will attest that gold, jewels and iron – yes, even iron – are not overflowing from our treasuries. I want my account of our home to be true to the people who live here and the lives they lead, Hapi; I don't want some imbecile to take up my stories several hundred years from now in exactly this same room, or its future equivalent, and suggest that this was a world of monsters and heroes and magic. That wouldn't be true and it would sever future generations from the stories our voices will cease to tell. When I am gone, Hapi, you will recount these stories too and you must not let the fantastical distort the faces that will fade as your own limbs weary and your mind clouds.'

Hapi closes his mouth, which had fallen open, and looks up at the ceiling, hands massaging his cloth-cat. Of course, the boy is enchanted with the thought that one-eyed monsters might have built the town's walls, or that secretly, somewhere, a hall full of the world's treasures weeps for the injustice of not being able to make music with light for the enjoyment of a child's eyes.

The trick to oral storytelling is repetition and rhythm, two concepts from which Hektor derives great pleasure, even transferring their satisfying comfort – *quite appropriately, I might add* – to the rigours of his political office and daily life. The *well-crabbed* and *seal-songed shores, coasts* or *tides* of his verse find their equivalent in the way he lays his clothes in exactly the same spot in precisely the same order – tunic; then kilt; then belt; then, finally, sandals (upside down to protect the aforementioned items from dirt) – whenever he undresses. Or the way in which he will line the stable lads up in height order when discussing horse-preening records, so as to effect a human graph demonstrating growth in the Wilusan people. It is a matter only of small consequence that the tallest stable lad is of Sehan origin.

The only difficulty with repetition, he finds, is trying to decide upon something firm to remember. It is often a familiar flow of words, an epithet of significance, or a long-favoured recipe of description that comes to mind with the least cajoling. Right now, he is, *well, let's say 'desperate'* to find the right way of describing Wilusa – a way for it to sink into memory, to lock into his metre with the mere familiarity of its presence. *Big-walled, high-walled, well-walled Wilusa* – he cannot decide. Others are easy. *Highly stacked tablet shelves, always-fretting commoners* or *forever-questioning Hapi.* But Wilusa itself deserves an epithet of magnitude and he cannot decide upon a fit decoration for the name.

'Where's the *hasawa*? I thought she'd come to see me…'

Hektor snaps back to the moment.

The *hasawa*, yes. The afternoon after he met with his father, Hektor managed to add poison to the *hasawa*'s herbal drink and she became violently ill. He made the suggestion to the acropolis healer-priests that the demon must have jumped from Hapi's body to hers and was liable to jump again once it had sucked the old crone dry. This, naturally, alarmed the healer-priests, as the threat of a demon that could leap, on a whim, between bodies was not to be understated. Consequently, they arranged for the *hasawa* to be transported out of Wilusa to a small community for the sick, the crippled and the mad that lay a two-day ride east of Mount Parraspeszi.

'I'm afraid the *hasawa* fell ill. Miserable, I know. And she had to be taken to a special place to get better again. I'm sure she's very happy there.'

'Oh, when will she be back?'

'I don't know, Hapi. Terrible as it is, she may not survive and then we would never have the enjoyment of seeing her warm, wrinkled face again. Still, that's life. Now, if that is all, I have to return to work.'

He kisses Hapi on the head and makes to leave.

'*Tati?*' the boy says.

'Yes?'

'You wouldn't let anything happen to me, would you?'

Hektor manages a smile, just. 'My only interest is in keeping us safe, well and fed, here in the acropolis. Nothing bad is going to happen to us. I promise.'

Tablet Five

'To the left, Hapi. Yes. Yes. No, wait. There's a big stone. No, I said "stone". To the right. Good. Now, straight on. I have your shoulders. Don't worry.'

Hektor shuffles the boy down the dirt-track hill, steering him out of the path of rocks, shrubs and tree roots alike. The blindfold is tight around his eyes, *I made sure of that.*

'Where are we going, *tati?*'

'You'll see soon enough. A surprise is not a surprise if I tell you what it is.'

It has been a moon since Hapi's surgery and the boy has been regaining his strength, pacing up and down the acropolis corridors, then hobbling about in the gardens and, finally, intruding upon the *tuhkanti* when he is working in his own private quarters. He would not admit it, but he has enjoyed making time, duties permitting, to recite some of Hapi's favourite stories to him in the evening, and they have dined together more than once.

Every now and then Washa's face appears in his mind's eye, usually at night, when it is quiet and Hektor is lying there looking up at the ceiling. He pictures the physician somewhere out there, his presence pushing the frontiers of this reality to break back in upon the *tuhkanti*'s world. And then there is the continued unrest in the lower town. *Dwelling on it will not undo the problems. These people are not to be understood, only controlled – their passions funnelled to work. Enjoy this day with Hapi, you don't get many.*

'This isn't another visit to the tablet-house, is it? That was really boring before.'

'No. Very different.'

Behind a clump of olives and cedars: the rickety wooden scatter of stables. In a central courtyard, stable-hands patter about with brushes, saddles, hay impaled on pitchforks and pails of water. The occasional horse is also led away, *clip, clop, clep,* to one of the paddocks where they routinely enjoy their exercise. Further off, other stable-hands work their way up from the gate leading into the lower town, pulling shiny stallions and foamy mares, having enjoyed lengthier journeys across the plains beyond the city borders. The air is a mess of chatter and whinnies, so Hektor has to cough in time with every sound, to try and hide their destination.

'Are you alright, *tati*? You haven't got a demon have you?'

'No. No. Just some dust in my throat.'

Hektor can see them now: Kummi and Aras, her foal. One of the stable-hands is holding on to their reins, face downcast. *He could try cheering up.* Kummi has lost her fat belly, and her brown coat is winning back its sheen. Aras's legs, as with all foals' legs, are almost the length of its mother's, so it looks as though it stands on stilts. But it is balanced and seems to possess that same arrogant expression that, inexplicably, Kummi often wears.

He draws Hapi to a halt a man's length from the horses.

'We're here.'

'Can I take my blindfold off?'

'No. Hold out your hand.'

'Why?'

'Just do it. I'm not going to cut it off. You aren't a thief, are you?'

'No.'

'Good. Hand out then.'

Hapi stretches out his right hand, warily.

'Good. Now, move forward. Good. Keep going. Keep going.'

Hapi chuckles; the *tuhkanti* has always thought he has a very odd laugh, *but then again, Hapi is an odd child.* He collects feathers, empty snail shells, rocks he thinks look like faces; picks his nose, keeps the dried snot in a line by order of size on a table leg in his bed chamber; sleeps with eyes half open; talks to Kuressar the cloth-cat about how he shall wage war on ants when he is big because they are an enemy to all peoples.

'Halt!'

Hapi stops. His hand trembles and a big, black nose lifts up, snorting hot, damp air over his fingers.

'Eurgh!' Hapi yelps, drawing his hand back. 'What is *that*?'

'Hand up. Trust me.'

A pause, then: '... *Dek*. I trust you.'

Hapi lifts his hand. Aras's nose meets his fingers again. To the foal's right, Kummi whinnies – perhaps with a hint of warning.

'It's the foal, isn't it? It's Aras!'

Hektor says nothing, but enjoys the various emotions tidal over his son's face.

Hapi's hand stretches out a little further, more eager this time, and runs with the bristly delve of the foal's cheeks. Up his hand goes, sweeping across the bony jut of forehead, gently clasping on to a single malleable ear. Hapi strokes, scratches – the foal tilting its head, eyes half-closing and then opening again.

'He likes that. Like his mother. You can take your blindfold off now.'

Hapi removes his blindfold and adds his other hand to the manic stroking to which he subjects the foal.

'When can I ride him?'

'Not for a while yet. He is too small. But he is all yours, Hapi. One day he will also be a warhorse and if he is a proud animal he will be a breeding horse too. He will be proud when he does this with his head.' Hektor lifts his head up and away with a superior look in his eyes by way of demonstration.

Hapi looks delighted. 'All mine?'

Hektor nods. 'Aras will be crucial to your training. We Wilusans are horse breeders and breakers – it is a reputation that stretches from Mykenai in the west to Hattusa in the east – and it is a tradition you must uphold.'

Hapi continues stroking Aras, quietly.

Oh, Hapi, you cannot stay a boy forever.

'Hapi, do you notice anything about Aras's legs, compared to Kummi's?'

Hapi tilts his head to get a good look at the foal's legs and then looks up at Kummi's. He looks back and forth several times, shakes his head.

'They are nearly the same length, yet Kummi is much older than her foal, obviously. Why do you think that is?'

'I don't know.' Hapi continues stroking Aras, runs his hands through the animal's willowy mane.

'A foal faces many dangers when it's born. Mountain cats. Bears. Wolves. They are weak, vulnerable – easy targets. The young, the old, the sick and the weak always are. But a foal needs legs to run, to flee any predators, and so it's born with strong, long legs.' The *tuhkanti* steps forward, trails a hand along the foal's back. 'The stable-hands tell me that Aras tried to canter inside the stables the day after its birth. Even young, he has to be fully prepared for the very worst. His life is uncertain and he lives in a dangerous world, even if he does not know it... But he has Kummi, at least, for now. Though that will change as he grows.'

He slaps a hand on the animal's rump and watches Hapi, the boy's expression lost in Aras's eye, a clot of primal mystery for him, as yet.

Further off, in a square, a small complement of guards, beige kilts catching in the breeze always present on the city's bluff, stalk purpose-fully towards the lower town. Hapi notices too.

'Where are they going?'

Hektor's eyes follow them until they are at the huge wood-and-bronze gate.

'Disturbances in the lower town. Again. Nothing you need worry about.'

'Sometimes Kaluti talks about that.'

Kaluti: as one of the *naptartus*' daughters, she is free to come and go as she pleases. *And Father has still shown no sign of preparing her for sending to Masturi.*

Naptartu: concubine of the *labarna*, of which there are many – not that Priam can do much with them these days. The harem is not too far from Hektor's and Hapi's quarters; *they make a lot of noise and it's not once I've yelled at them to shut up in the middle of the night.*

The *labarna* has quite a collection of wives and breeding women, Hektor notes. There are a number of *esertu* wives – secondary to the *tawananna*, Parta. *And these wives have always been ornaments, offerings to add honey to tablet-recorded dealings and pacts made with other* labarnas *and lords within the wider Aegean region.* Priam has a small collection – testament to the alliances he has formed over the years. The *naptar-*

tus though are greater in number and live solely to produce children; they often die in childbirth and are replaced efficiently, lords all over this and neighbouring regions queuing up to offer sisters, daughters, cousins – *and once an out-of-favour wife, as I recall* – in the hope of winning some small semblance of favour.

'Do you know what I think, *tati*?'

'No.'

'I think everyone in the lower town doesn't think Broken Grand-dad is the sun god's deputy anymore. They think it's the man who came to the temple.'

Hektor glances up, briefly catches the stable-hand's eyes flickering away, as though feigning disinterest.

'Go,' he commands. 'Take the horses.'

The stable-hand *hmphs*, draws the animals away with a few clicks and gentle tugs on their reins. As soon as he is out of earshot, the *tuhkanti* walks off, Hapi's feet scuffling behind in his attempt to keep up.

'Firstly, what have I told you about calling him "Broken Grand-dad" in public? There are disturbances in the lower town right now. But disturbances pass and… and what you say is true. But the people are wrong to think the *labarna* does not have the favour of the sun god.'

'Why are all the people saying that he doesn't then?'

'A lot of people are angry. The *labarna* has a lot of demands placed upon him that the people do not know of.'

'Memai told me that he heard his dad say that Father was "squeez-ing the fuck out of him". Is that what you mean?'

'Hapi! Mind your tongue! Hmm. Did he really say that?'

'Yes. Looks like we have a problem, *tati*.'

Hektor smiles, despite himself. It amuses him when the boy tries to add a decade to his voice, *as I have been told precocious children tend to do.*

'Maybe, Hapi. Maybe. All you need to know is that the *labarna* does stand for all the sun god is: fair judgement, wisdom, justice—'

'And if he ever didn't stand for that then you could just get rid of him and send him to live in a village somewhere, and things would be okay again and Memai's dad could stop being so upset.'

'... Yes, Hapi. Enough of all that for now. Would you like to watch the stable-hands run a canter with the horses for a b—'

He breaks off as a yell leaps up from, perhaps, down by the gate – *hard to tell exactly where it comes from* – and waits a moment, hushing Hapi, hearing the yell again, followed this time by laughter. Along the path leading up from the lower town, two guards drag a ragged fidget of a man, bloody, bound, tossing his weedy torso about like a speared worm.

'You know it! All you shinies,' he growls. 'Your time is coming. Appaliunas Himself watches over His people. The half-*labarna* will be judged— Ooh!'

A guard removes his fist from the side of the prisoner and tells him to shut up.

'Shut up? Shut up? No. You shinies don't know what's coming. Do what you want with me – I am Appaliunas's!'

Hektor keeps a hand on Hapi's shoulder as the man is led out of sight and then out of hearing. Looking down at him... *He may only be a matter of feet from the man, but he is still ten years away.* This is only going to get worse. He has heard of the shrines that have sprung up in the lower town, populated with pomegranates and apricots, being knocked down by guards at his father's command. And guards being attacked for their trouble. *Washa, in the temple, he did something to that crowd – such a brazen act, the kind that brews dissent, disorder, petulance in a people. That's all it takes: one action, to tilt the scales.*

He kneels in front of Hapi and takes the boy's hands.

'Hapi, we are taught there is a natural order to things, and people like *that*' – he flings an accusatory finger into the distance – 'contest that natural order; it isn't allowed and it cannot go without punishment. At the top are the gods, then there are the people in the acropolis – the "shinies" as he called us – and at the bottom are the people in the lower town, the commoners. This is the way of things. Always a separation. When *they* die – the commoners – do you know what happens to them?'

Hapi lowers his head, as though he has committed some misdeed. 'No.'

'They travel to the Under-Spring through the cave in the lower town – you know the one. They come to a grey place, where no one recognises each other. Fathers and sons. Brothers and sisters. Friend and foe. And they toil there, Hapi, just as they did in life, putting their backs into tilling ash, planting rotten bulbs and grazing silent cattle. They are shades, shadows of their former selves, because their souls are not so beloved of the gods and they persist until they fade from all memory, until even the gods cannot recall them.'

'A–and what about us?' Hapi's voice is equal parts fear, wonder.

'We? We are the "deserving". When the *laharna* leaves us, say, he does not die – he becomes a god and joins Appaliunas forever. And the deserving – the deserving come to a meadow that stretches beyond sight, where grass does not die and we no longer feel pain, or upset or fear. We come to meet our great-grandfathers, our blood becomes nectar and we each tend horses that are the offspring of the sun god's seed. Only demons can drag *us* down into the Under-Spring. The sun god loves the deserving – we are His children. To suggest otherwise is blasphemy.'

Hapi knots his brow, clearly thinking over what he has been told. 'But the commoners believe the sun god cares about them. They really believe it.'

This conversation is becoming uncomfortable for Hektor. 'Hope can mock any of us. And their hope is desperate.'

'I feel bad for them,' Hapi sighs, dramatically. 'I do.'

'Why?'

'Because we have meadows to live in and horses to love and old men to talk to when we die, but they'll only be shadows. All the farming and trading and dirt is everything for them. If they can't smile now, they never will. And they recognise each other, even if the gods don't. I think that's why they really want to believe this stuff about the sun god. It's because their lives are shiny to them, even if we don't think so. Am I right, *tati*?'

Hektor smiles, roughs Hapi's hair, tries to put all thought of desperate commoners aside. And *Washa*.

'Come on, I promised you could watch the horses canter.'

'Actually, can I go and play with my friends instead?' Hapi points up to where a ramp leads into the acropolis grounds – three children who Hektor vaguely recognises are skipping down the hill, leading… Yes, it is Kaluti.

The *tuhkanti* smothers his disappointment with a grim smile. '… Yes, okay… If you want.'

Hapi grins and bounds off, not quite at full speed again, but he is recovering well.

The *tuhkanti* looks around, aware of the fact that he is alone, and decides that he had better go and cancel the surprise he had planned for Hapi in the horse paddock.

But this is one precious afternoon beyond duties, where he has time to himself, to attend to the Hektor that exists beside the *tuhkanti*. But there is nothing; in his frustration he tries to envisage something more and all that returns is a hole in which his life is surely being consumed. He goes to his quarters and lies back on his bed against the wall. His breath comes heavy and he burrows his forehead into a blanket, telling himself to get a grip.

And then the building starts to shake…

Tablet Six

... But the tremor passes.

A dash of dust falls from the ceiling. One urn topples, smashes. Outside: several screams, tense yelling. *The Earth giant, Ubelleris, stirs. Hapi, where is Hapi?*

Hektor jumps up, throws himself through the door, charges down the acropolis corridor, buffeting the shoulders of both servants and men of importance as he goes. He comes to a large, pillared room which leads out to one of the exits. And there he is: Hapi, stamping in, the sunlight dropping from him as he goes.

'*Tati*! What was that?'

He slams right into Hektor, who grabs him by the shoulders. 'Are you okay? Not hurt?'

'No, no. I was with my friends. Some pithoi fell off a roof and we got scared. What is it?'

The *tuhkanti* exhales deeply, allows himself to accept that the danger has passed. 'Every once in a while, the giant beneath our feet, Ubelleris, moves in His sleep and shakes us all, because He is so big.'

'I remember Ubelleris – you mentioned Him in a story once.'

'Quite right. Usually, it is that a god is displeased with us and prods Ubelleris, making him fidget in discomfort.'

Hapi's face is pale. 'Have we made a god angry?'

The *tuhkanti* tilts his head from one side to the other. 'That is for... the *labarna* to divine.' Hektor looks up. 'Speaking of which...'

From another entrance a man Hektor recognises to be one of his father's regular messengers comes in.

'*Tuhkanti*, my Sun demands your presence in the throne room.'

What, now?

The throne room has suffered only a little damage, fissures having opened several frescoes, including the face of a deity who now appears to be cackling quite insidiously. Priam is on his throne, an array of people around him – all of whom seem to be in quite a state of disarray.

'Leave off Us, woman!' the *labarna* slurs, waving his good hand at the *tawananna*, Parta, who stands next to him.

'Be still and let me fix your robes,' she growls back, never a woman to cower before her husband.

'Damn the robes, woman! There are more pressing—'

'Pressing matters, yes. But it will not do for the court to see you in such a state. Plus, it's insulting to talk with the god like that. Would you have a beggar supplicate before you in the acropolis? No, of course not! Ah, look who's here.'

'Mmm? Ah! *Tuhkanti*, W-We...'

'You sent for me, my Sun,' Hektor says, stepping forward with Hapi beside him.

'Yes, We know that! Mmm, not good, this, this movement. Not good. You know what it means?'

'No, my Sun.' *I can guess.*

'Bad omen! Yes. The sun god, He disturbs Ubelleris, makes him shiver. To remind us He is watching, that He is *irked*. Yes. You know what that means.'

Hektor grimaces. He knows very well what *that* means. Such events as these: rumblings from beneath their feet, shooting fire across the sky, thunder, the churning of the sea – they are testimony to the gods' displeasure. And all it takes is one individual to rouse a god, to bring calamity down on his community. The *tuhkanti* swallows hard, thinks back to Washa... letting him free. *But I bought the life of my son, a transaction between myself and Kaskalkur.*

'Yes... Father, I—'

'Father?' Parta shrieks. Her voice: an angered goose when she loses her temper. 'Did you just call my Sun "*Father*", in his presence?'

'I-I apologise. I don't know what came over me.' *Idiot, Hektor – why did you do that?* The dignitaries, officials and even servants around the throne look awkwardly, disapprovingly at him.

'My Sun is our one link with Heaven, the deputy of Appaliunas Himself. And you want to *lower* him by reminding us all of his earthly ties? Words have power, boy. No wonder the ground trembles – with indiscretion like that on our tongues.' Tears roll out across the kohl constricting her eyes.

Hektor holds his tongue. He has always considered his mother obsessive and cloying when around his father. She has a dramatic personality, a horrible temper and a neediness for which he has little time. Sometimes he can remember those early years, those long, arduous lessons with his mother, when he shuts his eyes. 'You are my blood and I will *not* have my blood disappoint my Sun. Now, pick up the tablet again and read it. If you get it wrong you will be hit again. Do I make myself clear?' *At least Uru was a reprieve from Mother's scolds…*

'It will not happen again.'

Parta raises her head, glares down at him.

'*Tuhkanti*. We have spoken with the god, in peace, alone. And He is angered by this… this commotion within the lower town. Yes, yes. *Tuhkanti*, one of your primary duties is to ensure, yes, ensure this does *not* happen.' He turns to his wife. 'Parta, Parta. Tell him the latest trans… transgression. Yes, oh dear, oh dear.'

'Certainly, my Sun.' Parta nods wildly, fresh tears slipping out of her eyes. She turns to her left. 'Come forward. Come forward. Let my boy see you.'

From the small crowd of dignitaries, an aged ball of a man scuffs forward, eyes red with… *yes, with crying*. Parta beckons him into her arm, she leans her face towards him as one might with a child.

Hektor presses Hapi back as the child peers forward.

'Now, my boy, you look at this man. Look at him. Do you know what the commoners did to him? His two daughters were riding back to the upper town. A group of men – of *commoners* – confronted them, said – said *something* to the servants who were meant to be defending the girls, all except one loyal man, who they killed. They beat the girls, all took their turn at r— at soiling them and then they— They cu— removed the girls' heads and dumped the bodies at the south-west gate.

'What this poor man has suffered' – she indicates the man next to her, who is crying afresh, one hand shading his eyes – 'no parent should suffer. Imagine if something happened to your little bastard there.'

Hektor tenses. He has never liked Hapi being referred to as a bastard, though, indeed, *that is what he is in their eyes.*

Out of the silence, Priam clears his throat. 'You see, *tuhkanti?* There's a poison, a demonic influence in the lower town. It needs cutting out from the inside. If you don't do anything then the tremors will come again – We've been warned. That's why We command you to go into the lower town, disguised, and smoke out this evil. You are an accomplished fighter and We trust you to look after yourself.' He splutters into a fit of coughing.

Parta's arms swim back to embrace her husband. She cocks her head to look at her son once more. 'You heard my Sun.' Tears are, again, streaming down her face, washing her makeup away in a black current. 'We must learn of the rotten heart down *there.* And we must make an example of... of whoever it is, whoever they are. Before the sun god shows any more displeasure.'

The *tuhkanti* makes to leave.

'Oh, and one other thing, boy,' his mother says. He turns back to her. 'Your face, your head – recognisable. You will have to change it.'

The *tuhkanti* nods stiffly, takes Hapi's hand as the two of them walk off, his teeth working from side to side, his humiliation complete. He can feel their eyes on his back and he breathes deeply once he is outside.

'*Tati,* why does Grandma think there's someone in the lower town doing all this? I thought they just want their lives to be shiny. And what's "making an example"?'

Hektor does not reply. He is too busy trying to work out how one makes an example of an entire population.

His face is orange-brown and warped in the honeycomb reflection of the bronze dish. He tilts his head, looks at the beard he has maintained for all his adult life. The razor in his hand feels cool, potent. But the beard has to go. He cuts into it, watches in the bronze as clumps of it come away, feels the crisp judder of blade over skin. He will not let someone else do this, will not go to one of the acropolis's barbers.

If I'm to be brutalised in this way, if the necessity is there, I will not be seen. Besides: better that no one familiar sees his new face if this task is to work. There is also his own safety to consider. The skin under his beard is lighter than the soil-brown skin on the rest of his face. It is also softer, less victim to the high sun of summer or the shock of snow in winter. At his feet, the hair is a mess, and soon it has all been transferred from his face to the floor. *But I can't stop here.* His fingers run through the twisted threads clinging close to his shoulders. He scratches at the occasional tickle from a louse and is thankful, in the least, that he is unlikely to be clawing at his head so much from now on.

When he looks into his reflection, into his eyes, he asks if he sees what everyone else sees. Or if he has some private view of himself that the public cannot understand – he hopes so. All his life has been defined by duty. Duty to the *labarna*. Duty to the *tawananna*. Duty to the gods (most important, he is told). Duty to the acropolis. Duty to administration. Duty to the officials of the upper town. Duty to the upper town itself. Duty to... Duty to the lower town, yes, that as well. And, of course, duty to Hapi; duty in fatherhood – the most acute, persistent and demanding of duties. *Funny: I would rather face an army of people like Xturi the landowner than tackle one issue that Hapi might have.*

Schwip, schwip, goes the razor through his hair.

But once he has tackled all of that duty, exhausted his bones in travelling to and from rural communities, exhausted his mind in legal technicalities with administrators, exhausted his emotion in frightful confrontations with the *labarna* and the gods, what is left? He feels like a rock that is being washed upon relentlessly by a rampaging river, cut and refined to a perfect uniform smoothness, blending in with a bed of similar stones. *Ura always tells me I work too hard, that life is only worth living if you are enjoying yourself.* But perhaps behind such carefree words there is something quite serious and relevant that he has missed all these years. In the passing of just a few more moons he will reach his twenty-fourth year. And when his father dies – *no, becomes a god* – he will take his place as *labarna*. And this was never his choice, never what he had fashioned for himself; it was a fate chained to him from the moment of his conception, a mechanical absolute to which he has no option but to adhere and from which the only escape can be death.

Schwip, schwip, goes the razor through his hair one more time.

He looks again into his reflection, now at the close-cropped file of stubble running over his skull. He is surprised at the difference, confident that no one in the lower town who might have recognised him before will do so now. He grunts, satisfied.

Outside, the night is its usual inky indulgence of cicada song, starlight, rustling leaves. He throws on the trader's clothes in which he has decided to disguise himself and hisses out the flames in their sconces with spit-moistened fingers. Next door, Hapi is asleep, the boy's mouth a solid line of concentrated repose. He kisses Hapi once on the temple, slips out of the door.

By day, Wilusa's lower town operates through the complicated channels of marketplace trade, but by night it understands only one simple equation: a man's itching groin, trembling hands and/or fluxing pupils translates into a haul of silver for every merchant competent enough to manipulate his customers.

The sights of a Wilusan night are enough to delight the most avaricious of opium dealers, and horrify the severest of the purity goddess Nash's servants. Hektor has always been fascinated on a masochistic level with the lower town: here he finds the bawling of intoxicated men; epic conflicts between stray dogs for fly-licked chunks of meat; cats chanting poetry, simmering for love; and lung-rattling babies plundering the night for its natural peace. So far, he is unregistered – *not that I should be recognised, for I am no more than a trader, with which the town is replete.*

Further on, into the shadowed streets, Hektor discovers: girls, twelve-year-olds, strolling in twos or threes, their miniature breasts slipping over cheap bodices, anticipating sales of intimacy to whichever drunk stumbles upon them first; balding men with grating voices selling skewered chunks of hissing meat, fresh from outdoor grills, to passing strangers who, having spent the evening drinking and smoking, have an overwhelming urge to feed; men holding large trays, upon which are scores of luck charms, poorly devised items of thin metal with – so the traders promise – the miraculous ability to protect the bearer from muggers, hangovers and the inevitable verbal assault of a wife angered by her husband's late-night drinking sessions. In the grinning ooze of drunkenness, the *tuhkanti* has found, a man's superstition certainly can be manipulated with ease and, inevitably, these charms are always popular. But in the sobriety of daylight, a man can appreciate the artfulness of these vendors, and the tasteless nature of their product. So it is that one can witness many a horse, cat and dog emblem, all of tin, handed down by fathers with appalling headaches to children, who use them as a form of juvenile currency, if only one looks hard enough.

Hektor traces these nomads of the night to a particularly murky area of the lower town where taverns and *arzanas* are located. *Arzana*: entertainment house, brothel. It was deemed prudent years before, he has heard Father mention, for such places to be grouped together, away from housing, as though the lives of domesticity and ribaldry were siblings that could be excluded from one another. Officially, these areas are designated, euphemistically, as the 'Entertainment Quarters', but colloquially they are referred to as 'Shamhat Burrows', after the famous prostitute of the Gilgamesh epic. *A part of the Gilgamesh story I am always uncomfortable reciting for Hapi.* It seems to Hektor that the precaution of segregating the Shamhat Burrows is ineffective for the most part, as there naturally comes a point in the night when men commence a wayward pilgrimage back to their modest mud-brick homes, bringing chaos for companionship. From the heights of the upper town the view of the lower is comprehensive and, come sunrise, the streets are visibly speckled with shards of clay pots, forgotten items of clothing and estuaries of urine. More than once, the *tuhkanti* has seen women tutting, shaking heads at the occasional man who, having failed in his mission to make it home, has nested himself within linen, which he has removed from one of the many clotheslines webbing the streets.

As he has walked, he has noticed a wealth of shrines decorated with pomegranates and apricots. In his mind, Hektor speculates what the effect might be of sending guards in afresh to simply tear the shrines down. *It didn't work for Father, so probably not the best idea...*

After walking about for a few hours, Hektor comes to a stop at a crossroads, sighing and wondering how on earth he is to fulfil the *labarna*'s command. *What am I to do? Find a scapegoat?*

That is when he sees *him*.

Walking blithely along is Washa. There is no mistaking that distinctive moustache, that slouched, awkward movement as he sways down a major thoroughfare. Hektor thinks to run over and grab the man, arrest him, kill him, *something*. After all, he did command Washa to leave Wilusa upon pain of death. But he holds himself back, curiosity getting the better of him, *and besides – it would not be the subtlest way of giving myself away to the commoners*. Why is he still here? What is he up to? Perhaps he is getting himself into a drunken stupor each night, leaping into bed with every harlot within a two-mile radius. Or perhaps he is looking to set up... What was it? His experimental physician's surgery. Perhaps he is not doing any of these things. The *tuhkanti* throws a hood over his head, slumps his face, tracks Washa from a distance.

Before long, Washa comes to an *arzana* with a crude name painted above the large doors. He enters, the doors releasing a wave of noise as he does so. Hektor stands across the road, mule and carts passing by, drunks, prostitutes, widows selling spells; after a few minutes, he follows Washa in.

The *arzana* is dimly lit, the smell of opium invading his nostrils, cries and laughter scolding his ears. Here and there, sconce-light throws impressions of reds and browns this way and that. In a central room: men – drinks in hand – sat at tables or standing, indulging in conversation, laughter, the occasional fight. Girls walk about delivering drinks and fresh opium, naked save for jewellery and heavy makeup. The *arzana* is cramp personified, the stink of sweat and musk suggesting intimacy beyond the casual.

At a table on the far side of the room, Washa is sat. With Ura. Ura? *They are familiar with each other? And why is Ura here? My gods, she doesn't work here, does she? No one needs to see that. No, wait! Perhaps this is the* arzana *Ura owns – she mentioned it once or twice.* He slips through the girls, telling several, 'No, I'm alright for that,' and squeezes into a seat with his back to Washa and Ura. It is particularly dark in this corner and he tells a passing girl to fetch him a drink.

'I was beginning to think I wouldn't find you,' comes Washa's voice, the inflection of something foreign or simply wrong still present.

'I was hearing through various contacts you were asking after me. Some of us have to do the work though, eh?' One of the nude serving girls addresses Ura as 'Madame', whispers something to her, receives a response Hektor cannot hear, then makes off again. 'What's wrong? You look like an eel's trying to wriggle up your arse or something. You should be happy to see me. It's not every day a man is getting to treat himself to looking at *this* body, eh?'

The *tuhkanti* risks a glance over his shoulder – Washa seems to force a smile.

'But seriously, I'm happy to see you; it settles my heart to know you're alive, and well, I hope. Keeping out of trouble too...'

'Trouble is the last thing I want. I would like to say I have buried the past...'

'I don't suppose anything like *that* could ever be truly buried. I am remembering you at the height of your fame: Washa, the extraordinary physician! Sought after by everyone in the lower town. No wonder you were making enemies, eh? No wonder those guards were ordered to destroying your surgery.'

'But *I* burned it down. Finished the job completely. Could have killed people. I carry this up *here*.' Washa furiously taps his head.

Ura tilts her head. 'The farmer builds the paddock to contain the animal; we all must learn to do this with the animals in our heads as well, eh?'

'A year since I last saw you… All this time I just couldn't.'

'And only then it was brief, eh? I hear you are travelling about.'

No response from Washa.

'The man who always moves never sees things clearly, only catching glimpses as he rushes by. Friend of mine said that to me once. Funny really, as he's always rushing about himself.'

I said that! the *tuhkanti* thinks, smiling to himself before regaining his composure.

A stranger wishes Ura well, disappears.

'Seems like you're still just as respected as ever,' Washa finally says, the shift of tone in his voice suggesting he wishes to change the subject. 'I've heard your name mentioned more than once.'

'Yes. Ever since I was being expelled from the acropolis I have enjoyed common kindness. The lower town is home.'

Hektor recalls when Ura was told to leave and never return. She had been caught smuggling leftovers from acropolis meals down to the homeless in the lower town. *Gods, I even helped her on some occasions. I could only have been Hapi's age… She was likely ejected from her role as nanny because she involved me in her missions.*

'"Home" has always been the place that didn't kick me out for the night.' Hektor hears Washa swig his wine. 'And now I need to find somewhere that doesn't kick me out. I would buy you a drink, if I had any silver.'

Ura smiles. 'So why have you returned to Wilusa, finally?'

'My funds were near exhausted, and I can only steal so much before I'm caught or killed. After my… practice burned down I wandered for so long. I don't pretend to be more than I am. Perhaps once I could contribute something, but for some time I have been nothing more than a drunk. And then there were recent events…'

'Oh? What recent events?' Ura's voice brings to Hektor's mind a vision of her smile: toad-like but genuine, infectious.

Hektor risks another glance over his shoulder, finds Washa leaning in towards Ura. 'Alright. You remember back a moon to when Appaliunas possessed that man at the temple?'

'Yes, I do remember.'

'Well, that man… That man was actually me.'

'Ah! I'd heard rumours, yes, yes,' Ura bubbles in excitement. 'Of the *mad* physician. I have heard your name in passing too. How was it to feel so... inspired?'

'The whole experience was a fraud, clearly. I carried out my actions with the knowledge of the *tuhkanti*, that Hektor man. And if I recall correctly, you know him *very* well.'

Ura smiles. 'Hektor is the closest I was ever having to a son. Still, he is who he is and you are lucky to being alive, eh?'

'A superstitious man might say that the Fates, Istustaya and Papaya, are infatuated with me, and so keep me from harm. I saved his little boy's life, you know, and was released.'

'I... was having no idea Hapi was sick... Hektor, over these years he has hardened, become more distant. He used to laugh, but now I am seeing the weight of his father on his shoulders. His mother, Parta, she was always not liking me. Ah! I did so much with her boy. Played with him in the gardens. Painted horses on his walls with him. But Parta was always being caught up with the *labarna*. She used to look longingly over at me and Hektor – she thinking I not see, but I did! Then the *labarna* was having his *incident*. That broke her, I thinking.'

Hektor is ensnared in Ura's words. *Had I ever even thought of Mother like that?*

Washa bows. 'Hektor struck me as aloof and proud.'

'Ha! Did he now? I can't be faulting your impression, he's hard work, eh? Though, to be fair, it does sound as though you placed him in a... difficult position. What you did, well, it will have humiliated him.'

'If someone in his position can be stirred to any feeling at all,' Washa mumbles.

Ura leans forward. 'He is a human being, just like the rest of us, no? Not everyone in his position deserves hostility, eh? Hektor... Well, I am not thinking he is quite like the others.'

'You know him, and I do not.' Washa's tone is insincere.

'I am pleased he has spared you, of course. Pleased and, well, surprised. As you say, he does *seem* to live solely for his duty, and that is no good. He is making out like he has a turtle shell or something, but under all of that, I know there is more, and I catch glimpses of it at times.' Ura sighs with some exaggeration. '… So, he was making a deal with you for your life, is that it? If you could save his son, he would let you go free, eh? That is progress for him! Ha! And he did not tell you to leave Wilusa? He was not exiling you?'

'Well… he may have mentioned something like that, yes.'

Ura laughs. 'Yes, yes, that sounds more like him. You better watch yourself, no? But all these shrines now – all these pomegranates and apricots. There's a booming trade in the marketplace – Ura is not one to let opportunity skip her by. But… these people, they are taking the fruit for something more.'

Hektor twists his head around further, takes his first sip of the drink that has been delivered. He finds it revolting.

'But it amounts to nothing anyway, eh?'

'Why do you say that?'

There is a heavy scraping of a stool, and a huff from Ura. 'Some people say change doesn't come from the bottom up, it comes from the top down. They think nothing will be different till a shiny says so, no? I saying *no*! Change will come from the bottom up, but… Well, you are not knowing *who's* listening. Though… if you are possibly interested, come to my house on the third night of the fourth quarter-moon; there are some people I want you to meet… A group that *will* see change. Your antics in the temple have *empowered* the people. Yes, yes – so it may have being make-believe, but it was real to them. It is just what this group have been waiting for… Ha! But now' – she claps Washa on the arm – 'I am wanting you to enjoy yourself here tonight. My girls have many expertise, yes, yes. And my drinks produce a range of exciting problems in your head. Don't be a stranger, Washa, but watch yourself too.' She looks as though to leave, but shakes her head, leans back down. 'And Washa. You were a healer once. Be a healer again.'

A short while later, Hektor is outside, having fled from the nego-tiations of several women. He rubs his head, though he is not sure if the headache is the effect of the opium-rich air, the fact that the famil-iarity of the lice is no longer there, or something else. *What manner of meeting might Ura be conducting? What people is she consorting with?*

Across the street is one of the shrines. In the glow of sconce-light, the pomegranate and apricot juice dribbles down into rotten, greened remnants of the previous days' fruit. Leaning against it all are crude, home-sculpted horse figurines of the sun god. And weapons.

Tablet Seven

'I have already told you, my Sun does not want this hideous *thing* to remain here where he has to look at it on a daily basis.' The *tawananna* has hands on hips, tears in her eyes.

'There is no one who wants to be rid of it more than I. I have spoken with the priests at the temple of Appaliunas, but they are adamant they do not have room for it,' Hektor sighs, glancing with fatigue across at the figurine of the goddess Kaskalkur, expecting it to smirk at his displeasure. It is a simple statuette, yet the *labarna* has taken a profound and illogical dislike to it. *It is rather ugly, in truth.*

'And, of course, it doesn't belong in the temple of Tarhun. Well, I don't care how you do it, I don't care how many servants you need to pull from their usual duties – I want it removed. Today. I don't care where it goes, just make sure it is out of my Sun's sight. I only care about his comfort, he has plenty to distract him with problems in the lower town. The sight of this… *monstrosity* is unacceptable. Is that clear?'

'Yes, perfectly.'

'I certainly hope so. I don't want you to upset my Sun again; you have been a disappointment lately. Perhaps you've been disturbed by some demon of those commoners. Whatever the issue, we need to get back to our usual rhythm and our ability to do so will rest largely on your attitude.'

'I believe there is nothing wrong with my attitude.'

'Insolent now as well? I have no time to argue; my Sun needs me for his bathing. Make sure everything is ready for us to leave when he is finished. Understood?'

Hektor clenches his jaw. For one moment, he looks beyond the anger in his mother's eyes, finds something surprising beneath it: frustration, tiredness, misery. Yes, she is the *labarna*'s wife but is that all that defines her? Where he has questioned his own position lately, he wonders if his mother ever does the same. Perhaps she too struggles to recognise her own reflection, struggles to persuade herself that there is anything to Parta beyond her duties. 'Yes, *tawananna*,' he whispers, remembering himself.

She makes to leave, turns back. 'Oh, and one other thing. That boy of yours – he is too old for running about in the garden and swinging from trees like some monkey. When you were his age I ensured that woman, who… we don't mention' – *that will be Ura then*, thinks Hektor – 'had you studying every day, practising your athletics, taking in scribal duty. I have advised my Sun of your failure with the bastard and he wants to see a change. Clear?'

The *tuhkanti* bites back a retort. '… Perfectly.'

Hektor watches his mother make off towards the bathhouse, scratches his head. The lice are gone but the itch remains. His impulse is to yell at the servants who are surreptitiously taking glances at him, as they go about their responsibilities.

It has been half a moon since he overheard Washa and Ura's conversation in the *arzana*. Since then he has made his way about the lower town, listening in on a conversation here… a dispute there. He has, as he had suspected, found nothing to suggest a core character is orchestrating the population's general unruliness. And the unruliness *is* general. In the last few days there have been eighteen incidents in which a guard was injured, seven incidents in which an administrator was hurt and two further occurrences of rape – one of which was carried out on a six-year-old girl, the daughter of a prominent landowner. But his mind does keep returning to Ura's invitation to Washa, to meet this group of which she spoke. It is a lead, yes, but he has not informed his father – no, something has stopped him from telling the *labarna*… yet. *Besides, we are yet to reach the third night of the fourth quarter-moon, when this group meets.*

But today is a cause for celebration, a welcome relief from domestic unrest.

It is the beginning of the Parraspeszi festival, a particularly important event in the Wilusan calendar. Though it is only one of nearly one hundred and sixty festivals that take place over a full year, it holds the distinguished mark of being the single celebration of regional identity that Wilusa can look forward to. Hektor has been taught that the majority of festivals are held in honour of various gods or goddesses, inciting divine favour in most cases – or at least relief from divine wrath, where possible. However, Wilusa being the proud regional power that it is, the commoners had demanded a celebration of its enviable status. The Parraspeszi festival was established in response, taking Wilusa's iconic mountain, Parraspeszi, as a symbol of the region's character.

Wiping his head, Hektor looks darkly across at the figurine over which he was arguing with his mother and decides that, indeed, he'd better have it moved into his chambers before his father comes out of the bathhouse.

Besides, he has to prepare his horse, Kummi, for travel, as well as find suitable attire for the journey ahead. But before that, he has a harder chore.

The *tuhkanti* is incredulous at the general untidiness of his son's chambers. Small figurines are scattered over the stucco floor, and various tablets, wooden toys and musical instruments carelessly occupy other positions. Hapi himself lies on a bed staring into the ruddy, horse-fresco ceiling. It is clear to Hektor that the child realises his presence, but has nonetheless decided to indulge in juvenile silence.

Hektor leans into the wall, folds his arms, looks upon Hapi as a farmer might look upon a cart with one wheel stuck in a ditch. In all his governmental negotiations, he cannot conceive that there exists an ambassador with greater skills of diplomacy than a parent with unruly offspring. He shakes away several unpleasant thoughts, focuses his attention on the present. *I will have to tread as a moth treads the tip of a flame.*

'Your mouth is a goat's bottom screwed up like that.'

Hapi shoots angry eyes at him, makes a dramatic display of turning onto his side so his face is no longer visible.

Hektor runs one finger over where his beard used to be. 'You know, the Parraspeszi festival begins today and it wouldn't be the same without you.' That sounds better. He is pleased with himself.

'Don't want to go.' Hapi's voice is surly.

More effort required: 'Really? There'll be lots of banners and entertainers and people will be cheering. Exciting stuff.'

'Shows how much *you* know. Broken Granddad cancelled most of those things. Anyway, I wouldn't be interested even if that *was* all there.'

He really cancelled all of that? Why was I not informed? My son knows more than I.

Hektor decides upon a different tack. 'Well, I'm your father and I say you have to go.'

Hapi shrugs his shoulders. He has been quiet ever since the *tuhkanti* commenced his espionage in the lower town; he was quite upset when he first saw the change in his father's face.

'I'm not *asking* you, Hapi.'

'No, you're not! Why didn't you come to my bedside when my tummy wasn't well? Why haven't you given me a story in so long?'

This is more than Hektor has patience for. 'I haven't got time for your stupid stories and I *did* come to your bedside! Now, you listen to me: you stop looking so damn miserable and get up. Go on!'

Hapi starts crying.

'Don't you start crying either. I expect to see you out and ready this afternoon. You need to stop this behaviour... all this running about the lawns and swinging from the trees, like some monkey. I'll be watching.'

Hapi turns fully to his father in a show of rage. 'And where will you be? Doing some stupid duty!'

Hektor feels the fury fissuring his skull. 'I will be at your side with Kummi,' he yells. '*You* will take Aras out. That foal is old enough to feel some reins, learn some commands, take the whip. You can start brushing it, cleaning its hay out, feeding it. I have been too soft on you – I see that now – and you will *break* that damn animal in whether you like it or not. You will be my *tuhkanti* some day and I am disappointed in what you are turning out to be. You will follow our traditions, abide by our rules – else you are no son of mine.'

'I hate you!' Hapi squeals through his tears, covers his ears.

Hektor growls, flings arms in the air, storms out of the room. Children can be so insensitive.

The *tuhkanti* holds Kummi's reins tightly, the leather cracking in his fists, his jerkin cracking too in its clenching of Hektor's chest. Beside him, Hapi – red-faced, snivelling – draws Aras along by rope so weakly knotted that it threatens to fall away from the animal completely. *No matter, the foal will not leave its mother's side.* Around the *tuhkanti* a retinue of guards atop horses accompany him and, further back and to the sides, commoners stream forward as individuals and as groups, feet padding into the dirt. Hektor's hood covers his head so as to hide his face; it is clear for the world to see that this figure on horseback is he, but his features are not discernible and so his disguise for the lower town remains intact. There is a particularly loud group of women near him as he walks out along the Wilusan plains, sun flaying the long line of pilgrims. Just up ahead, the *labarna* is carried on his litter.

'I was surprised the *labarna* had balls to actually come into town; guess religious duty even outweighs his safety. One of my *arzana* girls, she says to me, "Limi, Limi, quickly come see him, he doesn't look as frail as I thought he'd be." So I say, "Silly girl, silly girl, you should remember our *labarna* has the eyes of an eagle, the head of a leopard, the penis of a bull," and we both laugh together.'

The women, collectively, shriek their appreciation. Hektor growls, shakes his head.

'Of course, I went to see him; I've only ever seen him once before. Many people have never seen him at all. That's why there are so many rumours about him and his family – don't you think so, girls? Looked weak to me, yes, sitting on his litter, holding his donkey-headed staff, one arm curled up like a bald chick's wing. Yes, they try to hide how fragile he looks. They can throw on armour and skins of big, big cats, but it makes him look all the more pitiable.

'The *labarna* is supposed to be a living god, adopted by Heaven at birth – that's what I've been told anyway. But Priam is not just half a man, he's half a *person*. If the gods really stick with him then he seems a funny choice.'

One of the guards asks Hektor if the woman should be confronted, but the *tuhkanti* decides to let it go.

Hektor clicks twice, communicating to Kummi that she must increase her pace. 'Come, Hapi!'

The boy trots to keep up but Aras bounds contentedly along, eager, no doubt, for his mother's shadow.

Mount Parraspeszi impresses the *tuhkanti* with its giddy spectacle. Looking up, he guesses it to stand a thousand horses high, slopping its gargantuan belly in all directions. He remembers the Mountain as it was last year in the winter, its snow-whipped peak staring across northern Arzawa like some – *how did I describe it to Hapi?* – like some 'pulped cyclopean eyeball'. Today there is no such snow.

The *tuhkanti* has created many stories about the inception of Parraspeszi to the delight of his son, borrowing from different tales prevailing in languages of people living on all sides of the Mountain. *But I feel I've concocted a tale as poetic as any other.* 'As Appaliunas shingled the original darkness with the first bars of light,' he tells Hapi, 'when the cosmos came into being, one such bar of light was mixed with the seed of Pirwa and impregnated the great Earth Mother – Parraspeszi is Her swollen belly and it routinely gives birth to the horses that populate the Wilusan foothills.'

Parraspeszi itself is half a day's ride from Wilusa, and Hektor considers it a disheartening prospect for a journey if you are either old or disabled. His father has informed him that the gods have seen fit to cater to his, the *labarna*'s, own difficulties by telling him that he need only travel to the near foothills of the Mountain to perform his duties for the festival – *and the response to the miracle I suggested.* Travel is nonetheless wearisome, a fact recorded by the heavy breaths of those carrying Priam's litter, for whom Hektor feels pity. He considers progress relatively fast, however, the party reaching the lower foothills shortly after Appaliunas finds His zenith. The *tuhkanti* notes that what had started as a group of no more than ninety people – the bulk of whom being professional guards to the *labarna* – has quickly ripened into a swarm of some three hundred pilgrims, consisting primarily of people from the lower town, who have turned inquisitive noses to Priam's advance. *Good – let there be a sufficient crowd of commoners for what is to come.*

Hektor is thankful when the call is given for a break in the journey.

He drinks from the river and splashes water discreetly over his aching face. The heat, as ever, is formidable, but the Katkatenutti's ageless flow, coupled with the woodland's leafy shelter, is a welcome sedative. He clears his throat violently, looks around for anyone familiar. Nearby, a guard is perched upon a rock, legs and arms folded, eyes shut, eyebrows turned down in apparent annoyance. Around him dance a small group of children. The sight amuses Hektor, despite himself, reminding him of a cat he had once seen batting its tail in agitation as five kittens rolled around it with maniacal determination.

Hapi sits sullenly beside him, fingering Aras's nose at intervals.

'Make sure the foal has enough to drink, Hapi. If it thirsts later on then you must bear the blame.'

Hapi turns his head away, but ushers – *discreetly; he clearly does not wish for me to see him acting upon my advice* – the animal towards the stream, where its rough, glistening tongue unravels to scoop up water and winch it back into its mouth.

A call announces it is time to move on.

People – bathing in the river, lying on the ground, collecting wild herbs so sharp in the close air – immediately abandon their activity and reform as a crowd. Hektor shuts his eyes, opens them, pulls himself up.

A morbidity breaks into the murmur of people's conversation. As several farmers move to one side in front of him, Hektor sees ten men swaying along, chanting, heaving a large wooden board between them. Upon the board is a conical rock, beautifully decorated with moss, flowers and a variety of small plants. The rock's peak appears to be painted white.

'What is that?'

The *tuhkanti* glances down at Hapi, surprised the boy has spoken. *It's been hours and not a word – perhaps he is calming down.* 'It's a statuette of Parraspeszi Herself. During the final part of today's proceedings, the *labarna* will invoke the name of the Mountain, and invite Her spirit down to inhabit the statuette. The statuette will then be taken back to Wilusa, where the deity can join in with the festival that we hold in Her honour.'

'So... that rock there – it's really important?'

'That's correct. So important that it will be placed in the head chair, next to the *labarna* and the *tawananna*— next to your grandparents—'

'Uh-huh.'

'—There the deity can enjoy the entertainment and the food, as well as the celebration being made in Her honour.'

'Food?' Hapi looks as though he is considering something difficult. 'Will the deity eat the food?'

'Of course not.'

'Why?'

'Because it is a rock.'

'*Dek* then... What river is this?' Hapi adds, after several moments, pointing at the stream *glock, glock, glocking* downhill.

'You know that,' Hektor growls. 'It is the Katkatenutti, which we are following right now.'

Hapi steadies Aras as the foal bobs its head a few times. 'Is the river important?'

Hektor's shoulders drop, relieved that the boy has stopped being so rude to him. *Now, all I need is for this headache to go away.* 'Immensely. Both the Katkatenutti and the Uwitar-Amiyaraza are living spirits. The Katkatenutti pours out of Parraspeszi at the Ayazma, a rocky clump of waterfalls and rapids some distance ahead. It is a direct current from Heaven itself, giving life to the fields, the horses and the town.

'Katkatenutti and Uwitar-Amiyaraza are benevolent spirits who began life as white horses. They were mates whose love brought tears even to the flame-stacked eyes of Appaliunas... You don't remember any of this? I've told you before in our stories. No? Well, I haven't done my storytelling in a while, I concede, and repetition is so important if you are to remember our tales. Where were we? Indeed, Katkatenutti and Uwitar-Amiyaraza could not bear the thought of dying and being separated from each other in the afterlife, so the gods took pity on them. They turned both horses into the rivers flowing here today, so that they could co-exist forever.'

Hapi looks away, perhaps considering all his father has said. From his position atop Kummi, Hektor cannot make out the boy's face, but does not sense anger. Aras starts pulling at the rope, drawing Hapi's attention, but the child – despite his coos – is unable to disrupt the animal's sudden irritability. Hektor tugs lightly on Kummi's rein, bringing her to a standstill. Hapi is being pulled further and further backwards by Aras, tripping over tree roots and bracken – attracting the quizzical glances of more than one commoner. The *tuhkanti* feels a smile tease the corner of his mouth, but he clears his throat instead.

'Hapi! What are you doing?'

'Aras... He... won't... do... as... I... want. Stop it!' Hapi grunts, digging his sandalled feet into the dirt.

At this moment, Aras comes to a halt, buries his head in a clump of parsley and commences lunch.

'Did you feed him before we left?' Hektor sighs.

Hapi glances up, looks back at Aras with hands on hips. '... No. I-I thought the stable-hands did it...'

Hektor wipes away some sweat stinging his eyes, sweeps one leg over Kummi's back, *duffs* to the woodland floor.

'And what did I tell you in your room? Hmm? You are responsible for Aras; I told the stable-hands not to feed the animal, to see if you would notice.'

Hapi's face is a mingling of anger, surprise, guilt. The boy seems to bite back his words, looks sulkily down at the rope in his hands.

Hektor folds his thick arms. 'You have learned two lessons today, Hapi.'

Hapi scratches a stone into the dirt with one toe. '... What?'

Hektor grabs at Kummi's reins, leads her towards the boy. 'You have learned that Aras *will* go hungry if you are careless with his well-being. He is a living, breathing creature – a blessing in time, but a burden for the moment. You must respect him, respect his needs—'

'I don't know his needs though,' Hapi interrupts.

'Then ask the stable-hands!' Hektor retaliates, exasperation creeping into his voice. 'Find out when he eats, what he enjoys, where he likes to be scratched, how long he can canter before tiring – does he respond to whoops, to clicks, to whistles. All these things you must know as surely as you know the skin on the palms of your hands. Hmm, you can even start now; Kummi responds to whistles: one for stop, two for go, three to come to me. Aras will probably do likewise eventually. Try it now, see if he does anything.'

Hapi knits his brow, arranges his lips around his tongue, blows... blows... blows. But only wet air escapes. Aras looks up at his young master with – what? – *is that pity in his eyes?*

Hektor shakes his head, hides another smile. *That is the second in such a short space of time.* 'You will have to practise whistling. It... took me a while too.' He remembers his father's tutting, Ura's laughter. 'It is such an easy thing, my boy. It is such an easy thing.' The *tuhkanti* looks up the hill, past the opal glint of the river. *We will be there soon.*

He turns back to his boy, still attempting to whistle. 'Come on, we must go. We have lingered too long. Though... I will walk beside Kummi as you walk beside Aras.'

Hektor moves off, but Hapi calls out. '*Tati!*'

The *tuhkanti* turns back. 'Yes?'

'You said I'd learned two lessons today... You only told me one. What was the second?'

Hektor smiles. 'That Aras likes parsley.'

At last, the flock comes to a near standstill as Priam's litter settles beside a large, moss-gnawed shrine, half-concealed in a scrabble of pine branches. The shrine itself reaches a good two-and-a-half times the height of your average man, its circular body reminiscent of some bloated animal. Numerous figurines, many of them knocked over by unknown forces, decorate the shrine, and outside, what once were flowers and candles lie in dismal clutters. Ancient inscriptions lend the shrine silent wisdom. Depictions of deities complete its reverential appearance.

Hektor moves forward – Hapi behind him – to where the *labarna* and *tawananna* are joined in prayer with several elderly priests – Hawi among them, whose eyes briefly meet his. He jumps down from

Kummil's back and ties her to a nearby tree — helping his son do the same for Aras.

'What's happening now?' Hapi whispers.

'The *labarna* will call upon Parraspeszi to bless all those who have journeyed with him to the Mountain. He will then ask Parraspeszi to continue watching over Wilusa and keep her safe and rich. After that, there will be the ceremony in which Parraspeszi will be invited down into the statuette from where She can watch the remainder of the festival back in the city.'

'Will She speak to us?'

'Not as such,' replies Hawi, overhearing the boy and *click, clack, clecking* closer. 'But if you close your eyes and concentrate really hard, you might hear Her voice breaking through to you – in here.' He taps his temple.

Hapi nods, closes eyes, clenches face.

After several minutes in which Priam and Parta continue to pray, the *labarna* turns around to face his people.

'Parraspeszi! Hear Us… Bless all these people who follow Our lead into Your realm where the trees are dense, and Your body stands above Us. Re-re-remember Wilusa now in her time of great trouble and help her to over-over-overcome her ene-mies who may, even now, stand before You. Now, accept this image of Your form.' The statuette is presented. 'Though it is poor, we ask it will suffice for You to enjoy the festival in Wilusa. Where You are loved.'

Priam is carried forward uneasily, Parta supporting him, her eyes, yes, still filled with that same depth as Hektor saw before. The *labarna* reaches the statuette, holds out a trembling hand, touches it, closes his eyes, murmurs another prayer. The priests stand beside the statuette; members of the crowd fall to knees, lift palms towards the heavens' attic blue. The priests, in time with Priam, chant.

The *tuhkanti* listens. The breeze vibrates with their unified voice, producing an eerily inhuman effect.

Priam lifts his head, clings to his staff, sways from side to side, as a willow branch flexes its elastic sinews when rocked in the wind. Slowly, the chanting builds, condenses.

To Hektor, there now seems something medicinal in the chanting.

Like opium, he feels the chanting might be a source of relief and release in minor doses, but in any great quantity it could be dangerous. He has not felt that way about it before and scratches his head, perplexed.

The chanting approaches a climax. And then...

Silence.

The chanting stops. The *labarna*'s eyes, closed during the chant, remain so, and he turns back to his people, raises his sceptre.

Hektor glances behind him to where the guards have formed a perimeter against the commoners, who look on, expectation etched in their faces. He looks back to his father. *You can do this. Be more than their miracle.*

Priam takes in great rattling breaths, each deliberate, a struggle. At first, Hektor thinks that something must be wrong and, indeed, his mother is creeping towards him incrementally. But then his head snaps up, eyes wide. There is a murmur from the commoners, muttering.

Expectation.

'Hear Us, Our people!' Priam's voice is changed – deep, gravelly, assured – booming out and echoing through the trees. Hektor is instantly gripped, as are the commoners, it seems. 'We are the sun, the sceptre and the judgement. Where there is injustice, We bring justice. Where there is hunger, We bring nourishment. Where there is chaos, We bring order. Where there is darkness, We bring light.

'For too long, Wilusa's ear has been bitten by the demon, Rumour. There is misgiving and ill-will, and a rot has set in that even now is foul in the nose, harsh to the ear and vile to the eye. Wilusa is greatest of the Arzawa states. Wilusa commands the very earth and the water, and the Mountain stands in protection. The gods gift us horses bred in Heaven itself. They answer our prayers and direct our good fortune, for Wilusa is precious to Them.'

Hektor looks back again at the commoners. Many are open-mouthed, hypnotised by the spectacle. He clenches his fist in celebration. Looking back at his father, even *his* mouth drops open, as the *labarna*, using the butt-end of his sceptre on the arm of the chair, pulls himself up to stand before his congregation. Hektor, Parta, Hawi,

Hapi and anyone else intimate with Priam gasp in unison. Priam is up, for the first time in gods only know how long, balancing firmly on his right leg, the butt of his sceptre still perched on the arm of his makeshift throne. He looks all the more regal, glorious and intimidating with his left side firmly concealed by the pelts of wild cats.

Hawi falls to his knees, turns his palms up in a prayer. 'Gods preserve us.'

There is a great commotion among the commoners. It seems as though this is not what they were expecting.

'The rumours were false!' – one voice.

'He is whole... Fearful and whole' – another.

Priam, apparently bolstered by the reception he has received, though his left eye is sunk and his left cheek droops, opens his mouth once more and insists, 'The God gazes upon you now. Look upon Us and despair of your vain fancies for false miracles, false gods and unrest. The time has come for, for— The time has come for or— For or— Or—'

But Priam's voice, swollen with inspiration, fails him. His grip on the sceptre wavers, it slips from his grip and rolls off the litter to the forest floor. As his support disappears, so too does his balance and he collapses back into the throne with a grunt.

All in a rush, Parta leaps forward, cries out; Hawi pulls himself awkwardly to his feet, shakes his head; Hektor takes a firm grip of Hapi's shoulder, turns to face the crowd; and the crowd itself pushes forward against the semicircle of guards who instinctively raise their spears and shields in a threatening manner.

'Hapi, stay close to me, no matter what,' Hektor commands.

'Yes, *tati.*'

The commoners are not yet menacing, but they are all yelling and shaking their fists as though they have been tricked in a game of chance and discovered the deception.

'You are no god!' – one voice.

'Broken old fool!' – another.

'Qu-quiet!' comes Priam's familiar, weak voice. It is dust against the din of commoners.

And in that moment, as the commoners heft their way against the shields of the guards, a single filthy boy from among the rabble breaks through the legs of one guard – preoccupied, mischievous grin on his face – and whips the short distance uphill towards the *labarna*. Guards turn, Parta points, Hektor watches, Hapi yells, Priam glares. The boy slips through the grip of one guard, then another and jumps up onto the litter. For one moment, he and Priam look into each other's eyes, then the boy has a hold of one of the pelts concealing the *labarna*'s ruined left arm and leg. He swift-steps right, ripping the pelt with him and reveals what Priam has kept hidden from the commoners for so long.

Hektor does not know where to look. His eyes are locked on his father, who is desperately trying to cover the left side of his body, voice hoarse with, 'Don't let them see! Don't let them see!' as Parta trips past the throne in a flood of tears, desperate to help her husband. But what haunts him is the collective scream of the commoners, the spits of revulsion, the *fury* at this shattered man-god before them.

'Stop that boy! Stop that boy!' Priam's command comes angry, his one good eye wheeling about to seek out his attacker.

It happens too quickly.

Hektor finds the boy, still brandishing the pelt like a trophy, still smiling mischievously, as he swivels and slides back towards the throng. He finds also the guard raising the weapon to shoulder height. Hektor screams out for him to stop, throws an arm instinctively in front of Hapi's face.

The vengeful bronze of the spearhead explodes out of the child's chest in a harvest of blood, rib and lung; he is dead before he hits the earth.

A particularly harrowing cry from the crowd is likely the boy's parents, and in a split second – once the shock of the kill has passed – the commoners throw themselves upon the guards, ravenous for the *labarna*.

'Get him back to Wilusa!' Hektor roars at, well, everyone he can, pointing to his father.

Fortunately for Priam, there is a sizeable number of guards, such is the importance of security. Hektor runs over to Kummi, unties her from the tree, heaves himself up into the saddle. He yells out for the guards to adopt a formation better suited to securing his father from all sides. Already, guards are being forced to cut down the more zealous of the commoners as a barrage of rocks hurtles overhead, and more guards have to take up a position in front of the *labarna*, shields raised, to protect him, as the litter is once more lifted into the air by servants. As the bodies stack up, the commoners become more cautious and hang back, not daring to get as close to the guards. Hektor continues to roar directions, telling Hapi to grab Aras – who is somewhat panicked – and stay close to him and Kummi.

Soon, Priam's entourage, defended by the guards is on the move and heading away from Parraspeszi, back towards Wilusa.

Hektor looks beyond the mutinous commoners, back to the shrine where a man and a woman are wrapped around the body of their murdered son.

Tablet Eight

Hektor is unused to feeling so angry, and though he dislikes this loss of coolness, he appreciates the strange cleanliness of the emotion. Too many feelings clash within his head, and they settle uncomfortably in the deepest part of his guts.

He has been back from Mount Parraspeszi for a few hours now. The great festival feast is well underway in the central patio at the heart of the acropolis, though it is a woeful affair given the events that have transpired. Hektor had suggested cancelling it altogether, but Priam angrily insisted that to cancel it would be to risk the divine wrath of Parraspeszi. It is the *tuhkanti*'s duty to attend, but he has taken liberty in readying himself. Right now, he is in his quarters, ripping through his various robes, tunics, kilts, all so neatly folded. Outside, the grounds are quiet, the sky a pale orange offsetting the black of the lawns and foliage. There is a smell of damp grass.

I can only imagine the fury in the lower town right now. The *labarna*'s stunning failure on the Mountain could not have been more overt and catastrophic. The commoners are looking for something – *anything* – to validate their claims, their confidence. *Father has just given them justification for...* For what? Hektor is well aware of the size of the lower town's population and how it eclipses that of the upper town and acropolis. *And then that boy... It could be the one spark to ignite them all.* Already there have been rapes, murders of the deserving, and, so he has heard, much in the way of retaliation by the guards, *and all this only in the space of a few hours.* He is under no illusion as to his and his family's fate should that divide between the two worlds be torn.

He decides upon a tunic the colour of an angry sea, with trimming the colour of waterlogged sand. *Yes, this will do.*

Hapi is at the feast already, as befitting the blood of Priam. Kaluti is there too. Hawi. Everyone he knows. Family. Priests. Administrators. The *mesedi*.

Mesedi: the *labarna*'s personal retinue of guards.

The feast is gluttonous – an excessive raid on the full storehouses of the upper town. It is show, boasting: *look at us, gods, look at what we have sown and what we may reap at whim. This is our control, the lock we hold over our domain.*

He adjusts his kilt, a limp wave of material in the expiring sunlight.

His days in the lower town come to mind. The commoners – even that word now feels acerbic on the tongue – had not been as he had imagined. Yes, he has always maintained his friendship with Ura, but she always seemed *different* from the rest. Those days in disguise among the people have been illuminating. They drink, eat, laugh, work, love, fight with a weightlessness that he has never experienced himself. And what is this weightlessness? It is the absence of centuries of tradition, practice and privilege condensed into all that expectation placed upon the shoulders of one man. And that man is... *me.*

Hektor grasps at his face, running fingers deep into the hollows of his eyes, the nooks of his cheeks, scratching his nose. He shakes his head, frightened by the untempered thoughts galloping about his head. Hapi should not see this weakness in him; Hapi would have to learn what life has in store for him. He would have to accept his future and fulfil it. Soon. No, *no one* could see this weakness in him.

Hektor breathes deep, stems the torrent behind his eyes with a simple clamp of his jaw. He then plods towards the door, but before he reaches it he feels a sudden jolt from the ground. A jolt that travels through him, leaps up into the very ceiling. He staggers; dust falls.

No, not again. Not another trem—

But the shake does come again, stops... comes, stops... comes, stays, stays, stays, *heightens.*

His heart is racing – the building, the ground, the sky, the universe itself shivers violently. He is on the floor, up again, down once more, up again. The ceiling is cracking, the walls fissuring. There is a terrible force at work and he is powerless to combat it.

Gaining half a moment's balance, he throws himself through the doors to his quarters, just as a screaming chunk of ceiling bites down behind him, digesting his room entirely.

Outside, the corridor is a travesty of flying chunks of stone, split walls and flailing servants, all masked in an aura of dust.

Hapi!

His son, being at the feast, is in the patio area, surrounded on all sides by columns, roofing, decorative stonework – *all of which is liable to break off and fall.*

The patio is *this* way. He shoulders past people running in different directions. In the distance: a salvo of cries and the dense *kih, kih, thunk* of falling stone. He breaks into something as close to a run as he can manage, occasionally losing his balance to smack against any wall that will offer him support. To his left: a complexity of tributaries flash across another wall, ripping through an expanse of frescoes. Red light blinks through a freshly opened hole in the ceiling and Hektor leaps instinctively to one side as another slab of stone stabs down on the exact position in which he had stood.

He comes to an open area in which a man is lying, one leg crushed by a column, begging for help or at least the reprieve of a quick death. The *tuhkanti* ignores him, breathes a faint prayer for the man, storms on.

As he comes to the next corridor, the world finally ceases shaking. It has felt like an eternity, but, as he considers it, the quake cannot have lasted more than, say, forty to fifty seconds. *And in that meagre blink of time, look what damage – what terror – has been wrought.* It is a chilling reminder of the gods' destructive capability.

The world seems to settle and the howl of torn stone transmogrifies into the wails of women, the yells of men, the screams of the injured or dying. The dust, billowing everywhere, is the final breath of a savage deity.

At last, he comes to the patio. What he finds is difficult to comprehend; he had somehow – despite himself – imagined that the catastrophe elsewhere would not have intruded upon the diners here.

Columns have collapsed across the extensive feasting table, food and flesh pulped into colourful stains over table and floor alike. He recognises an administrator's wife and sister kneeling over the body of the administrator, whose head is half caved in, though the man's twitches suggest he is still alive. There are several dead across the floor, the bodies covered in some way by stonework. His father is sprawled across the ground, blood over his legs, the *tawananna* weeping over him, screeching for help from a steady stream of personnel.

Father can wait. Where is Hapi?

He looks from here to there, to over there, to behind that. He is nowhere to be seen.

Hektor is seized with a familiar panic – the kind he felt only a short while back when returning from the rural areas with the medicine. He marches right up to his mother, barks, 'Where is he?! Where is Hapi?!'

The *tawananna*: shaking, face greyed with dust. 'G–Get away! I–I don't know where your bastard is. I don't care. My Sun, my poor Sun is injured, my poor Sun! You must help him, boy. You must.'

Hektor's head is swimming; he is reckless. He snatches away from his mother's outstretched hands and swings around the decimation that was once the patio.

'Hapi!' he roars, voice hoarse and potent.

He pulls through stone, bodies, the living, to find his son, but he is nowhere. *Gods, gods, gods, don't let him be under one of these columns...*

A rough pull on his tunic, he spins around.

'What?!' he snaps into the face of a dust-covered girl.

It is Kaluti. *Yes, my sister, yes...*

'I–I saw him – saw Hapi. When it started. He ran off. Ran off. Looking for you. He was calling for you. I tried to stop him but he wouldn't listen.'

A noise escapes his lips, his hand sweeps over his head, eyes dart about, tears surfacing.

'Which direction?'

'That way – o–over there.'

He turns, floods back into the acropolis, dimly aware of his mother's startled voice behind him. And how it turns to anger.

The acropolis is darker than it otherwise should have been; sconces have fallen to the floor, their fires snuffed out in the chaos. The bloody dusk-light bleeds into corridors, chambers, halls, profiling the faces of the dead, injured, bewildered. *But none of them is Hapi.* He calls for what seems hours but to no avail. No person he grabs has seen his boy either.

Eventually, he falls out of the acropolis onto the main porch, over-looking the upper town and, below that, the lower. He draws in his breath at the sight of Wilusa; it is not the city he knows, but a foreign world of disaster and nightmare. The screams and pleas for help that he heard inside the acropolis reverberate around the city on a mass scale. The lower town is a tangle of smoke, sporadic fire – *gods, fire* – and wreckage. The mud-brick houses though, being small and closely packed, do not look to have sustained much damage. The upper town tells a different story. The buildings, large and separated, look to have suffered extensively. All seem to have taken at least rudimentary damage, but a great many also have collapsed or half-collapsed.

He bursts down the shrub-lined pathway, quickly passing from the acropolis grounds into the upper town. The orange mixes with grey and white to create an otherworldly feel, and he is reminded – despite himself – of one of those heroes Hapi loves so much, perhaps descending into the Under-Spring, awaiting the lethal touch of Kaskalkur Herself. But now – here in the present – he cannot imagine where to start. Leaning out of the gloom, every shape and half-shape seems to bear a resemblance to children – to Hapi. Dislocated individuals passing by – he shakes them, 'Have you seen a child? Have you seen a boy? He would have come out of the acropolis.' But no, they only look confused, dazed, shocked. Eventually, he falls to his knees, looking about with no inclination as to what he might do. *He could be trapped somewhere, half buried under rubble. Dying. Dead.* He forcibly shakes his head – he cannot allow that mentality to go unchecked.

Soon, he is aware of several guards running up to him, yelling his name.

'Yes? What is it?'

'It's the wall, *tuhkanti*. A section has collapsed and there are fires in the lower town.'

Hektor feels the blood in his channels run frosty. He looks further down the upper town and gasps. The guards speak true: in one section, there is an enormous hole in the ground where an entire portion of the wall had once stood. There is no divide.

'Fires...' he murmurs. 'There's nothing for that. But the wall... The wall you *must* guard. See that no commoner gets into the upper town.'

'Yes, *tuhkanti*. But… what of the people? In the lower town, I mean. We are being asked for help. We don't have the men, but…'

Hektor curses, tugs his jaw to one side. His thoughts linger on Hapi – *I do not know where you are… What else can I do?*

Hektor takes a breath, deep with the difficulty of decision. '*Dek*, I will come.'

'*Tuhkanti*, that's not the worst of it…'

'I said I will come!'

The wall is as badly damaged as the guards suggested. Though the structure was of solid stone, it would seem the rigidity and lack of forgiveness in the fixture has been its undoing. Would it have bent, given a little, it might have survived with only superficial damage. As it is, the rupture emanating from the ground has been merciless, and the lower and upper town are now one. Through the hole in the wall, Hektor can make out a scene very much like what he witnessed in the upper town. People are tearing around, lonely children potter about, bodies lie disturbed only by robbers. There is a line of guards filling the wall with flesh where stone should be and, for now, it is keeping commoners at bay.

'Sir,' a guard points over to the right: a pitch void in the lesser darkness.

It takes Hektor several moments to realise that in the area the soldier is pointing to – a short distance off from the wall – there used to stand the single largest food store in the upper town. The *tuhkanti* jogs the short distance up to where the food store was and finds himself looking into a large crevice. Inside are the crumpled remains of the storehouse, lumps of dirtied food and several bodies.

'Sir, the lower town,' yells the guard.

Hektor drags his attention back to the line of men blocking the hole in the wall. There are several commoners pulling at the guardsmen, knocked or shoved back with the butt of weapons. The *tuhkanti* stomps downhill – still in the upper town – and the commotion gains in volume as he nears.

'What is this?'

'*Tuhkanti*,' one of the guards replies, 'these people are asking for help. But we cannot help them all with our small numbers.'

'Please!' a scraggy-looking man with a cut forehead calls, desperately. 'There's a house on fire. A woman and her children – they're trapped inside. Please help.'

Hektor meets his eyes. He sees the same terror there that he feels within himself. And then he thinks on the incident earlier in the day and how this could be an opportunity to perhaps make some amends. Though, in doing so, he would abandon his son. *But Hapi, what can I do? I don't know where you are.*

'I will go.'

Several guards turn in shock. 'But sir, you shouldn't!' and 'You can't!' echo out. 'Some are in need – maybe. But after what happened today…'

'Don't presume,' the *tuhkanti* growls, 'to instruct me as to what I will do. We're hated by those in the lower town as it is. Let's not compound that hatred when we can set it right. You!' – he points at a guard – 'Grab me the clothes there – off that dead man.'

Without contemplation, Hektor strips off his finery, and dresses himself in the beige tunic and skirt worn by the body of a nearby commoner, delivered by a mousy guard. Once he is suitably attired he closes his eyes, draws another deep breath and then looks ahead of him. With shaky resolution, he steps over the divide that had once been the wall and finds himself, once more, in the lower town.

Down here, he has always felt strangely nude: no guards, no armour, no weapon, only a small layer of material between him and whatever the night may hold, whether maddened traders and heat-crazed widows, or worse. However, tonight he feels especially vulnerable. The streets, such as they are – more funnels of dust, shit, dead cats and beggars – bear the displaced chuck of mud-bricks from homes, worm-tunnelled timber and lost, praying elderly.

As he approaches, he gets the smoke, flavoured with scalded herbs, and soon he cannot see more than a body's length ahead. The flames have consumed a row of shabby homes and caught another house, freestanding. The brightness and heat: the intensity of life and death warped together. There are people running about, some throwing buckets of water at the blaze, others pointing, yelling commands, pushing back those who are frozen with fear. Beyond the smoke, in the lungs of the quick-jumping flames, Hektor can hear the calls for help. The gruff cry of a woman, the non-understanding of children. He looks at the men – they are not approaching.

'Why are you doing nothing?' Hektor roars, just another simple victim of this horror.

One man mutters a response. 'We've tried – look.'

Hektor follows the man's finger to three men slumped on the ground and against a wall: one is hideously burned, lifeless; a second is whimpering, the skin on his face and legs half-melted; a third is gagging on water – coughs are knives, face charred.

'The shaking collapsed some of the houses, and many were burned alive when the fire spread. The heat is too much already for this house. It's too late. You want to try though, then you've got a funeral pyre ready-made,' another man wheezes.

Hektor shunts his lower jaw from left to right. This house has also suffered damage from the shaking and, for whatever reason, the people inside cannot escape. 'At least carry on fetching water!'

A number of men snap out of their daze and stagger off, westward, where the spring is.

Remember what the Chief of the Fire Watchers told you in your training. 'Fire breeds like distrust. In a foot race with flames, don't expect to win.'

At the time, he thought the Chief was exaggerating, but now – *I am not so sure. I only have a few minutes at most to save them.*

Hektor stalks around the building, aware of the crowd watching on, quickening his feet with every plea from the family inside. He yells words of comfort, but the fire is fierce and he knows the smoke must choke them soon. *Too soon for me to do anything.*

But then he sees it: a livid crack in one of the walls, trickling up from the ground to a small window. It is barely visible, but he finds it and realises immediately what it means. The wall is mud-brick – unyielding. But, like anything in the lower town, when damaged it will give way under enough pressure. He pulls back to a distance, finds a spot where there is already a faint fissure of damage, heaves a breath out. Then he has an idea – something else the Chief taught him.

'You!' he yells to a lad running past with a bucket of water. 'Yes, you! Throw it on me, now!'

The lad pauses, but only momentarily.

Drenched from head to foot, Hektor breaks into a run, accelerating towards the building, throws his body, side on, into the wall. The pain down his arm is great, but he clamps his teeth together, steps back. *It gave.* The crack is darker, deeper. He steps back again, heaves a breath out, accelerates. His full weight smashes into the wall; the pain in his arm is not so bad this time. *Definitely, it loosened.* Sure enough, more cracks have journeyed off like the fracture forks in a skull – a few chunks of mud-brick have gone through, leaving holes in the wall.

Then there is the scream. Colossal, mortal.

'It's... *cuh... creh...* in here! The fire's... *cuh... cuh... crah...*' a female voice coughs.

'Hang on!' Hektor yells.

He steps back into the beginnings of an alleyway. *Come on, come on.* He snorts the rancid air from his nostrils, levels his eyes at one particular part of the crack – *I'll throw everything at that single point.* He runs, runs, runs – flings himself from the ground, bends over, turns his shoulder wall-ward. The pain shoots through his shoulder and he feels himself falling. Scratches of mud-brick tear past his face, legs, chest and he crashes into the floor. He is inside, covered in dust, dry mud and the darkness of the interior. The smoke harasses his throat. Above him, the doorway is a hole in the night. He pulls himself up, yells a husky word of comfort, hoping the family will hear him, and stumbles deeper into the building.

It seems far bigger in here than it looked from the outside. But this cannot be anything more than a modest earner's home – perhaps belonging to a trader with several stalls, or an apprentice scribe. It is so dark, the smoke so disorientating that it is a struggle to breathe and a battle to keep his bearings. He is concerned by the lack of calls for help.

And then, there is the fire itself. A howl of heat, threatening to cook his flesh even from a distance, despite the water covering him. Tables are black sticks in the light; beds are pitch biers; pots are explosions. He throws his hands up to shield his face, but he can feel the hairs on his arms curling like the woodlice he has seen children throw on sconce flames. He coughs, ducks his head further down, hoping to find something cooler, fresher nearer the ground, but there is nothing. He staggers into a slim hallway, and there is a tattered mess of leather skins that would, until recently, have made for a door, crumpled in embers at the entrance to another room – small, smoke-soaked. Inside are trading goods – linens of all kinds: tunics, kilts, robes, throws, horse coats, skull caps. In the corner: a woman, baby and young girl huddled together, unconscious.

'Can you... *cruh*... hear... *cruh crah*... me!?' he coughs, voice toad-like. He can sense the fire scurrying up behind him.

But there is no response. The room itself is completely closed up, apart from the doorway he has just come through. He leans down, coughing all the time, stomach muscles cramping, and lifts the baby up, tucking it under his arm. He then grabs hold of the girl's arm and pulls her up, letting go and catching her around the waist. Panting hurts all the more and he is dizzy.

I have to get out of here.

The mother is still unconscious. He moves back towards the door, squinting, heaving up rotten chestfuls of smoke. Urging all remaining energy into his legs, he charges through the hallway and back into the main room, where the fire, in the space of a minute, has tripled in size. He grunts in pain, the heat unbearable and he staggers back into the room from which he originally came.

The night air, smoky even out here, is nonetheless as fresh as any summer day on Mount Parraspeszi, compared to the house's cindered guts. He lurches forward as many times as he can before the muscles in his legs refuse to co-operate. The ground hits him, but the two children in his arms are cushioned against his forearms as he falls. His head spins like a whirlpool and he feels stupid. He is dimly aware of the children being tugged away from him, and a stamping noise.

Was... one o' them on fire?

No one is paying him much attention, so he finds as he turns his head around.

The mother.

Slowly, his arms drag his weight up and he is faced once again with the fire – the building almost entirely engulfed. His legs support him, though he does not know how, and he staggers towards the building again. It does not feel like him; he is watching this empty figure from higher up. Then comes the lurch of failing timber, the crunch of giving wall. He is only vaguely aware of being thrashed by an agony of noise, fire, wood and mud-brick, before losing consciousness.

Tablet Nine

The silence is exactly as he had expected. When he opens his eyes he will be wading through deathless grass, cerulean skies, a forgiving sun, and there will be loquacious ancestors and horses with hair so fine that it does not even need brushing. Instead, as he opens his eyes, he finds himself looking up into the face, such as it is, of a woman so obese, hairy and astonishingly ugly that he could believe the gods must have competed at a certain stage in the distant past to give life to the most ghastly creature of which they could conceive. *I know that face, but the name…*

'You are lucky, eh?' the voice matches the face. Crackly, deep, foreign. *Familiar.* 'Yes, yes.'

She is pressing something pleasingly cool to his face, and as he responds to this sensation, he also feels other sensations across his body. His head is searing, his ears are ringing, his chest aches, his right arm burns and his face is still a detonation under the wet-cold of the cloth. Nonetheless, he feels strangely relaxed, probably owing to the familiar presence of opium in the air.

He coughs, heaves, finds a cup of water being pressed to his lips, so he ravenously hauls the liquid into his mouth, swallowing half, losing the other half down his chin and neck. He splutters, but soon calms again.

I wonder where I am.

For some reason he does not feel as alarmed or as curious as he might otherwise have felt in such an unfamiliar place. Though he is familiar with the smell of opium, he has never taken the liberty of drawing it in for any length of time – he has seen the effects it has on the sick, the mad, the addicts and Father, who regularly enjoys the drug to better commune with the gods.

'You are probably wondering where you are, yes?' she continues, her voice thick. 'You are in the house of Ura. You know Ura? Course you know Ura.'

'… No… What is an Ura?' *Ura? Ura? Ura?*

'I am an Ura; Ura is my name.' She stubs one millipede-fat finger into a colossal breast – Hektor is put in mind of the sheep stomach water bags used by exotic traders he regularly sees coming into the city. 'I am thinking that this fire and brick and wood – pop!' – she jabs his head painfully, but he can only smile – 'sends your wits to the Under-Spring.' She flourishes her arms – seals tangled in cloth and bangles.

Ura! Of course! '… No.'

'Hmm, you are hurt worse than I am thinking, Hektor.'

Hektor's smile disappears, realising his vulnerability. Part of him dimly recalls what happened. There was the shaking ground. The fire.

'But it has no matter, no, no. You are lifted to hero, yes. Many heroes that night – you one.'

Hero? 'What… did I do, Ura?'

'I hear from the people there that you went into the burning build-ing and were rescuing the little girls.'

Yes, I remember. 'Yeah…'

'Sadly, you were not getting the chance to save the mother – she was found later, she was found. And the baby, she is in peace now too. The shinies would be thinking she is in the Under-Spring – but we know that is not true, eh?'

'She… died?'

'Mm-hmm. Terrible. But you were trying your best, and we all know this. Little girl is living though. She breathed in lots of the smoke, but it was not getting into her channels.'

'Where is she?'

'She is safe. With friend. No shortage of orphans to be taken in by mums and dads who are losing their own children. Sad, sad.' She turns away briefly. 'But the gods are speaking with the earth, and the earth is angry with Wilusa.'

'Yes… the shaking. I remember…'

Ura steps away from the bed, lifting the cloth from Hektor's fore-head and waddling over to a corner of the room where a small basin of water stands.

The room itself is dim, sconce-lit. He only realises now that moonlight is coming in through a torn gauze netting which proofs the room against mosquitoes. Outside, there is a quiet quite out of keeping with the usual din and squabble of an evening in Wilusa's lower town.

'Were… many buildings damaged down here? Many fires?' Hektor persists. 'The walls, yes, how are the walls? What about the—'

'Is that all you are caring about?' Ura glares back over her shoulder at the *tuhkanti*, sunken, circular eyes glazed in disappointment. 'Who is caring about the buildings, the fire damage, the walls? Yes – a lot of damage in that. So? Lots of children are dead in the streets. Lots of orphans too. Men and women crushed by the houses, burned by the fires. So terrible. And is there help from the shinies? No. They are only guarding that hole in the wall, calling night and day, "*Tuhkanti! Tuhkanti!* Where are you?"'

Hektor swallows, more than aware of his own weakness. The effect of the opium is dissipating more and more with each word that comes from Ura's mouth.

'Still, we are keeping together and looking out for ourselves, eh? That is always our way. Let the shinies keep to themselves. Still, we are hearing some news from them tomorrow. The Public Speaker was saying this today in the marketplace.'

'He said what?'

'Hmm? He was saying your father have some news for us all, in regards to the earth shaking. Can't be any worse than we already have, eh? Stay together and we are alright.'

Ura brings the cloth over and places it on Hektor's face again. 'Ura… what have they been saying about… about me?'

'Hmm? They have been saying that they lost you and cannot find you. But between you and me' – she looks around, leans in to Hektor's ear; he can smell opium, herb and rot in her breath – 'I have contacts up in your big house still and they are speaking to me, like Appaliunas talking to your father, eh? The god is telling him that you ran into the lower town, leaving all the shinies to their dying.'

Hektor grinds his lower jaw from left to right. 'What is the… my father doing about that?'

'I am hearing that he is very upset. Still, he is wanting to find you, hear your tale. And they are searching now.'

'Did any of your contacts say if anyone else was... if Hapi was hurt...'

Ura narrows her eyes. '... I am hearing that everyone is fine, apart from one or two fat men and women with shiny titles. You need to be worrying about yourself right now.'

Hektor has not considered his own injuries, but is keenly aware of the various pains playing across his body.

'How badly hurt am I?'

'Hmm.' Ura moves down the *tuhkanti*'s body. 'Legs okay. Cuts and bruises, small burns. Manhood not burned away, either. Ha! Not to worry there – you will still make many lucky girls giggle. Chest okay. Few burns and bruises. Arm had lots of burning though and maybe the damage is inside – not sure. Your face...' She glances up at his face, smiles, looks away. 'No problems, no problems. Very pretty.'

Hektor gazes at the ceiling, thankful that he is okay. But the pain in his face is great – surely it cannot be fine.

'My face... hurts a lot. Are you sure it is fine?'

'Of course, of course,' Ura responds, with a flap of her hand, sidling away to a table.

'You are lying to me. I do not appreciate lying. Tell me.'

Ura sighs. 'Ura is thinking that you should concentrate on getting better. You saved a girl from the fires, who care what your face—'

'Damn the girl! I want to see,' he yells, suddenly panicked.

Ura sighs again, turns around. 'If I am showing you, you promise not to rage and break my house down?'

Now he is alarmed. 'W-What?'

'You are promising?' She is firm.

'Yes... Yes!'

'Keep your voice down, shhh!'

Ura looks around and finally arrives at Hektor's side, holding one of the clay urns women typically use to accommodate water taken from the spring in the lower town. The *tuhkanti* takes the urn, heavy with water and looks down into his reflection. He waits for the water to stop rippling.

The burn runs up half his face, from the chin, across his cheek and ear, narrowly avoiding an eye and ending on his scalp in an oozing patch where hair used to be.

'… No. No.' His voice is perfectly measured, as though his words can make the reality false.

'Remember, you are not breaking my house. You must rest.'

'I cannot rest! Look at me, you vile woman! I am a monster… I need to go. I need to go home. Leave off me!' He throws the urn down on the floor with a watery crash, throws the loose cover off his body. His arms and chest scream with pain as he pulls himself up, but he grinds his teeth in protest at his weakness.

'Please! You need to rest. Don't go down there!' Ura urges, waves massive arms about.

Panting, Hektor staggers towards the leather throws covering a doorway. His head swims with pain, opium, anger. He is vaguely aware of his nakedness, but does not care, and stomps jerkily down the steps outside the doorway.

The room downstairs is large and decorated with horse figurines, horse skulls, horse hair, candles. There are eight, maybe nine people – he is hardly sure – sat on chairs in a circle. They all look at him as he lurches forward, Ura thudding down the steps behind him, yelling something.

Who in the Under-Spring are these people?

Some of the people are standing, others speaking, holding out hands. Above his breathing and the ringing in his ears, he cannot hear what they are saying; however, one face he recognises instantly – Washa. The world grows purple, then prickly white and, finally, black.

When he awakens, he finds himself back in bed, alone. The pain is worse than before; the effect of the opium has near completely worn off. Moonlight occupies the room.

He wonders what is happening in the upper town and in the acropolis. *Hapi, he will not understand any of this, if he is alive…*

But no matter how he tries to turn his mind to his family, his thoughts always return to the scene he witnessed in the upper town: the enormous fissure where the wall had stood; and the food storehouse – gone. Perhaps that is what this announcement from the upper town will be about. With the lower town in disarray and gods know how many dead, the people would require firm leadership and assurances that everything would be done to help them. But he knows Father's mind. If the food is all gone, there will be only one way of ensuring the storehouses are made full again... The commoners are already protesting, and are bold after Washa's performance at the temple – angry after the death of that child on the Mountain.

Distracted, he hears voices, murmurs, conversation coming from downstairs. *That group must still be there.*

Sitting up, his muscles complain and he has to suck in breath to plug the yell driving up from his lungs. In the room's dinginess, he can make out a small pillar of wobbling light shooting up from a patch of floor. Hektor slumps out of bed, this time giving himself several minutes to allow his head to clear, before stepping as delicately as he can over to the light, though the floor creaks more than he would have liked. Below, he counts ten people; Ura is the only one he recognises – no, there is Washa, still.

'... and with the damage to the port I won't be taking the *Sea Bee* back home. Lucky she wasn't destroyed, I suppose,' says a gruff, one-eyed man, scratching a gold-and-silver beard, his voice heavy with the twang of Middle Ahhiyawa, the land to the west across the Aegean.

'Your trade won't be happening, Basil. They'll need them horses for dragging timber. Mark it.' Hektor can only see the balding top of this speaker's head, yet his voice is, strangely, familiar. 'Anyway, Ma, what have the horses told you this last quarter-moon?'

What have the horses told you? Who are these people? Wait, that's Xiuri the landowner!

An old woman clears her throat, noisily. Hektor looks closer. *And that is Xiuri's mother.* She is the high-priestess over in the Bones of the Dead God, the rural community to the south-east. *What are they doing here?*

'Suppose you'll be wanting to know if I saw this earth shaking coming, hmm? If I had, I'd have howled – you know the way of it. I looked in the entrails of only one horse – poor old mare knackered to death – but the Dead God didn't have anything for me. However, we are favoured by Him – as is our cause – remember that.'

So this must be the group Ura mentioned to Washa in the arzana*! But what is it? A secret meeting? And what is their cause?*

'Was there much damage to the Dead God, Ma?' a young woman asks, her voice brash, arms folded. 'Its bones are vulnerable, set out on the hill as they are.'

Ma turns her eyes on the woman. 'No, Three-Shekels, His bones are tough. Maybe He sent the shaking to begin with. Maybe He wants to swallow up rude little twerps like Manis here.' She playfully slaps the younger man.

'Err, in Mykenai, we have a god called Poseidaon,' begins Basil, scratching his gold-and-silver beard again. 'I pray to Him every time I take the *Sea Bee* out, 'cos he lives at the bottom of the Aegean and I don't want his farts shaking my ship. But He shakes the earth when He's angry – might be that He's angry with you lot worshipping your false gods here in Troy.'

The older, balding man whose voice Hektor recognises – *sounds like Xiuri* – turns to Basil. 'That's as well as may be – but if it's true, then He didn't seem to mind fucking up your trade and irritating your mistress in Mykenai. No, all this earth shaking isn't because of gods or us misbehaving – it's because of things we don't understand. The earth is deep and I wager there are things going on down there we can't even imagine, well before we reach the Under-Spring. Yes, laugh if you want, Manis – if I'm so daft and still your master, what does that make you?'

There is appreciative laughter, then...

'And how has the shaking affected... the plan?' This is Washa speaking.

Ah! Now we come to it, thinks Hektor.

'Washa, thank you for coming here as discussed in my *arzana*, but we are now on the sixth night of the fourth quarter-moon and you know my feelings on the plan by now.' Ura's voice is sad, tired.

'We are,' replies the young woman they earlier called Three-Shekels. 'But we also know that it cannot continue. Think how bad it will be now that their food depot is gone. It's obvious what the Public Speaker will say tomorrow.'

Ma breaks into a watery cough. 'The Dead God gives me no counsel on these matters. No, no, no.'

'He won't,' Three-Shekels replies. 'This is a matter for men. The gods are with the shinies and can be excused from any plans of ours.'

Ma laughs, unattractively. 'Where death is concerned, the gods are *always* involved. And the Dead God is pleased with our plans.'

Hektor pulls himself up as quickly as he can and looks around. *Death? I need to leave...* There is a tunic and kilt in a corner, so he pulls them on. The window is small, but he can fit through it.

Kicking the gauze net from the window, Hektor clambers out onto a ledge, loses his footing, falls into a crate of apricots at ground level. An open-mouthed, silent scream of pain, but he raises himself and staggers off into the night, fruit juice trailing down thighs, face and arm burning.

'I am the *tuhkanti* – look at me.'

The guards look closely at Hektor, then one of them says, 'If you are the *tuhkanti*, tell me the names of your mare and her foal.'

'Kummi. Aras. Now let me in.'

The guard nods cautiously after a few moments. '*Dek*, sir. We are under orders to take you straight to the *labarna*. Please come with us.'

He has made his way through the lower town as quickly as he could manage, considering the pain. The sun has come up and it is now mid-morning. *I need a physician.* Briefly, he wonders at Ura having not enlisted Washa to help treat him, *but if he were to do so he would recognise me. Ura cannot have told that group who I am... But why?*

His thoughts are now of Father and Hapi. Until this moment he has tried to block out all thought of his son, for fear of letting his feeling overwhelm him – his emotion is a dark country, unknown and dangerous, a country to avoid whenever possible. He imagines his boy in all manner of circumstances – all manner of injuries, deaths, calling out for him. However, it would seem duty will, once again, trump any attempt he might now make to locate Hapi.

The upper town is in a worse state than the lower. In the truth of daylight, the shaking's damage is not to be disguised. Buildings are collapsed, half-collapsed. At the very least, every structure has suffered damage. There are bodies, lined up along the paths, covered in sheets to protect their identity and dignity. Near off, he can see the stables. There are groups of men gathering around stray horses, attempting to capture them.

'What are the casualties for the horses?' Hektor asks one of the guards.

'Several dead, sir. One dead stable-hand as well. And...'

'Yes?'

'Your son is in the stables with Kummi and Aras.'

The *tuhkanti* lets out a gasp, hobbles off briskly towards the stables, gritting his teeth against the burns. There are tears in the corners of his eyes, *but that is because of the pain.*

A small crowd of personnel gathers around the stable entrance; there are holes throughout the structure where several of the horses have escaped. Hektor shoves his way through the crowd and looks long and deep into the stable itself. At the back, in Kummi and Aras's joint pen, a little boy is curled up in a corner. One of his two equine companions sniffs at his curly hair, perhaps bemused at the presence of this curious intruder. It is, indeed, Hapi.

The *tuhkanti* breathes in deep, feels a terrible knot slipping from his chest – as though a second heart had taken residence there, but is now redundant.

'H-Hapi... Hapi,' he starts, stepping cautiously forward. 'It's me... It's – it's *tati*.'

He slips into the pen, closing the creaking gate behind him. Kummi comes over to investigate and he runs his hand along the animal's cheek, then behind her ears.

'So, were you looking after Aras, through the shaking? Hmm? ... Scary, wasn't it?'

'Where were you?' Hapi's response comes from behind folded arms, sullen, accusative, heavy with tears.

'I-I... well, I looked for you,' Hektor replies, stepping nearer as though approaching a rogue predatory animal in the wilds. 'I couldn't see you in the acropolis. I called. Gods, how I called. I was on the central patio. I thought one of the columns had…' He turns away, closes his eyes, steadies his breath. Hapi is silent. 'Hapi, where were you?'

'You don't listen to me. You should have known where I'd be.'

'What? How could I—'

'I told you. I *told* you. When I was poorly, I told you where I was – in my head, I was in the stables. I told you it's where I felt safe. I told you. I told you. You should have known.'

Hektor makes to speak, but the breath escapes in a gust of incredulity. 'But, but Hapi. I can't remember everything you tell me. My mind is so taken up with—'

'With your *duties*.' Hapi snarls the word, whipping his head around. Still, he does not look up at his father. 'I ran here when it started. I covered my ears and closed my eyes tight – like *this*' – he closes his eyes tightly, then opens them once his demonstration is complete – 'and I whispered to myself, "*Tati* will come. *Tati* will come." But you didn't.'

Hektor is uncomfortably aware of his own inability to counter this indictment. He can sense the eyes on him at the stable entrance. Hapi's eyes: large, demanding, confused – finally they lock on the *tuhkanti*. He jolts hard against the stable wall.

'W-What happened to you?' His voice trembles.

'Sir, my Sun was expressly clear that he wanted to see you as soon as—'

'Shut up!' the *tuhkanti* yells, the guard behind him slinking away. He turns back to Hapi, tramping forward, kneeling down in front of his son. He grabs the boy's hands tightly in his one good hand, shaking slightly. 'Look at me, Hapi! Look at me. Don't be afraid.'

'You look scary. You look like a monster.' He starts crying.

'Do you know how this happened to me? I tried to rescue people in the lower town. There was so much fire. *I* was frightened. What could I do, Hapi? I didn't know where you were and there were people in trouble.'

'You should have known. You should have known. You never know. You're never there! I hate you! And now you're ugly!' Hapi tears himself from his father's grip, runs off out of the stables.

Hektor looks at his hands – the one burned and searing with pain, the other empty, where his son's hand had been. He lifts himself up from a squat, quickly wipes at an eye and turns to the guards behind him. *They cannot see me like this. I am their* tuhkanti *and I must be more than a man, more than a father.*

'*Dek*. I'm ready to see my Sun now.'

Tablet Ten

'Come. Come sit down.' The *labarna*'s voice is stern.

On a simple wooden table is a proliferation of fruits, breads, cheeses, meats. Parta presides over Priam, and, opposite her, Kaluti sits rigidly, clearly in some emotional discomfort.

'Have some food. There is plenty. You must be hungry after your time away,' Priam continues, as Hektor greets his family with customary bows, taking a seat next to his half-sister. The *tuhkanti* tugs at some bread. Priam looks on with an unchanging expression, wavering delicately, but maintaining a pose that suggests he has been locked into a single moment in time.

'Gods, boy. What happened to you?' Parta gasps, dropping a plate.

Hektor looks briefly up, then across at Kaluti, who is crying.

'Burned. I was attempting to save—'

'And now you are *spoiled*,' she spits the word. 'My Sun,' she continues, turning to her husband and clasping his shoulder. 'You can't send him now, not like *this*. Who would have him?'

Priam raises a hand, silencing his wife.

'I trust none of *you* were hurt,' Hektor says, remembering the last time he had seen his parents – his father bleeding.

'The gods do not harm those they favour.'

Hektor flinches. *What does he want? Co-ordinating the clear-up? Defending the lack-of-wall?*

'Have you seen the food stores?'

'I have, my Sun. I am concerned.'

Beside him, Kaluti snivels, folds her arms. Parta leans across and smacks her on the back of the hand, holding up a single finger, dangerously.

What's wrong with the child?

'And your horse: it is safe? Well?'

'... Yes, my Sun.'

'Mmm,' Priam grunts in a fierce bass. 'Good. Good.'

The *labarna*'s contribution to the conversation devolves into heavy breathing through thick nostrils. A distant smile cracks purple lips. Priam is prone to moments of contemplation, as though he is in a continual process of composing attempts at thought.

Hektor patiently sustains guerilla raids upon food and water. Gods, he is hungry and thirsty both.

'Indeed,' Priam says quietly, to himself more than anyone.

Parta seems to understand, and leans in closer to him, tightening her arm around his back and placing her hand on his wrist. 'Are you sure? You know how much speaking drains you, I'm perfectly capable—'

'Woman – no. Let Us say this.' He looks across at his son. 'B-boy, your mother doesn't think We should say all this. But for you We make an exception... You are Our prized *tuhkanti*. Of all surviving, you are a rock for Wilusa and for Us—'

'Really, I do not need to hear any—'

Priam closes his eyes, raises a hand. 'We said We'd say this and We will... We have watched you grow into a good public servant. *Tuhkanti*, you remind Us of Our self when We were younger. You obey as Appaliunas and Tarhun decree a *tuhkanti* should obey his *labarna*. We value this more than We suspect many others might.' Dramatic pause. Kaluti picks her wrist. 'You have kept the people in order. Mostly. Despite recent events. Of us, you have kept with Us in all we decree... But recent events have not gone your way. No. No. The incident at the Mountain was your fault. Your idea. You have disappointed – angered the gods. Upset Us. This shaking shows the gods will not tolerate any further...' He coughs, Parta holding him tighter.

Hektor feels a blade of anger. 'My Sun, I do nothing but my—'

Priam again closes his eyes, again raises a hand. 'L-Let Us – let Us finish. Please. We are almost done... You said you saw the storehouses. Early indications are that We will have to tax the farmers further to make up for *Our* shortfall. This will not be accepted calmly by the commoners. *Tuhkanti*, We are in danger. Our numbers are fewer. Now, Our guards are fewer. Now, the wall is weakened. We need help. Help. Now. That is where you have the chance... The chance...'

'You're tired now, my Sun. Let me finish,' Parta interrupts. Priam sighs.

The *tawananna* turns to her son, affecting the same blank expression with which Hektor has always felt uneasy. 'We have waited eagerly for you to return to us, and knew you would. We have taken the liberty of planning for such. Well, anyway, the heart of the matter is this: as you know, when Masturi visited recently, my Sun refused to negotiate a joining between you and Luha—'

'Terrible girl. Terrible.'

'Indeed. But now the situation is different; it is *severe*,' Parta says with exasperation in her voice, pushing grey hair back from her forehead. 'Seha can offer us additional men to defend ourselves in a heartbeat – they are, geographically, very close to us, after all. It would be enough to save us from whatever barbarity the commoners might concoct, at least for now. This is our only chance and you must do your duty.' Parta lifts her head, clears her throat. 'Hektor, you are to travel to the heart of Seha, to the Four Forts where Masturi holds Gate. You will offer the man gifts which are even now being prepared and you will say that you have come to take Luha as a wife. Additionally, you shall take Kaluti here' – her open palm extends towards Hektor's half-sister – 'as we need to fulfil our promise to Masturi of her becoming his *esertu* wife. We hope that he will not be offended at the time it has taken to… prepare Kaluti for him, as this should have been done sooner—'

'Nonsense. Nonsense. There was no rush.'

'With a contract agreed, you must make Masturi aware of our plight and… and beg, if need be, that he offer what we require. We can only hope that he did not take too much offence when my Sun refused you joining with Luha. That is your task, Hektor, and a way of redeeming yourself in my Sun's eyes.'

'Mmm, yes, yes. We have faith in you.' The *labarna* raises his head.

Parta looks at her husband, opening and closing her mouth.

The *tuhkanti* digests this information as stolidly as he might digest the announcement of a new taxation law. He is entirely unprepared for joining with a woman, though he has always known the day would eventually come when he would be required to perform this particular duty. It seems the most natural thing to accept this dictate, to jump at the possibility of redeeming himself. However, within him there is something rebellious screaming not to do it. But this is his truth. Despite everything he has seen recently – and learned – he is still the *tuhkanti*, and that is all that is realistically his. This he feels, and though it seems entrapment, he lacks the will and the courage to free himself.

Hektor sets his mouth firmly, swallows hard. 'Indeed, my Sun. I am the servant of Wilusa, and Wilusa needs me…'

Priam attempts a smile.

Parta squeezes her husband's wrist. 'As is the custom, you must make an initial offering to Masturi for his girl. Fortunately, my Sun has already arranged for a gift to be readied. You'll find gold, rugs – freshly dusted – and good stallions all gathered ready in the portico of the acropolis, which should be quite enough to satisfy Masturi.'

The *tuhkanti*'s mouth falls open. 'Gathered, as in, already? You mean I should leave for Seha today?'

'Don't be ridiculous. Tomorrow at dawn will do just fine. That shouldn't be a problem, should it? Only your duties take your time, and my Sun has seen to it that they are handed to others for a short while. Now, your best clothing has already been loaded onto a cart with the gifts and – I know you won't like it but you'll just have to accept it on this occasion – I have seen to it that kohl, henna and jewellery have also been packed; you will have to' – her eyes rove up and down his face with contempt – '*look* your best in the Sehan court. A show of our strength.'

Hektor stares vacantly down at the table. '… I understand.'

'Good. You will be escorted by a small number of guards to ensure your safety. You should think about preparing too. My Sun has seen to most things, but, clearly, you'll have to ready your own horse and your own supplies. You will help your sister too; you will be able to tell her what she needs to take for a long journey far better than any servant or stable boy.'

A servant signals to Parta, who turns to her husband and whispers in his ear.

Priam clears his throat. Parta helps him up.

'Well, *tuhkanti*, we hope your mother has made that all clear enough. We're sure you'll do very well. We have to go now though. It seems the commoners have started surrounding the food depots in the countryside. The farmers, they seem to guess our plans. They are not slow. Remember, boy, this is your chance to redeem yourself. Do Us proud.'

'Oh,' Parta adds, as she stands, 'see a herb widow or something about your burns. You look horrible.'

The *tuhkanti* breathes deep once his parents have gone, massages his forehead, turns to his half-sister, who is staring tearfully up at him.

'I'll catch up with you later, sister. And… I will help you with your packing.' He pats her on the shoulder, walks away towards his personal quarters, only remembering once he arrives that they were destroyed in the shaking.

Finally, he finds a stranger's empty bed chamber, where he relishes the rare moment of physical isolation, and half-collapses into a divan, clutching his face, breathing violently, muttering indiscriminate prayers to gods he is struggling to comprehend.

Tablet Eleven

Hektor opens his eyes at the sound of a servant's firm whispers; night is in labour with dawn.

'*Tuhkanti, tuhkanti.* Cicadas are already singing in the grass, and Appaliunas is rubbing His eyes.'

'Ah, yes. You can go now.'

Groggy, he pulls himself up, and looks indiscriminately around the dim, blue quarters he has had to call home this past night.

The memory of yesterday instigates misery. He sighs, clambers from his bed. The servant leads him to a bath already prepared, stepping over small piles of rubble as he goes.

Duty does not inhibit his emotions, as many privately, or even publicly, joke. News of his arranged joining has, though he would scarcely indulge the feeling, mortified him.

Having grown up in a community that emphasised his political position in the structure of the city, Hektor found himself isolated at an exceptionally early age. He could not partake in the common activities of childhood, and had to quickly learn that much depended on his ability, especially since the incident that left his father paralysed in mind and body. In the *tuhkanti*'s presence, every person, from the gardener to the *labarna* himself, had to adopt a certain propriety, Hektor recalls only too well, thus negating any natural affection or interest they felt towards him as a person. Although he has never been truly alone, the thought of accepting another person so intimately into his life is mind-rending. He knew this day would arrive though, but what the mind avoids deliberating will not bother the heart.

The bathwater is searing heat – his preference, though he grits his teeth against the pain from his burns, stoic as ever – birthing beard-lengths of steam, wriggling upwards, swallowing air, regurgitating vapours. The water is stained with oils, embalming the atmosphere with scents of lavender, honey, lily and orchid. Petals span the water's surface. Lanes of moisture collect across close stucco walls.

Hektor's muscles tense, spasm. His heart is loud in his ears, his lungs shrinking, bulging, shrinking, bulging. He bites down so hard his teeth ache. It takes several minutes for him to acclimatise to the pain – the punishment – but once he does so – and has controlled his breathing – he becomes near-limp in his relaxation. His eyes close in red darkness under a cloth. He spent much of the previous evening explaining to Hapi the duty that his father had placed upon him. *Hmph, and didn't that go well.* It is clear to him that the boy is not destined to embrace the life he leads; for his part, he simply cannot understand why the child has such difficulty in this. Their upbringings have been dissimilar, but they are in the same building, with the same teachings and same expectations. Hapi cried when he told him the news, perhaps fearful at the perceived loss of his father to another person's love, and cried further when he told him that he would be staying in Wilusa while he travelled.

In his daydream, he has dawdled into semi-consciousness, but is startled back to vigilance by a feeling that he is not alone. He jumps, pulls the cloth away from his eyes, and finds the bathhouse occupied by his mother.

'Wh-what in the Under-Spring do you think you are doing?' he growls, leaping up.

His mother glances away.

The fact that Hektor stands naked, with rose petals attached to him, does not bolster his attempt to appear dangerous.

After his initial anger, Hektor remembers his nakedness and sits, swiping at stray rose petals still clinging to his chest. He clamps his mouth shut, looks grimly into the water.

Parta is silent, but looks back again at her son.

Hektor tries to avoid her eyes, clears his throat, turning red from the embarrassment of his outburst. 'Is there anything I can do for you, *tawananna?*'

'I wanted to apologise,' she finally says, her voice oddly gentle as she settles down on a stone block. She looks towards the door, seemingly nervous.

Hektor searches his mother's eyes. They are tired.

'What do you want to apologise for?' *I sound suspicious. I suppose I am.*

'That this is happening to you. That you must be forced to marry against your will.' She appears close to tears as she looks up into the rafters of the bathhouse.

'Why should you care, *tawananna*?' Hektor blurts out, his jaw twitching. 'I must do this for the good of my people – for the good of my Sun. It is a sacrifice I must make because that is who I am and that is… that is *all* I am – all that is of consequence. What do you know of sacri—?' But he regrets it at once.

Parta's eyes flash angrily. 'What do I know of sacrifice?' Her voice sounds dangerously close to breaking. 'What do I know? You think this is the life I wanted to lead? I grew up not so far from Wilusa. I used to run about in the gardens – in the woods – playing with friends and indulging in imagination, much as your boy does. *My* father was a good man. He treated me well, gave me attention. I used to sit on his knee and he would name the cities of our world: Hattusa, Myke-nai, Heliopolis… It was well until he pointed Wilusa out on a map. He told me of its horses, its gold, its importance. I wish he hadn't been so kind to me; it made it that much harder when I was married off to your father. I was only thirteen.'

Parta pauses, breathing hard, the anguish in her eyes bearing out in her face. Hektor continues to watch her, struck by such an uncharacteristic outburst.

'I have watched so much of my life – *myself* – leak away, like rain draining in soil. What am I now? A husk. A husk propping up centuries of tradition, propping up a god. My one blessing has been that I have only ever birthed you, that I have not had to watch child after child taken from me as *I* was taken from my home.'

'I am still here,' Hektor manages, trying to keep his voice soft.

Parta makes eye contact with him. 'And I feel you trickling away too. Every day. Ever since you were a child, with that woman Ura as your nurse. It is so hard to bear. But who gives a thought to a mother's anguish?' she spits. 'Who cares for us? We are forgotten, as though our influence was of no consequence. After your father – after the demon tore through him, in Seha, he forgot *everything*. I had to teach him to read again, to give him the meaning of numbers – he used to look at me and say, "Who are you, woman?"' Parta runs a hand through her hair, a tear escaping at last. 'It is a question I have asked myself ever since.' She looks at Hektor, eyes suddenly fierce again, then stands, jabs a finger at him. 'So when you question what I know of sacrifice, know that it is all that has defined my life! And if you feel that duty is all of any consequence that defines you, then you have my pity. Safe travelling, *tuhkanti*.'

Hektor hardly registers his mother leave the bathhouse.

Hektor hears the disturbance before he reaches the courtyard. He recognises the precocious tone of Kaluti among several other voices. In the courtyard, numerous horses stand idly, Kummi included, chewing expertly cultivated grass, while systematically excreting over the flowerbed; a large wagon sits with its protective sheet half-open, supplies neatly piled up inside, though a number of boxes holding gifts for Luha lie unceremoniously across the ground; guardsmen assigned to this entourage are standing about with dumbfounded expressions as, standing at the centre of a heated argument, Kaluti screams up at a woman – her mother. A little behind Kaluti stands the reserved figure of Hapi, arms folded.

'I won't go anywhere without him! You can't make me. *Hektor* can't make me.'

'Why do you have to be so petulant, child? Do you see other children acting so disrespectfully? You've been given this opportunity for a future most people can only dream of, yet still— Ah, look, here's your brother now. Perhaps *he* can pinch this attitude out of you. Peace and light on your path, Hektor, though with my daughter acting the way she is I can't see there being much chance of that. She was meant to be all ready for you to leave. I'm very sorry.'

The *tuhkanti* does not want a headache. 'I am sure we can resolve whatever problem my sister might have. Now, Kaluti, in your own words, tell me what is wrong.'

'It isn't fair. I don't want to go anywhere without Hapi... Go on' – the girl huffs, grabbing Hapi by the shoulder and pushing him forward – 'tell them!'

Hapi shuffles forward, head bowed, hands linked.

Hektor folds his arms. 'Well, Hapi, what have you to say for your-self?'

'P–Please can I go with you, *tati*? I promise I'll be good.' His head remains bowed.

The guardsmen chuckle.

Hektor growls. It is enough to spend such a journey with one child, but two will probably push him over the edge.

'Why do you want to go with us? You are hardly in an appropriate condition for travel. In case you've forgotten, you have only just had a demon removed from your belly.' Kaluti's mother and the guardsmen lift palms upward, muttering protective prayers. '... And' – he lowers his voice – 'I thought you didn't like me anymore.'

'I–I know, a–and I don't... but I'm feeling much better. Honest! I've even got my things together, and... and... and I'm going for Kaluti, yes, not *you* – Kaluti's my friend—'

'Best friend, Hapi, *best* friend.'

'—best friend, a–and I want to see her safely to Seha.'

The guardsmen make sounds of mock sentimentality, but stop when the *tuhkanti* raises a hand.

'I won't go without him!' Kaluti pouts.

Hektor sighs, lifts his arms and drops them. 'Well, it appears I have little choice. Hapi, if you come, you can spend time with me learning some of the things you will need for when you are *tuhkanti*. You can take Aras with you—'

'But, *tati*—'

'No "buts". Hmph, if you come along then... at least I can keep an eye on you – make sure you don't get into any trouble – not that I want you to come or anything, with your behaviour.'

'And I'm only going for Kaluti,' the boy retorts.

'Very well. At least we understand each other... We are late to start, so come on let's ready your foal, then we can get moving.'

Kaluti leaps up, cheering, patting Hapi furiously on the back. The *tuhkanti* grunts disapprovingly, and stalks off towards Kummi, who is busy investigating a shrub. *At least she seems happy.*

Arrangements are soon complete, despite the mess, and despite Hektor's insistence on a final, thorough cataloguing of all the gifts. The entourage collectively kneels, and incites the storm god, Tarhun, to grant clear skies; Appaliunas to offer protection to the company and stamina to the horses; and numerous minor deities of travel, roads and even wagons, to condescend to support the journey in various other ways. Kaluti suffers a tearful farewell with her mother (argument forgotten by the end). The *tuhkanti* gives Wilusa one final moment of reflection, feeling somewhat dislocated with the knowledge that the next time he looks upon this city his political standing will have undergone dramatic and irreversible changes.

The group thunders out of a postern gate, through the wide streets of the lower town, past the wooden palisade that surrounds it, and over a bridge spanning the defensive ditch, the horses digging south, deep into the red-black stain of the Wilusan plains.

Hektor busies himself by reflecting on the route that has been charted by Wilusa's chief cartographer. He recalls that, by direct cloud-path, there is a great distance between Wilusa and Four Forts, the capital of Seha, despite them being near neighbours. This distance is clogged with snow-capped mountains, which means a far more circuitous route is required for the group to travel. Hektor understands that he must continue south for some time, hugging the coastline, drifting past small settlements until they reach the westernmost tip of the Wilusan region, near the fishing colonies, known collectively as Wida-Harwa. Here they will set up camp somewhere around the nearby woodland. The *tuhkanti* wishes to avoid places with any real population, as it will be a concern if news were to spread that he is travelling in only a small group alongside a wagon laden with valuables. He will look to cover a good distance each day, setting up camp in an appropriate location every evening.

Wilusa, as looked back upon by the *tuhkanti*, occupies a craggy hill gazing out over the Aegean Sea, which is only a short ride away from the city itself. To the north runs the diminutive river, Uwitar-Amiyaraza, but, to the south, the far larger Katkatenutti flows inland from a large estuary, sitting at the mouth of the Hellespont. To the east, a plentiful mountain range isolates Wilusa from the land of Hatti where Muršili II reigns as Big *labarna*. Wilusa has, for some thirty years, fallen under the jurisdiction of the expansive Hattian authority, fulfilling the role of vassal state – one of many vassal states that make up Hatti's bloated geopolitical map. Further down the Aegean coast, the regions of Seha, Assuwa and Mira unite with Wilusa to collectively form Arzawa, which, after many decades of political disturbance and social unrest, has become more and more compliant with Muršili II under his awkward peace. However, Arzawa is home to rebellious factions, incompetent Hattian puppet-magistrates, ambitious local rulers and small centres of Ahhiyawan authority.

He pulls himself from his daydream and surveys the lands around him. It is pleasing to feel the violence of Kummi's thudding beneath his legs again. He considers it likely that, in his union with Luha, he will not be allowed as much time for this simple indulgence, and will instead have to attend to duties required for a successful relationship.

Hektor assures himself that he and Luha are not being fused into one identity – that they are not like the single god who is Appaliunas by day, but also Arma by night. *No, this is not my oblivion; I will not let it be. But even if it were, I would walk into it willingly, as it is my duty,* and though he values his own individuality, he would willingly see it extinguished for the greater benefit of Wilusa.

Irritably, he acknowledges he will have to overcome his anxiety around women – especially beautiful women – at least to a certain degree. He offers a prayer to Ishtar, asking that Luha might in fact be decidedly short, plain-looking and timid, or if she were not that way now then might it please the goddess to alter her appearance and personality suitably inside of the next quarter-moon.

Appaliunas reaches the apex of His cycle and Hektor pulls his horse up near a stream, calling the group to a halt. They have journeyed solidly for many hours, reaching a respectable pace, despite the accompanying wagon's bulk, stopping a few times along the way where the shade of woodland invited. Though the sun is high, the wind blows with a noticeable chill.

Hektor takes several guardsmen with him into a patch of woodland to collect various nuts and fruits for lunch, though a small quantity of cheese is also pulled out of the wagon, as the *tuhkanti* feels a craving for such.

Everyone settles down to their meal. The guardsmen chat and share jokes between themselves while the *tuhkanti* takes both his son and half-sister away from the group.

'It's not appropriate for us to eat with the guards,' Hektor explains to the children, who are naturally curious as to the motive for separation.

The three sit in silence, the two children adhering to this apparent need for calm and segregation. They soon become restless.

'*Tati*, can we go and play, please?' Hapi asks, in a wheedling tone.

Hektor shakes his head.

'My bottom has gone stiff from all that riding. Please can we go and play?'

Hapi has ridden with a guard so far, Aras being far too young to be mounted; the foal has cantered beside Kummi instead.

'No, I want to speak to you.'

'Is it going to be one of your lessons on duty again?'

'What? No, no. Well, in a manner of speaking, yes, but it is different this time.'

'It's never any different though. You always tell me that I have to put my responsibilities first before I can play. But I don't have any responsibilities.'

'You have Aras. Besides, you are at an age where you are ready to learn some more. And I shall be the one to tutor you. Understood?'

'Yes, *tati*.'

'Well, I certainly hope so. You have always been as a magpie among swallows, disturbing the nest without a care – no wonder that demon chose your body to live in; that is what happens when you are ill-disciplined. But no more. Your wildness must be refined. There will be no simple task or goal; we must keep our aim high and never waver.' Hektor crosses his arms and closes his eyes briefly, appreciating the silence before continuing. 'Right. Aside from daily physical training, you will continue mathematical and language studies with your current tutor in the *eduba*; it is imperative—'

'Why?'

Hektor sighs, leans back on his hands. 'Because most of your duties, when you are an adult, will revolve around regional politics. That may include anything from drawing up trade negotiations with foreign rulers to monitoring agricultural tribute from the countryside settlements. Following on from that, you will have to learn how to conduct yourself propitiously in your dealings, both face-to-face and written, with dignitaries inside and outside of Wilusa. Do you understand?'

Hapi scratches his head. 'I-I think so… It sounds boring though. Can't someone else do this, and I'll just do the rest?'

Hektor pauses. 'Whether you like it or not, Hapi, the position you shall one day inherit calls for excellence in all your studies, which brings me to perhaps the most important education you shall receive.'

'Does it involve swords?'

'Not if it can be helped. I am talking of your spiritual training. My Sun, as you know, is high-priest over all our religious establishments. He is supreme judge over all issues of contention brought before him, acting on behalf of Appaliunas. To appreciate the magnitude of my Sun's duties, you must become a faithful disciple of the temples, as I have, and verse yourself well in the nature of our pantheon. You must understand this of all things, as it is chief among your priorities.' Hektor explains, glancing up at Kummi and Aras – mare and foal close by, grazing.

Hapi apparently absorbs all he has heard, nodding unconsciously before looking back up and smiling. 'Will I learn to ride Aras as well?'

'Yes, you will learn to ride Aras – but not yet; he is too young. You will have to continue breaking him in to begin—'

'Wh-what is it, tati?'

Hektor looks up at a nearby hill. Running down it: a group of men, numbering somewhere between twelve and fifteen. Though unarmoured, they are well armed. The guards, at the foot of the hill with the wagon and their horses, see the attackers too and leap up in a breath, ready for combat.

'Stay here, both of you,' Hektor commands. He pulls himself up also, drawing his sword in a gleam of bronze.

The *tuhkanti* dashes towards the guards and wagon, entering the fray, which is already a squall of blade, blood and brawling. First, a large man in a cloth tunic throws himself forward, a clumsy swipe with his sword leaving him open to Hektor's counter-attack, which tears the man's belly open in a rupture of gore and guts. Next: two more men, both smaller than the first, but they compensate by launching themselves at him at once. Hektor parries one attack with his weapon, weaves under the second, kicks out with a heavy foot into a knee, bringing one man down. The other man he hacks at, but the attack is parried, so he ducks under the next assault and rends tendon from thigh in a butcher's display of meat. With his next attack, he has the man impaled on his sword and is alert enough to withdraw it immediately to defend himself from the man whose knee he had kicked. After a brief exchange, he punches out at the attacker's nose and, in the man's momentary frailty, Hektor brings his sword up through his lower jaw, into the roof of his mouth, embedding it in his skull: bone, tooth and eyeball bursting forth.

The guards easily contend with the other aggressors, taking only the one casualty, but a cry from Kaluti draws Hektor's attention to the children. A lone man runs at them, so the *tuhkanti* pursues. *He will reach them before I do.*

'Children! Get behind the horses!' he roars.

Hapi and Kaluti have already scrambled to their feet, and dive behind the nearby Kummi and Aras – mare and foal tied to an olive tree. The attacker reaches them, jabs and thrusts at the children with his short-spear to the right of the tree, between the horses, to the left of the tree. Kummi rears up, narrowly avoids stamping on Kaluti. Hektor arrives just as the man launches a final attack on the children, which misses, but severs the rope tying Aras to the tree instead; the foal, already startled, spins about and runs off into the distance. Hektor parries a spear thrust and jams his sword in between the man's ribs. He screams once, hits the ground – dead.

Panting, Hektor looks from Hapi to Kaluti, who both run forward and hug him around the waist.

'You two are okay.' He nods through heavy breaths, more to reassure himself.

Hektor looks back at the guards who have dispatched the last of the attackers. He looks down at the dead man. He is just a farmer, fisherman or a merchant, perhaps – not a gritty bandit. There is something around his neck. Hektor pushes away the children, not unkindly, crouches down, pulls what he can only describe as a necklace from the man's throat. Coarse thread, running through dried apricot and pomegranate chunks. *These two foods again, just like the shrines in the lower town... What was this attack then? Opportunism? Retaliation? Zealotry?*

'*Tati*, w–what about Aras?' Hapi stutters, his face pale. Next to him, Kaluti is equally pale and wiping a hint of vomit from the corner of her mouth.

Hektor looks about for the foal and sees him – still running away in a blind panic. He smiles.

'We go after him, Hapi – seems Appaliunas challenges you already. Kaluti, you stay here with the guards.'

Kaluti looks up. 'I thought we were meant to stay away from the gua—'

'Just do as I say!' He turns to Hapi. 'You ready?'

'I–I think so.'

'Good, let's go and get your foal.'

Hektor looks over his shoulder and, sure enough, in the distance, the guards are all slung back over the wagon or the grass, watching the *tuhkanti* lead Hapi out towards Aras, who has approached a group of wild horses, perhaps instinctively searching out his own kind in his separation from Kummi. His heart still thudding, Hektor tries to steady himself and turn his thoughts to something more prosaic. *When was it I last spent time with Hapi? Yes, think on that.* Invariably, the boy was keen for his father to join in with his silly, childish amusements – like hiding in the garden, leaving Hektor to find him. *I remember when he got stuck up a tree doing that once. Took an hour to get him down.* The memory draws a smile to his face. Or playing 'market day' with all Hapi's toys, Kuressar the cloth-cat being the deep-voiced trader who always ran out of aubergines. *Were those days really such a chore?* Even looking down at his son now, he feels a sense of pride, a sense of wonder that a miniature remodelling of himself could be walking about, growing and both emulating and assassinating the character traits he recognises as having existed in his own younger self. The thought of his own failings as a father suddenly fills him with a desperate sadness, and anger.

'Why did Aras run from Kummi so far?' Hapi asks.

'He was spooked,' Hektor replies. 'He needs to learn discipline and for that he must be tamed. You must tame a foal, like Aras, because one of the most important relationships in your life is that which exists between you and your horse. Most people see horses as tools for travel and burden. But we each have the ability to energise that sacred link which has always existed between man and beast. Breaking the foals of Wilusa is no easy task as here our horses grow rebellious and coarse. The challenge is not only to break the foal, but to unite your own spirit with that of the animal. You must then guide it on its path through life.'

Hapi pauses... then: 'Yes, *tati.*'

'Good. Enough talk for now. I want us to concentrate on the task at hand, if we're going to actually do this.'

Hektor leads a trail across the plains. The wind blows blue notes. Cicadas chatter; other animals perform their usual routines within the trees and swamps. The track on which father and son walk is quickly absorbed by weed-smothered rock. Nature reveals its nudity.

Finally, Hektor and Hapi arrive at a field, secluded from the plains by a curvature of pine trees. In the field, a large group of horses graze, Aras among them.

'They're moving into shelter... Are you alright?'

Hapi rubs his belly. 'Yeah, I'm okay. Just aches a little. But... I barely feel it. So, what happens now, *tati*?'

'Follow my lead.'

Hektor rubs at his face where the burn still sears away – the sunlight livid. He is thankful that no one has – *yet* – mentioned his appearance. *Except Hapi. And Kaluti. And two of the guards. And Father and Mother.* At least his arm is not as bad as it might have been. He can move it with little discomfort and the sun has not exaggerated the pain too greatly. He wonders how Masturi will take him, looking as he does. *Or Luha, for that matter, if she is as picky as Mother says.*

'Yes, *tati*. Hey wait!' Hapi runs a few paces to his right, rips up some parsley. 'The second thing I learned back on Mount Parraspeszi, remember?'

The *tuhkanti* smiles, rubs the boy's head. They move into the grass, the horses a good five hundred paces ahead. Hektor opens his legs a little. Hapi copies, parsley swinging from his outstretched arm. The horses, proud and poised, do not seem to regard the approaching figures with any interest, and so carry on with various discussions in the rolling of their own language.

Hektor watches Aras, lingering by a mare's flank.

... The space between them closes quickly.

Hektor and Hapi phase through the lengthy grass. Hektor is careful not to make direct eye contact with any of the horses, but allows his gaze to rise and fall over the neck and haunch of each animal. Hektor pulls a length of rope from his belt, hands it to Hapi. 'Now, ready your rope and parsley, and pay close attention to the reaction of Aras.'

The horses graze in silence, tails and necks occasionally swishing. 'Are you excited?'

'I'm not sure. Maybe. I do feel something.' Hapi sounds troubled, *but I'll ignore that – just nerves.*

They slip sideways. Hektor blinks in response to the gaze of several horses, assuring them he is not a threat. Aras prods forward, still near to the mare's flank. Appaliunas's oil-light trickles through his hair. Hektor clicks his tongue, mutters praise, trying to settle unthreaded nerves. Several horses murmur, perhaps with concern. Aras faces him, nose twitching maybe in recognition of a familiar smell. Hektor catches his eye – one glossy dome as deep and as distance-swallowing as summer constellations. Hektor's hands slip into the relative positions along the rope. He ensures his boy does the same.

'When we're in a hurry to get back home, we tend to burst along the final stretch of the journey in our impatience. When we catch a foal, we must not be so impetuous. Instead, we must slow down, right to the final second.'

'Yes, *tati*.'

Ten paces.

'This is your moment, Hapi. I want you to take the lead in the final approach. Trust your instincts. I will support you, but I want you to make the first attempt.'

Hektor allows his son to step in front, creeping at an angle, towards the side of Aras. The foal looks at Hapi, encouraging the mare beside it to do likewise. Hapi freezes, blinks, turns his head deferentially from the potency of the horses' gaze. Hapi moves, attempting coos. Hektor follows, aware that the horses are on edge.

Five paces.

The animal breath is audible; only cicadas muffle the force of their nostrils.

'That's good. Keep it slow, almost at a standstill. Keep your rope ready for his neck – you may only get a single chance. Move up so that you're level with his head, and walk forward, swaying gently from right to left – that will help confuse the mare behind our mark. If the mare is spooked, she will upset Aras – keep the mare calm.'

Three paces.

Hektor senses his son is desperate to reach out a hand. Something is wrong. Hapi's breath is not calm. His cooing is stuttering as though he is fearful, or distracted.

'Hapi, control your breathing.'

Two paces.

The mare snorts incredulously, flicks ears, brays deeply. Aras back-steps.

'I said *control your breathing*.'

'I can't. I can't.'

'Yes, you can.'

Three paces again.

Hapi stops walking completely, raises the rope into position, holds out the parsley. Hektor watches.

'What are you doing? Do not stop. They know we are here; they will think we are hostile.'

The mare grunts, forward-steps, eyeballs betraying no certain emotion.

Frenzy of action: Hapi leaps forward, throws the rope over Aras's face. The foal whinnies in fear, surprised at the attack, bucks upward, sweeps away from the rope. The mare runs off. Aras makes to run back in the opposite direction from which he is facing, but barely covers a step before he is strangled by the forceful grip of another rope. Hektor tugs. Hapi's distress is sewn into his face. Aras throws his head around – screams, kicks. Hektor quickly circles rope about the foal's neck with a tensed forearm. Hapi backs away, his eyes locked on the terrified foal – the screams are frenzy, panic. Hektor has glee in his eyes. Heavy breath churns in his mouth. Hapi is staked to the ground, his horror undisguised.

'We have him! We have him!' Hektor yells, tautening the rope with a sickening squeeze of Aras's neck, the animal's channels bulging beneath the skin.

Hapi staggers back, collapses.

Tablet Twelve

The afternoon slinks away. Craggy outcrops and lonely vegetation find their forms mimicked by excessive shadows. The sun is liquefied, stale. The approaching night promises coldness, threat.

In the saddle, Hektor glances across at his son.

Hapi has been melancholy this afternoon following the violence of the attack on the company and the recapture of Aras, though he has at least stopped shivering following his faint. *Perhaps he is pained that his childhood is reaching its conclusion.* It hits the *tuhkanti* that the boy's vivacity, which has directed so many games and experiences, is to be redirected, as a natural stream may be artificially channelled. And this redirection is draining that exact vivacity. *Hapi loves and worships me – I'm not blind to that,* as any young child is liable to do with a parent. Nonetheless, Hektor, perhaps for the first time, fears the fresco his boy has painted of him, fears the shades with which his son has coloured him. *The shades that I have allowed to be readily available to paint me with.*

He pictures Hapi in the acropolis gardens, climbing trees, trailing insects, running across flower beds, encouraging the chief gardener's hostility; numerous treks down to bronze-smithies to talk with workers, laugh at jokes, listen to wild tales of the lower town; sneaking down to upper town gates to watch friends slip into the lower town and come back with assorted tin charms – charms that the poor children apparently collect from drunken fathers and then trade among themselves.

From the earliest age, the *tuhkanti* informed Hapi of his position in society, and how his only superiors in Wilusa are his father and grandfather. And this doctrine in turn came from Parta; it is the *tawananna*'s chief role to ensure that the *labarna*'s children are spiritually attuned, and wholly aware that they are far more eminent in birth – and far more receptive of divine favour – than any other person in the region. *Where I have accepted this doctrine without hesitation, Hapi wonders at its merits; Ura would have found a worthier apprentice in him than she did in me. Maybe in his heart is discomfort at the thought of being superior to another person. And now the fear of losing himself entirely to this fate, to this… this manufactured existence where there is no life but what is made for us. He sees it. He sees it.*

Night subdues sunlight to a glaze. Bluebells, sunflowers and daisies interrupt the flow of darkness with prickles of purple, yellow and white respectively. Cacti snatch at shadows and ring them out over greater stretches of rock-face. Goat conversation scrapes with cicada chorus against unfamiliar bird calls. Early bats flail silently across the lower sky, exploding after indistinguishable insects.

'Hektor, I've been thinking,' Kaluti begins, hands clenching the saddle. 'You know how Father and the priests have always said it's important for us to look for the direction of Heaven in our lives?'

'Yes.'

'Well, maybe what happened to us earlier with those men is a sign from Appaliunas.' Her voice is delicate, far more subdued than her usual boldness.

'How so?'

'Well, I think that if the gods really wanted you and me to be joined to Luha and Masturi, then they wouldn't have allowed those men to attack us.'

Hektor tightens his lips. 'I understand…' He tries to confront his own feelings on the joining, and it comes to him: *Kaluti is so young – how frightened must she be? I have no words…* 'It may seem unfair, but it must always be remembered that it was the will of the Fates, Istustaya and Papaya, that we be joined.'

Kaluti goes quiet for a little while, then: 'I think to make our own fate would be worth the wrath of gods…'

Hektor opens his mouth, but immediately closes it. He does not trust himself to reply. He is put in mind of his mother, Parta, in the bathhouse this morning. All those years ago she too was just a girl, like Kaluti, being given to a man she met perhaps only once – sent away from everyone she loved and everything she knew to desolation and the distraction only of her own hopeless reality. And then, when Father was attacked by the demon, she had to make the ultimate sacrifice – *gods, will that be Kaluti's fate also: to nurse an old man as his body disintegrates and his mind unravels?*

Several silent minutes pass before he notices the sniffles. Suddenly, he is uncomfortable and wishes to be anywhere but with his sister and her torment – for this, he feels shame.

'I'm scared.'

'... I know.'

'I don't want to join with Masturi. I don't want to be alone in Seha.'

'Unfortunately, I... I do not think there is anything I can say that will make you feel any better. But, I do know how... how "scary" it is, facing such a strange new prospect; I am more than a little apprehensive of taking Luha as my wife.'

'But at least you'll still live at home. What have I got to hope for?' Her voice is desperate, accusative even.

A slight, tingling cold shifts from Hektor's temples to his lungs. 'You have to remember that the gods are with you, so long as you keep your mind open to Them. Yes, yes, They are there. You have to remember that you are serving the greater good of your family – of Wilusa itself, in its hour of need. This is our way. I am sure... I am sure you will find Masturi a loving husband and his family quite accommodating.'

'But how can this be right when I feel so awful? How can I just be given up so freely by Father and Mother? And you are just the same, Hektor, you are just the same. Don't pretend you're not.'

The *tuhkanti* sighs once again. There is no response he can muster.

The party has not encountered a single person for over an hour now, the last having been an elderly sheep-shearer guiding an alopecic donkey towards his village home, the animal encumbered with several creamy fleeces. The man had seemed preoccupied with private mutterings, but had been aware enough to recognise the group and yell, 'Bad men! Bad men here! Ger'off!' much to the amusement of the junior guards. Hektor is in no mood for amusement, even less so than usual, as with lighting at a premium, every person has to keep his wits about him.

The terrain is treacherous. The *tuhkanti* knows the moonlight has witnessed many travellers meeting with unfortunate accidents for lack of geographical knowledge. He knows that even in the intermittent assemblies of woodland there are concealed dangers. Sheer embankments, where earth and rock have broken away over aeons, are not an uncommon danger amidst trees, nor are rocks made slippery by sleeping pools and purring streams. The *tuhkanti* is also aware that the lands above the woods are the haunt of wolves that go in search of sheep, goats and the occasional herder too.

Hektor rubs away the loose tiredness in his eyes. Hapi has been yawning for ages and Kaluti has started too. Aras slopes along beside Kummi, quiet after the commotion earlier that day.

The party delves deeper into woodland. Hektor intends to take everyone through, with the aim of finding a suitable place for camp on the other side. Progress through the woods is frustratingly slow, despite the sparseness of the trees. More than once the wagon becomes stuck and they spend the better part of an hour, overall, getting it free. Light has altogether failed, rendering the trees brawnier in appearance than is real.

Suddenly, a *swish, thwip, thook* and three guardsmen fall from rearing horses, arrows chest-embedded.

Hektor ducks immediately, as several more arrows whistle past his neck, turning once more to see a further two guards fall from their mounts. He yells to the guard captain, who is riding with Hapi, 'Get out of here! Go now!'

But as the captain shakes the reins, sending his horse into a burst of acceleration, two arrows lodge in his chest and he crumples forward with a groan, a dead weight in the saddle. Hapi yelps but clings on tight as the horse pulls him blindly on into the darkness.

'Hapi! Hapi!'

But he is gone.

The *tuhkanti* leaps from his horse, ripping the sword from his belt – *cavalry manoeuvres among trees are clumsy; I am a harder target on foot.* Through the trees a group of men on horseback come charging. One rider makes directly for him, a small blade outstretched, spinning around. Hektor rolls to the side, narrowly avoiding a strike to the throat, and swings his own weapon round into the calf of the rider, who cries out. He glances over at the other guards. One has been struck down, and two others are scrambling about. Close to them, Kaluti is sprawled out in the dirt. Still.

'On your feet!' the *tuhkanti* roars at the guards. *No time to check Kaluti now...*

The rider he injured is grabbing at his wound, the horse he is riding stepping about haphazardly. Hektor runs at him and plunges his weapon deep into the man's chest, blood spitting as the man screams his last.

The other riders – *there are four more, yes* – have circled about, dismounted, perhaps realising that the lack of space between the trees does not lend itself to charges on horseback. In the darkness, he cannot make out any uniform or distinguishing marks. *Are they like the attackers earlier in the day?*

He watches the remaining two guards charge into all four of the attackers, swords meeting with *clangs* and *dacks*. He races forward, both of the guards cut down before he can reach them, though they take one of the attackers with them and injure a second in the process. Hektor chucks his weight into one of the men, knocking him to the floor. In the same movement, he brings his sword through the neck of another, but not before taking an almighty hit to the head with a shield, and comes to a stop above the man he has knocked over. Without hesitation, he jams his blade firmly between the attacker's shoulders.

Behind him comes the trampling of the other guards, who are covered in blood – but not apparently their own.

'*Tuhkanti!* Other riders made off with the gifts on the wagon. Shall we pursue?'

In the dirt, the one remaining attacker writhes about, clutching his belly, black fluid draining through his fingers.

Hektor raises his foot with a roar.

'*Tuhkanti*, sir, don't! He must sp—'

But it is too late. Hektor has brought his foot down on the man's face. And again. And again. Bone and flesh rolling into pulp. With the final stamp, he grabs at his aching head and collapses to his knees, falling backwards, the darkness trickling into his eyes.

Hektor is aware of inestimable black.

What follows is the claustrophobic pummel-of-heartbeat cloying in his ears, even as he becomes aware of the surrounding woodland noises. He opens his eyes. His arms, his legs: he cannot feel. He has the sense of hanging over a vast expanse of weightlessness, much as a water spider sits atop a shallow pond. He wrestles with his body for what seems an age, pulse inflating all the while, but no matter how surely he wills it, he is powerless to help himself.

After a time, he discovers he can at least move his head. It is repulsive, twisting his neck up, the pine-filth of woodland floor scraping cheek and temple. In so doing, however, he is able to recognise the body of Kaluti, lying like a fallen branch several metres away. She is still unconscious – perhaps dead. His first instinct is to try and wake her, but his broken calls provoke no response. He attempts to rouse his limbs. Frustration. He pants, submits to paralysis with a groan.

Where in the Under-Spring are those guards?

Hektor looks up. The woodland canopy is a galloping mesh of branches set against a moonlit sky. *Must be, hmm, four hours before dawn.*

The events that led to his unconsciousness froth into mind. His first thought is one of utter shame and contempt for himself. If he had maintained his concentration he might well have recognised the danger, saved some lives. And then, of course, there is the wagon, until recently loaded with gifts to be presented to Masturi, the Sehan *labarna*. *The attackers must have been more of those peasants from earlier. Are we being tracked?*

The image of Hapi stains Hektor's eyes, brings memory into scalding clarity. He prays to Kurunta, tutelary stag god, to walk by his son's side until he himself can find the boy. He must put faith in Hapi and try to accept, at least until some evidence contradicts, that his lad is alive. Warmth moistens his arms.

The sudden thought of Kummi causes Hektor pain too; she will doubtless have run off deep into the forest by now. *And Aras – where will he be?*

He drags himself onto his belly, faces Kaluti. Willing any surviving reserves of strength into his forearms, he drags himself forward, earth scraping stomach, until he reaches his half-sister. He leans his ear against her mouth and is relieved to discover her breathing. He whispers urgently, shaking her shoulder. Eventually she stirs, moans succeeded by hazy questioning. The *tuhkanti* explains quietly what has happened.

A familiar noise courses in from a clutch of trees. Moonlight reveals a figure holding the reins of two horses.

'*Tuhkanti*, sir, you're awake!'

'Y-Yes. Is that, is that Kummi you have there? And Aras?'

'Yes, sir.'

The *tuhkanti* grunts, nods, smiles to himself. 'And my son. Where is he?'

'Sir, we... We haven't found him. Yet.'

His heart plummets.

'What?'

'We've been looking. We've been looking for half an hour now. But we can't see him. We're still looking though, sir. We're not going to stop.'

'I need to find him... immediately.' The *tuhkanti* tries to pull himself up, but collapses in the process.

'You're in no state to stand, let alone wander off into the trees. Umm, begging your pardon, sir. Please. Let us help you. We'll find him. Don't worry. He can't be far.'

Hektor lowers his face, bites down hard.

'Which direction did he go, do you remember?'

The *tuhkanti* twists his mouth. 'His horse rode off up there.' He points in a direction that pushes off uphill. 'Please find him. Please. If he...'

'I will, don't worry. May I use Kummi? It will speed up the search.'

'Yes, do so.'

The guard ties Aras to the nearest tree, jumps up on Kummi and disappears back into the gloom of the forest.

Hektor drags himself up, back to a close-by rock; Kaluti does the same. Aras snorts, whinnies. The siblings are sore and exhausted, having decided through omission of speech to enjoy the respite while they can.

An hour passes. All around them, unseen creatures maintain their nocturnal conversation. Every now and then, Hektor imagines he hears footsteps, clenches his weapon, heart skipping a beat. But no one shows.

'Hektor, do you think Hapi will be okay? He's only little and we've been waiting here for a long time now.'

'Hapi is a resilient child. I'm sure he's fine.'

'If you say so.'

Hektor tries to erase several intrusive images from his mind. *Kaskalkur, please do not put me through this fear again – please do not take him from me.* Silence returns.

Some time later, as the first red of dawn picks out the wrinkles of the bark on the trees, Hektor distinctly hears the *crrck* and *keh* of breaking branches, the *th-dop* of hooves. His heart drops. He pulls himself up, drawing his sword; Kaluti rises too, held back by her brother's arm. Through a clearing comes a rider... It is the guard, and he has Hapi.

'Hapi!' Kaluti screams, leaping upon her sorry-looking nephew, who only manages a weak smile by way of greeting.

Hektor feels his heart rise back into his chest. He hugs his son – once Kaluti has finished suffocating him with kisses – who grips him determinedly.

'He's terribly shaken, as you can see,' the guard says, smiling. 'Found him beneath a tree, *tuhkanti*, gripping his knees. He spoke for a bit but has gone rather shy again, haven't you?'

'Thank you for finding him! Thank you. Thank you. Thank you!' Kaluti latches on to the guard's waist.

'My! Sir, I'm sorry, I-I...' Hektor waves away his embarrassment. 'Emotions are running high. How is your head, sir?'

Hektor rubs at his head, the dull ache dissipating.

Kaluti pulls Hapi away, telling him how brave he is and how fortunate he is to have survived the night's horrors.

'Thank you,' the *tuhkanti* manages. 'Thank you for bringing back my son.'

'That's okay, sir. But... what do we do now?'

Tablet Thirteen

It is the day after the woodland attack and the sky has whistled out a tune of coolness that, even now, only three hours past Appaliunas's zenith, lifts goose-pimples over Hektor's arms. The air is delightful on his burns and his headache has been less severe. But, pleasant as this is, it is no distraction from the imminence of the decision he must make and, perhaps, the task he must still complete.

After escaping the forest and finding a small cave to take refuge in, Hektor told the two guards that he would take watch as they and the children slept for a few hours. Once they were asleep he woke one guard to take over the watch, and rode Kummi back into the woods to find the wagon. He knew it would be a risk, but he also knew that the success or failure of his mission rested on the reception given to him by Masturi, *and gifts are a good prelude to negotiations*. When he located the wagon, he found that it had been picked clean and, upon examining a few corpses, discovered that the attackers had been wearing necklaces of dried apricot and pomegranate chunks. *We must have been tracked from the moment we left Wilusa*, the *tuhkanti* reasoned, *and set upon at our two most vulnerable moments*.

Hektor returned to the cave and meditated on what to do. *Clearly*, he thought, *to carry on and go before Masturi as I am with no gifts save myself and Kaluti is insulting*. But the alternative was to head back, and that would mean putting them all in danger, if more commoners were about who would be willing to attack. *Besides*, Hektor reasoned, *I would be failing Father and consigning the upper town to the prospect of being overrun*. He was surprised to find that this latter thought had not felt quite as traumatic as he had imagined it might; the thought, however, of Hapi and even Kaluti being put in harm's way again was the deciding factor.

They would proceed with the mission.

A half-moon passes. The company – depleted in size to just three men, two children and four horses – has now been moving steadily uphill over increasingly rocky terrain for the last two days. The lack of a wagon, which had held the gifts for Masturi, has been ameliorative to their previous slow progress. From the toes of the mountains, Hektor has led the party through the clefts of the Biting Peaks, past settlements surrounded by palisades painted white, and up the Riven Staircase, home to goats with bushy hair and twisted horns. One of the horses slipped along the way and fell to its death from a precipice, smattering red against the chalky landscape. Twice they almost lost one of the guards, rocks that deprived them of a horse almost claiming a man. This is not the main road to Four Forts, but it is the quickest, and the Sehan capital does eventually present itself to Hektor's eyes.

Occupying a hillside, Four Forts is suitably named for its colossal, tower-like structures of stone sitting at each corner of a square of fortified wall. Beyond the wall, sloping downhill, is a vast settlement akin to Wilusa's lower town in its general shabbiness and poverty. Plateaus spanning the surrounding mountain face are vivid greens against the pallid rock and the hills are busy with agriculture and wind.

'Where do we go now, *tati*?' Hapi asks.

Hektor narrows his eyes, looks once more towards the fortifications. 'The acropolis is hidden behind those walls.' He points at a particularly busy road leading up from the lowlands towards a gate. 'We can join there and Masturi will admit us once we explain to the guards who we are.'

Kummi makes a groaning noise, shakes her sweaty head. The *tuhkanti* strokes her mane, reassuringly. *I know. I never like coming here either.*

The entrance hall is a geometric triumph of co-ordinated reds, yellows and blues: the mosaicked floor curling waves of colour and the walls fresco-full, paintbrush strokes disciplined into deities, past *labarnas* and creatures that only foreign travellers dare claim to exist.

The doors to the throne room open up, revealing a court full of people, at the end of which, sat on his throne, is the familiar, spidery form of Masturi. Hektor feels the eyes on him, hears the whispers. In his wake come Hapi and Kaluti, and the two remaining guards. Masturi is clearly attending Gate, judging by the number of commoners in the room, conspicuous by their grime and tacky clothing.

'My messengers tell me Hektor of Wilusa approaches,' comes Masturi's gnarled tongue, speaking in the common language traders use as opposed to his native dialect. 'I see only a burned man and children. Identify yourself, stranger.'

Hektor swallows a sudden flush of anger. 'My Sun, I *am* Hektor, son of Priam, *tuhkanti* of Wilusa. I come before you to—'

'It is true then... Yes, you have travelled far,' Masturi interrupts.

Hektor pauses, weighing the *labarna*'s tone on internal scales, finds the balance unfavourable. Glances to the left and right assure him that he has the court's full attention, which is of further discomfort to him. Once more, he has the uncomfortable feeling of nakedness, as he did when he first went into the lower town in disguise back in Wilusa.

'... Yes, my Sun, and it has not been a journey without incident. I come before you now so suddenly and unannounced with a matter of grave importance for all Wilusa, a matter of the utmost urgency and... and a matter of some delicacy.' He looks around the court again, studies the faces with suspicion. 'I appreciate you are at Gate, and my entrance is rather... bold, but might we speak in private?'

Masturi smiles, moves his head from side to side. Then his smile becomes a scowl. 'No! Look at you. You bring two men, two children. No retinue. No gift? What insult does your father make me? I suppose that whatever residue of his brain is still functioning is incapable of thinking clearly.'

Hektor twitches, clenches a fist, reddens at the open insult. Some of the better-dressed men in the court chuckle. 'My Sun, were he here in my stead, my *labarna* would offer apology for the poverty of my situation.' *No he wouldn't.* 'However, if you would hear my tale then perhaps you would not be so quick with your' – *I can't say 'criticism' and I can't question his judgement* – 'assessment, which, owing to my abrupt appearance, leaves you no scope or time to consider our state, such as it is. No, you do not see the wealth – the gifts – that would otherwise come to you as tribute for attendance because we were attacked and robbed, but as it stands the true gifts offered are *not* linen, or gold, or horses. But that is getting ahead of ourselves—'

'*Ourselves?* Oh no, no, you stand quite alone, Hektor. Keep talking, if you will. Know that my ear means the ear of all in court. If you don't wish to talk then go back on your way.'

Hektor knew his reception would not be warm. There has always been suspicion and snapping tongues between Seha and Wilusa, but there is usually cordiality, though tense, when representatives of one visit the other. The *tuhkanti* has visited Four Forts on six separate occasions: twice as a representative of Wilusa during the nuntar-riyashas festival; once for discourse on a border treaty that had been mediated by Muršili II himself – the Big *labarna* who governs Hattusa to the east; twice to establish a code of conduct for a military alliance against raiding Ahhiyawan pirates along the coast; and, finally, today, to beg for aid.

Hektor deliberates once again on how he should describe Wilusa's situation, as well as how he must portray the attack made on him in the woods. He has given thought to this on the journey to Seha, but decided, ultimately, that the tone and telling of his dialogue must invariably be determined by the mood in which he finds Masturi.

'My Sun, as I have touched upon, we set out from Wilusa with full retinue, gifts for you to know our good faith and in a presentable state of repair. *Twice* we were attacked on our journey by' – *I can hardly say furious commoners* – 'bandits who caught us unawares, killed many of my men and took possession of the great gifts we had for you.'

'And you didn't think to turn back? Instead you come before me like *this*?' Masturi spits.

'I would not have had it so, had I been in a position to make a better choice,' Hektor hurriedly replies, as the court buzzes with condemnation. 'As it is, Wilusa has suffered the shaking of Ubelleris. There is damage to the wall that protects the upper town, many are dead and our primary food store has been destroyed. I do not hide the fact that our situation is desperate. I come to negotiate aid.'

'No!' Masturi snaps. 'You slither into my lands – uninvited – to beg like some common pauper. Your father has never respected me but expects help when he needs it.'

'I am disappointed, my Sun,' the *tuhkanti* sighs – tired, filthy, thirsty, irritated. 'It was not so long ago you came to *my* home, enjoyed *my* Sun's hospitality. You were admitted to our temple... observed the – the miracle and—'

'And I recall the promise of a delicious young *esertu* wife but she never materialised!' Masturi retorts, standing up, pointing accusatively at the *tuhkanti*. 'I also seem to recall that when I came to your city I brought with me a retinue one hundred strong, offered wines, gold, silks, urns, jewellery, pomegranates, apricots. What do you offer me now? Eh?'

'She is here,' Hektor concedes. 'Your future *esertu* wife, I mean.' His hand indicates Kaluti, who closes her own over her belly and looks around the court.

Masturi does not respond. Knobbly fingers spring up towards his mouth, playing over pale, chapped lips, a tongue darting out. His eyes are filled with lust. 'Well then,' he finally manages, his aggression gone. 'That is something, at least. Come forward, girl.'

Hektor turns to Kaluti and clenches his jaw, his half-sister's face offering nothing but fear and resistance. However, she obeys, holding the attention of the entire court as she shivers soundlessly towards Masturi standing by his throne. She is tiny, and her size is exaggerated by the magnitude of the hall and its audience members who stand poised like cats watching a mouse. The *tuhkanti* reflects upon the theatre of the situation. It is uncomfortable not to play the key piece as he is so used to, and the lack of control – especially in front of the Sehan commoners – is humiliating. He wonders at the games he plays – the games that so substantiate who he is and what he is – and imagines a quieter, private space in which he and Masturi might communicate without the need for flourish and ostentation – a place where only the gods could intrude. As he watches Kaluti parade about, as Masturi demands of her, he accepts that he must remove himself and the children from the public eye that the custom of Gate so indulges.

'She is a charming, charming girl,' says Masturi, smiling lecherously. 'Your father knows how to temper my *just* anger.' He clicks his fingers, settles back into his throne. A servant brings him up a drink, which he noisily consumes, holding his court in suspense. Once he is done, the same servant dries his mouth, removes the cup. 'Now, you spoke not of a gift, but *gifts*. And as you have already testified, I am not to receive gold or any of those prize horses your people are so fabled for nurturing. So, the girl is one gift and as good a gift as she is, she is but one. I see only yourself, a boy and two common guards.' He pauses, placing one twig of a finger upon his mouth, tapping away, evidently enjoying the labouring of his point. 'I conclude then that any further gifts have either not travelled with you, or... we are looking upon them.'

Masturi smirks, as though he guesses what the offer will be.

'Now, I presume you seek to barter for my aid with some, as yet, unspecified goods that you hope I will be unable to resist. The girl, mark, was already promised and so I accept her as tribute that is due following my last discussion with your father. She is not to be part of any possible exchange and I declare her mine forthwith.'

Hektor holds Masturi's gaze, his mouth stern, his heart unwilling to give the *labarna* the satisfaction of seeing his frustration, his anger. *And there was Father forgetting his visit, insulting him at our own hearth.* His position here in negotiation, he knows, should be far stronger and he balks under the very real consequence of his father's failings. He senses Kaluti's attention on him – can almost feel the heat of her anguish – but cannot bear to meet her eyes. 'All you say is fair,' he grinds, trying not to let his discomposure wrestle through. 'All you say is right. I do come looking for your aid and you do look upon certain... *goods*' – the word is grime on his tongue – 'that my Sun offers in trade for men to aid us now.'

Masturi grins broadly, appears to be on the verge of speaking; however, one of the dignitaries behind him steps forward and whispers long into the *labarna*'s ear. As he listens, Masturi's smile falters, eventually setting into a defeated crag across his wrinkled face.

'Very well,' he concedes, eventually, to the dignitary, before turning back to Hektor. He claps his hands together. 'Forgive me. You enter under my roof and all I do is press you, question you, when I can see you are weary. The rock of Seha does not allow for mercy to those unaccustomed to it – or, indeed, to those unfit to conquer it.' His lip curls slightly at this. 'You are the son of my neighbour *labarna*, who I love as I love a brother. I should not open your hardship to the ears of commoners.' He nods, sweeping his hand towards a section of the room's audience. 'Go. My servants will see you to quarters and to baths. Tonight, you will join me at the feasting table and we shall celebrate the love we share as neighbours. Then, and only then when it is fit to do so, we will discuss the terms you present for a trade agreement... We look forward to that immensely.'

Hektor stands facing out across the Sehan landscape. From the guest quarters, he can see over the fortified wall that encloses the acropolis, beyond the lower town and out towards the distant muddle of haze and blueness that constitutes the horizon. It is the same horizon wherever one goes along the Aegean coast, distance so vast and unknowable that it takes on a dreamlike quality, as though if you were to look hard enough or pinch yourself it might suddenly disperse and reveal something more real. At this time of day, the horizon is tinged with yellow, like sweet wine poured into water, and the sun slips ever further towards a place where it can no longer observe the workings of man. Hektor, for one, will be glad when the severity of Appaliunas's glow has gone, as the thoughts playing out in his head are not thoughts he would wish to share with a deity so associated with judgement.

It has been a few hours since his interview with Masturi and he is struggling with the prospect of what he must do this evening. He is perfectly comfortable with the concept of selling trade deals back home, but there is a difference – he must acknowledge – between forcing through an exchange of coins for cows and an exchange of himself for guards. *And how will I broker a deal in the face of such open hostility and determined humiliation?*

Where other men pace corridors when deep in thought, Hektor stands perfectly still, straight-backed with fists tucked into the small of his back as though to hold himself up by the sheer threat of self-harm. He has checked his face once or twice over the last twenty minutes in a beaten bronze plate hanging on the wall – a gifted item judging by its pride of place, as Masturi, so he learned from his father, is wont to adorn the guest quarters of the acropolis with supplicatory gifts from other regional *labarnas*. Hektor is surprised, with each viewing, to find the ugly burn down one side of his face, the missing hair at the scalp.

He has never cared much for physical appearance, but he knows that girls in the acropolis back home have always whispered of his angular handsomeness. Now that has gone and he no longer looks such a prize for Luha, or any other *labarna*'s daughter. *And it isn't as though I was maimed in battle; I don't even have some heroic story to relate to others.*

He grinds his teeth together, irritated by the sensation of his foot tapping the floor, his lips twisting, quite out of synchronicity with the rest of his disciplined body. Something further – something deeper – is bothering him. His thoughts flit back to the conversation he had with Kaluti all those days ago, before the second attack. She had questioned how she could be given up so easily, as an item of commerce, by her parents – how it could be the right thing when she felt so bad. And the realisation in her voice – the hopeless realisation of her future, of the loneliness that would constitute her life. *My gods, it shook me to the core.* He cannot forget the tone in her voice: a broken voice of terror, of pleading. But again, how could this be wrong? This is centuries of tradition, commands given by the gods Themselves. *We are Theirs to use as a scribe handles a stylus, and our stories are Their authorship. What right have we to change the plot? That madman, Washa, certainly saw fit to try and change his plot, and he was puni*— Hektor pauses in his thought. He thinks on the decisions he made, such a long time ago it seems now. Washa was spared, spared because he, the *tuhkanti* had chosen that fate, chosen so because Washa had saved his son's life. Washa was not punished. It has eaten at him for a time, but he now accepts – not without some discomfort – that what he did was contrary to the commands of Heaven. He is disappointed that this realisation does not, in fact, harden his philosophical point of view on the subject; instead, it feels as though a density in his chest has been relieved and the feeling is liberating.

Overcome by a sudden flush of sadness, Hektor turns on his heel and leaves his quarters. He wanders down the corridor to his son's room. He makes to throw the door open, but pauses and, with an obscure sensation in his hand, knocks at the door instead.

'H-Hello?' comes Hapi's voice from within.

Hektor opens the door, gently, and slips inside, closing the door behind him. Hapi's face develops from anxiety to relief to tiredness in three quick movements. He turns away from his father and the *tuhkanti* cannot help but smile.

Hektor clears his throat, self-importantly, then shakes his head, cursing himself as though he has done something wrong. 'It seems we have been away from Wilusa a lifetime, Hapi, and you have grown.' He lets the words work what he hopes will be a delicate magic on the atmosphere, but Hapi does not move. Instead, he carries on playing with some toy horses. 'There is an ugliness to this world – no, to *our* world that I did not want you to see. You remind me of something I once was, something that seems distant to me now – like an island behind haze on the Aegean horizon. I have viewed you as a problem to resolve and not as my son. And then when we caught Aras out in that field... I realised that something in you broke. You were no longer a boy, and that is at once an inevitability and a tragedy. I want you to know that... that I do love you. I have always loved you. And not a day passes that I am not proud to call you my son.'

He pauses after this, not knowing whether he should continue, but decides after a few awkward moments not to, as he can feel a build-up of pressure behind his eyes that may result in an undesirable conclusion if he does go on. He waits a moment longer, clears his throat, makes to turn and leave. At least he tried to put things right, even if he is not very good at it. But as he reaches for the door handle, he feels arms around his torso. He looks down to find Hapi's face buried in his belly, light sniffling sounds coming from somewhere inside the mess of his hair and face.

Hektor does not speak, nor does Hapi, but, for once, the moment does not require it.

Nightfall, and the darkened acropolis is lit with sconces, the fire within dancing to the lively music of lyres and various woodwind instruments. Hektor makes his way through corridors busy with servants and guests of Masturi, the men loud and, to the *tuhkanti*'s ears, obnoxious, women giggling at their elbows.

The feasting hall itself is resplendent in colour, the walls fiery in their depiction of scarlet gods, auburn beasts and sepia *labarnas* of ages past. The tables are arranged in a square with one side missing, filled instead with lascivious dancers who, draped in so much jewellery they could be mined for minerals and metals, wriggle and swoop to the slow beat of a drum, all other instruments, for the moment, in a state of rest.

'Hektor! Hektor!' shouts Masturi from the head of the table, sitting in a high-backed chair as beautifully decorated as any of the walls. 'Come, sit beside me. You are the guest of honour!'

Hektor looks from Masturi – who appears already to be quite advanced in a state of drunkenness – to the chair his spindly hand is tapping by way of invitation. He sighs and takes in a deep breath, preparing himself for an unpleasant evening, once more reaffirming an internally worded pledge not to assault the man who calls Seha his own.

'You look much better for a bath and some fresh clothes, Hektor. I hope my hospitality has been to your liking.' Masturi's tone has a tinge of mocking.

Hektor draws his chair forward, taking the time to devise an answer, careful not to look at the *labarna* yet. Once he has weighed various replies, he decides on a response, turning for the first time to Masturi.

'Yes.'

With his response made, Hektor turns back to the empty plate in front of him, reaches for some of the food that is piled so – as he feels – ostentatiously over the table. However, he succumbs to the temptation of skewered lamb, freshly barbecued. The smell is of charred flesh, lemon and a herb to which he cannot quite put a name.

'Hektor, forgive me, but may I ask what happened to your face?' This is the enquiry of Massanauzzi, *tawananna* of Seha, Masturi's premier wife. She sits on the other side of her husband, leaning forward a little to make herself heard.

Hektor swallows a chunk of lamb, conceding as he does so that the acropolis chefs are skilled in their profession. He meets Massanauzzi's eyes, aware of Masturi guzzling back yet more fragrant wine.

'After the shaking of the land, there was a fire and I was injured in my attempts to rescue a mother and her two children from the lower town.'

The *tuhkanti* had carefully prepared himself for this meal before he made apology to Hapi, but now all his preparation seems worthless and the work of a weaker man. He is feeling reckless instead.

Massanauzzi raises her thick eyebrows in surprise, her dark eyes stretching like fresh wounds. 'Oh, well… that was most admirable. Do you not think so, Luha?'

Hektor looks up, mouth full, to find Massanauzzi addressing an attractive young woman to her right. Luha's mouth is open, her face a twist of revulsion as she looks upon the *tuhkanti*.

'Nothing admirable about saving the life of some commoner bitch or her two brats,' Masturi cuts across his wife, looking out over the mountains of food and drink before him, so vast and rolling that it might require a cartographer to navigate. 'A man should only be wounded in battle.'

Hektor looks long into the side of Masturi's painted, bejewelled face, little bells and chains of gold constricting the wayward coursing of his long, grey hair.

'I only saved one child. I couldn't carry the mother to safety and the baby died of smoke inhalation.'

Masturi applauds as a dance routine ends, the women quickly replaced by fire breathers who commence their own dangerous act.

Whispers to the *labarna*'s right: Luha saying something to her mother, eyes flicking over to Hektor, her face still filled with that same revulsion.

'So, your face is a ruin for the life of one child. Your father must be very disappointed.' Masturi takes another long draw of his wine. 'However, it does not surprise me that you should act so. You are a product of your father and your father is a man whose very appearance confirms the presence of' – his mouth purses in distaste – 'demonic contamination.'

Hektor closes one fist in anger at this outright insult, but stops himself from saying anything in response. *Perhaps I am not feeling so reckless…*

Masturi seems annoyed when he next speaks; maybe he had hoped to provoke a reaction. 'We will speak, in a little while, of a suitable trade, Hektor.'

The *tuhkanti* slips further back into his chair, unable to consume any more food, his appetite quite extinguished by Masturi's barbs. He sips at water – never touching wine – as act after act fill out the evening's quota of performance, and the sky is soon quite full of stars, Arma gazing down with Her one, milky eye. He could sleep right now, sleep for days that pass into quarter-moons and into years, until all the world has changed through the carnage of time. But he is, to his immense disappointment, quite alive to this moment and he cannot extricate himself.

Eventually, the entertainment comes to something of a finale and Masturi manages – after a struggle – to stand in appreciation of what he has seen from the various actors, musicians and dancers who have brought ribaldry, eroticism and showmanship to the table, populated by men and women of consequence in Seha.

'W'have one more act b'fore – well, b'fore w'reach the purpose of this evening,' the *labarna* yells out to his guests, his words slurring with the drink. 'And it is an act I'm sure w'shall all enjoy.' He claps again, settles back into his chair with not some little difficulty.

Hektor, keen for the theatre of the feast to end, only watches half-aware as a man and a woman step into the centre of the room. The man is old and short, dressed in the regalia of a *labarna*, donkey-headed sceptre in one hand, his other hand held by the woman who is tall, fearsome and also old. She is dressed in clothes befitting a *tawananna*. Together, they walk on the spot, looking ahead somewhere behind Masturi's chair, as though searching for something in the distance.

'Woman, woman!' the old man yells.

The woman makes a show of looking surprised by the sudden outburst. A few of the Sehan guests laugh.

'Woman, woman!' the old man repeats. 'My feet are bleeding on these damned Sehan stones!' He hops up and down.

Hektor shifts up in his chair a little, paying attention to the pantomime. Next to him, Masturi chuckles as he chomps on a lump of strong-smelling cheese.

'No man, no man!' the woman scolds, putting one hand on her hip and coming to a standstill. 'Your feet are too soft for Sehan rock.'

'Then carry me!' the old man pleads, dramatically, jumping, in one movement, up into the arms of the old woman.

The guests cackle at this amusing development in the routine, as the woman runs all the way around the hall carrying the old man, who uses his sceptre as a tool for direction – taking them in between pillars, round and round in circles and behind Hektor and Masturi's chairs before coming to a stop back where they began. They have been joined by a third actor – a younger man dressed also in the full regalia of a *labarna*, holding a sceptre that is colossal. He is far more dignified and rouses the guests to applause and cheers.

The old woman collapses to her knees and drops the old man, who rolls along the floor into the feet of the younger actor.

'And who comes rolling into *my* halls in such a shabby state before a *labarna*?' The man's voice is strong, his gaze baleful.

'No man, no man! Get up!' the woman hisses, her 'husband' comically scurrying behind her, his arms around her shins as he peers out from between her legs. 'We are your neighbours, my Sun; do you not recognise your neighbours?'

The younger man holds his arms out towards the guests, as though to invite their sympathy. Everyone laughs.

'I see the one who rules my neighbour's lands, but I do not see her husband!' the actor quips.

Next to Hektor, Masturi claps, roars with laughter. The *tuhkanti* reddens; the appearances of the characters are too defined now to be coincidence.

'My Sun, my Sun! Do you not recognise' – the woman pulls the old man up from the floor, though he struggles against her – '*my* Sun, my Sun?'

She pushes the old man forward and he bows extravagantly before the younger actor.

'*This* is my neighbour? The man I call brother?' the younger actor demands, positively spitting scorn. 'If you truly *are*, then you should be able to lift a *real* sceptre!' He holds his own gargantuan sceptre aloft and the guests cheer him on. 'Drop that child's toy you hold.'

The old man looks blankly at his counterpart, then blankly down at his sceptre, then at his stage wife – who nods – and then back at the sceptre, which he drops. The younger actor holds out his own sceptre and lays it along the floor with a flourish.

'There, my *neighbour*! Lift! Lift for all these good people to see!'

Soon, all around Hektor: a chorus of 'Lift! Lift! Lift!' The *tuhkanti* continues to watch, glances briefly at Masturi, who is fully engaged in the pantomime.

The old man looks around hesitantly, one finger to his lip, before grinning stupidly and grabbing hold of the enormous sceptre. He strains and strains but cannot move it.

'It seems *labarna*ship is too heavy a burden for you!' the younger actor laughs.

The old woman stomps forward, pushes her 'husband' aside and lifts the enormous sceptre with one hand to a raucous cry of celebration from the guests. She chases her 'husband', beating him about the hall, then hits him once more on the head. This time, the old man stumbles forward, distress etched into his eyes. One side of his face he lets droop, tongue lolling to one side as he makes obscene noises. Then his arm slumps uselessly, as does his leg.

'Oh, my lion, my wolf, my bull!' the old woman cries dramatically, throwing herself behind the old man and catching him as he topples.

Hektor scrunches his face up, shocked at the scene. The insult cannot be misinterpreted. He looks around at all the fat, reddened faces, the howling women, the guffawing men, Masturi wiping tears from eyes running with kohl.

As the old woman carries the old man away to deafening applause, Masturi settles back into his chair, sips some wine, turns to Hektor. 'Is something the matter? Are you not familiar with this sketch? It is well loved south of the border we share.'

Hektor takes a moment to compose himself. He tries to keep in mind the reason he has come to Seha in the first place. 'I am unfamiliar with it. I do not recognise it,' he grinds out.

Masturi leans in towards Hektor's face, close enough that the *tuhkanti* can smell the sweetness of wine on his breath and the rot of something else altogether more offensive.

'Are you certain you are not familiar with this sketch in Wilusa? Is it not well loved there?'

Hektor leans away, but turns to face the *labarna*, whose eyes hang heavy with drink.

'Is this how a guest is treated beneath your roof? If I offend you so then send me away. You let wine control proceedings where your wits are wanting,' he hisses, loud enough only for Masturi to hear.

The Sehan withdraws back into his chair, mouth twisted horribly, eyes awakened by a clot of hate.

'Then perhaps we should come to the business of the evening.'

'Soberly would be my preference,' Hektor agrees, glad that his host finally seems ready to move past distraction and venom.

Masturi stands, unsteadily, pushing away the hand of his wife who, judging by her expression, is becoming increasingly uncomfortable with the situation. He raises his cup and looks around the room as much as his declining vision allows.

'M'guests,' he begins, with a slur, apparently not paying attention to the *tuhkanti*'s request for sober negotiations. 'Tonight has been filled with good food, good wine and good – no, *excellent* – enter-tainment.' He stops to allow for appreciation, which is readily delivered by the diners in the form of applause and drinks being bashed on wooden tables. 'But I called this feast in honour of Hektor, M'guest, who rides – who's *ridden* here from Wilusa, which, unfortunately, has suffered of late.

'Now, I was promised' – he jabs a finger into his chest – 'a lovely *esertu* wife by Priam, who I love as I love a brother, and Hektor has brought her here. All the way here. But – you heard him earlier, some of you – he said I looked upon certain *other* trade goods too. Now, Hektor, what would those trade goods be? What will yer offer? Yer wanted aid, didn't you? Wilusa wants Seha's aid, doesn't it? Show me the goods. Let me put them to tablet. Let me make this deal in the manner of custom. In the manner of good traders.'

Masturi, swaying, clicks his fingers. A scribe enters the room with stylus and tablet. The Sehan looks at Hektor expectantly.

Hektor breathes deeply and stands, taking his time, as though to acclimatise to so many eyes. He does not like being forced into this public display. Trading is not a sport fit for the dining table. But he will have to play this game. '*Dek*, my Sun. My *labarna* offers me as a

husband to Luha, as you have wished for, as you have tried to negotiate before.'

'I'm not marrying *that!*' Luha scoffs.

'Be quiet, girl! *I* will decide what is to be done with you – it is
high time you were married,' Masturi barks before cooling. He looks
at Hektor, smiles, indulgingly, nodding his head. 'Very good. Very
good. And what does your father wish in exchange?'

'He wishes... He wishes for trained men who might assist us at a
time where force is necessary.'

'To aid you in recovery from this earth trembling?'

'Yes, the upper town sustained severe damage and we lost food
reserves. We must now protect ourselves from the commoners. The
wall that divides the upper from the lower town is breached.'

Hektor would lower his head, but he keeps it upright and proud as
is befitting a man of his position.

Masturi chuckles. 'Very good. Very good. Then let us chart the
wares.' He clicks his fingers again, and the scribe raises his stylus in
preparation.

Hektor looks from *labarna* to scribe to guests and back to *labarna*
again. 'I do not understand. I *am* the... the wares.'

Masturi grins. 'Precisely! Pre–cisely! And of what value is a man?
Does not each man equal out some estimation that traders, such as
ourselves, can calculate? Or are we all worth the same? Am I more or
less valuable than... than him, say?' He points towards a particularly
rotund individual who raises his cup in toast. 'So, you see, Hektor, I
must discover exactly what you are worth if I am to agree a deal. Let's
begin, shall we?' He turns around, eyeing diners one by one. 'Look at
him, would yer? Look him up and down, weigh him in yer minds.'

Hektor grinds his teeth, not for the first time, arms tense with
anger. He watches each diner's face, and they are looking more and
more uncomfortable, one or two even embarrassedly looking anywhere but at him. However, Masturi does not seem deterred.

'He is handsome, I grant. Look at those arms – those *are* a fighter's
arms, despite the burns. He can hold shield and spear. I grant five
guards for those arms. And those legs' – he pauses to take a gulp of
wine – 'are a rider's legs. Would yer expect less of Wilusa's *tuhkanti?*

Would yer expect less from a horse-rearing people? For those I grant... yes, I grant ten guards more. That is fifteen for just yer limbs, Hektor! Now, his chest – broad, manly, the kind of chest any woman could lay her head upon at night. For that I grant ten more guards. You're at twenty-five now. Shall I keep going? I am not done with the estimation. I hope you're getting this, scribe!'

'Yes, my Sun,' the scribe replies in a hurry, tendrils of clay curling up with every cuneiform symbol he impresses on his tablet.

Hektor holds Masturi's gaze; it is now a battle of wills and whether decency shall be outdone by humiliation. Few of the diners are laughing, he can see; the majority, in fact, are looking elsewhere – at the various breads on the table, the mosaicked floor, the wall frescoes of men doing battle with impossible creatures.

'Now, that face. The burns have undone much of it. But we can salvage something; I am not without compassion. Those broad, square cheeks breathe masculinity. I offer yer a further five men for those ch—'

'My Sun, please stop this now!' It is Massanauzzi who speaks. Her face is contorted with both fear and desperation, but resolute nonetheless. 'Hektor is a guest beneath our roof. This goes against the laws of hospitality as set down by the gods. This is enough now.'

Masturi looks at his wife with something close to shock beneath the drunken smirk. Hektor looks from the *labarna* to the *tawananna* and finds her face still resolute. The hall is still.

Out of the silence dribbles Masturi's voice, unable to hide just a sliver of irritation. 'Fine.' He licks his lips, wine-wet though they are already. His gaze shifts from his wife to Hektor, mouth trying to hold the smirk, but eyes betraying uneasiness. He drains his cup and tosses it to the floor with the deftness of a praying mantis releasing the extraneous body parts of an eviscerated insect. 'Fine,' he repeats. 'I grow weary of negotiations anyway. I think I will make a final check of the goods I have already been delivered.' He motions towards a servant at the door, who bows in response, then leaves the hall.

Hektor takes his seat, slowly, watching Masturi all the while as he too returns to his chair. The music starts up again, a piece with deliberate pacing raised from the careful plucking of a lyre. The mood palpably transfers from one of discomfort to wary relaxation, diners shifting about in their chairs, some audibly exhaling.

Hektor knows what is coming; he has been waiting for it since the evening commenced. Sure enough, before long, Kaluti steps gingerly into the hall, keeping pace with the music – to an extent – as though she has already been taught some manner of decorum for when she approaches the *labarna*. She is draped in a light gauze cloth, held aloft by two servants walking with bowed heads behind her. But something is not right. It takes Hektor several moments to properly discern his half-sister's appearance, layered in a whisper of shadow as she is. The first ceremonial appearance of an *esertu* wife, this is not. Underneath the cloth, Kaluti is naked, as one might expect from the showcasing of a fresh *naptartu*.

Hektor glances at Masturi, who is smiling with evident satisfaction.

'What is this, my Sun?' the *tuhkanti* demands. 'This is not what was agreed.'

Masturi, smile intact, leans gently towards his guest. 'It was agreed that your father would provide me with an *esertu* wife. This did not happen. However, I accept the girl as a *naptartu* by way of apology. Before, I loved your father only soberly; now, I love him fully as a brother once more.

'You see, a girl such as Kaluti is a prize product. She is younger than any other I possess. She is at a wonderful age. I love them at that age, d'you not? You can enjoy them at each stage of their growth into womanhood. Appreciate how the definition of their skin changes with each new development. The delicacy of a child's hands shifting with the confidence of maturity. The smell, the taste, the experience. Oh, Hektor, it is like taking a fresh bite from an apricot each day as it swells and strengthens.'

Hektor feels a familiar tightness in his chest. He cannot bear to meet his half-sister's eyes, which he senses on him.

Masturi turns, finally, to Hektor, his expression having lost its serenity, instead adopting a grim conclusiveness. '*Dek*, Hektor. You came here to trade and I see you are not to be riled. I will make you an offer – one non-negotiable offer and it might just be enough to protect you, your family and all those who reside in Wilusa's upper town: you will join with Luha and Luha will live at your side in Wilusa. For this, I will give your father fifty spearmen, twenty-five archers and twenty-five chariot teams. They will answer to your command, or your father's, and you may utilise them for as long as it takes to rebuild the section of wall that was destroyed by the earth shaking.'

Hektor's eyes widen in shock at this apparent change of heart, swallowing back his fury as quickly as he can. The offer is incredibly generous and this number of men should easily serve to protect the upper town and acropolis from any social unrest. *Father will be very pleased with me.* This is better than he had dared hope and would certainly restore him to favour in his father's eyes.

Masturi smiles – not an unpleasant smile, but one with genuine warmth.

'How does that sound to you, Hektor?'

'It... It sounds good, my Sun,' the *tuhkanti* replies, nodding because he is unsure of what else he should do. 'Thank you.'

Masturi takes a sip from a cup of wine brought freshly over by a servant. 'I trust your father will remember who his allies are. Seha and Wilusa have long been friends – let it not be said that Masturi acted contrary to that alliance.'

Hektor actually laughs, vaguely aware that Kaluti is still being paraded about, but never mind her – he has achieved something he never thought he could: salvation for Wilusa. *Salvation for Father.*

Masturi takes another sip of wine. 'I trust you will find Luha a worthy wife.' He glances to his right at Luha, who does not look impressed. 'She has womanly hips and will provide you with many children. You will no longer have to be embarrassed by your bastard – what is his name? Hepa? Hupu?'

Hektor's laughter disappears like so much mist over an early-morning sea. 'His name is Hapi,' he replies, quietly.

'Well, whatever his name, I know from your father he is an illegitimate child and brings no small degree of trouble to your life.' He leans in, conspiratorially, and, again, Hektor can smell the reek of wine, of rot. 'But with Luha you can disown him – send him to train as a guard or something. Of course, with *legitimate* children, your bastard will not be able to stay with you.'

'… Why?' Hektor asks, dumbly, once he has recovered himself.

'Why? Why?' Masturi laughs, as a parent who laughs indulgently at a child. 'Because his very existence will bring shame to both your family and *mine*. And that cannot be. Oh, but I see you have some passing attachment for him. No matter – the sooner you have sent him off, the better. Shortly you will have children you can be proud to call your own.'

Tablet Fourteen

Hektor had just seen his fourteenth harvest when the stable-hands took him to the *arzana*; they had had a lot to drink and he was still reserved and suspicious of anyone of a lower birth. The stable-hands had likely thought that a little whoring and drinking would bring them closer together and loosen the boy, who was already *tuhkanti*. It was in the *arzana* that he met the prostitute Piha-wiya.

It was just a common *arzana* in the lower town, filled with the usual ruckus of drunken men, cackling women and attempts at music. The place was redolent with the sweetness of opium, the sharpness of urine and another odour, pungent, that Hektor could not identify. He felt somewhat harassed into this expedition and more than a little concerned that his father should find out. His mother had already made him well aware that he was not to consort with the like of stable-hands – though Ura encouraged it in secret – and he hardly cared to imagine how the *tawananna* would react if she knew where he had been led. And been led he had, but to be led is not to show unwillingness; rather it is to exhibit a cautious intrigue.

Hektor was not impervious to the charms of women about the acropolis. The *naptartus* were confident in their womanhood, and never afraid to display it so or tease him in ways particularly sensitive for a young man. Some of the serving girls would smile at him in passing, a flicker of the mouth that would make him, however temporarily, feel invincible and assured in the fact that they must be in love with him. Once, he had caught a guard and one such serving girl up against an olive tree, the man ramming into her from behind with all the technique of a spearman playing at thrust. But what the *tuhkanti* wanted was to run his hand over a girl's skin, to place his hand against her chest in its rhythmic ascension and decline. He needed to taste a girl's lips, to run one thumb over the roughness of tongue. And so cautious intrigue overtook his better judgement that one night when he was led by those stable-hands to the *arzana*.

His girl was paid for by the eldest stable-hand, a youth named

Tarkasnali, and, after the transaction of six shekels, Hektor was shown to a small hall in which cubicles were afforded privacy by the provision of curtains hanging from awkward wooden rails. Behind one such set of heavy curtains, Hektor was shown, and awaiting him on the other side was Piha-wiya. At first, he could do nothing but stare at her as though enraptured with some celestial apparition, though in truth the girl was sunken eyed with opium and sweaty from half a night's toil already. She lay as something of a 'ra' symbol Hektor had seen on scribal tablets, her legs folded, knees bent and arms spread across a small hillock of cushions. The unidentifiable smell he had noticed earlier was quite concentrated here, and something about it suggested the possibility of excitement and the need to obey less refined instincts.

'I am Hektor, son of the *labarna*,' he said, deciding that the rules of officialdom could be extended to his current circumstances for the purpose of introduction.

'Piha-wiya, whore,' the girl replied, almost as a challenge.

Three-and-a-half minutes later, Hektor was standing outside the *arzana* reflecting on what had been, perhaps, the single greatest experience of his life, feeling assured also that the girl – whatever her name had been, for he no longer recalled – would be feeling the same. He looked up at Arma in the night sky and felt instantly glad that it was She and not Appaliunas, Her male counterpart, who shone down on him at that moment, for he would not have wished to be judged if his thoughts were known.

Hapi, when the *tuhkanti* first saw him, was bawling from within a swaddling blanket on a step leading up to the acropolis. Several officials were gathered around him and one was holding a wooden tablet bearing a crudely carved message:

> Property of Hektor, son of the labarna at a cost of six shekels. He is yours by the birthmark you share across your heart.

Of course, Hektor understood the message immediately and, ever willing to prove himself in no way a coward, confessed to his father later that morning his exploits in the lower town nine moons earlier.

The *labarna* was not angry, as Hektor felt he would be, but disappointed that his son should embark upon a venture so unbecoming of a man in his position; the disappointment stung more than anger.

'He will be taken by a serving woman, raised as befits his station.'

However, Hektor – already keenly aware of the need to take his responsibilities seriously – could not look upon the baby without feeling something unique and, as yet, unfelt, something warm and fulfilling being coaxed out of his already hardening personality.

'No. The deed was mine and I alone must shoulder the burden of the child's upbringing... But, more than that, he is my blood and I owe him everything,' the *tuhkanti* had declared.

'You owe him nothing,' his father had returned, his voice cold. 'He is a bastard and always will be a bastard. He will bring shame upon you and will be reviled by all deserving.'

'He is still my son,' Hektor concluded. 'And I *will* look after him.'

Hektor's eyes are fastened to his son, and in this instant he can see a whole world within the child. Moonlight falls across Hapi's sleeping face and Hektor runs one hand through the boy's hair, savouring the moment, smiling to himself at how peaceful the lad looks. His eyebrows, so dark and flimsy, float above eyes wrested from reality into the territory of dreams. Kuressar the cloth-cat is fastened under one arm, an island to the body's continent. The delineation of his shoulders suggests frailty, dependence. Hapi is not divinely ordained; he does not drive a chariot of pearls across the sky, nor will his favour grant plenty or pestilence; he is not the spoken praise of a temperamental father; and he is not made of walls that only a deity could have constructed. In Hektor's oral history he has always valued the everyday through storytelling – whether the everyday be the taste of earth on a farmer's field or the silver of terrible rocks crashing out of Heaven itself, igniting the sky in their wake.

He realises it now as though stirring from a life of sleep: the everyday triumphs all else in its immediacy, and there is preciousness to the transience in which his mind only can exist to love a child who defines, and always has defined, the man he is. All else must be superfluous and he is seized with a sudden desire to kiss Hapi on the cheek, to put an arm around him and whisper that everything will be all right till long after it has ceased to be so.

'In ages to come they will sing of men at arms, of jealous gods and wonderful creatures that can never leave a trace of their existence,' says Hektor, smiling and sitting down on the bed, running his hand along Hapi's curly fringe again. 'They will revel in our courage and damn us for our cowardice. Villains will be painted blacker than the deepest coal and heroes will be such that they cannot be human alone. Our faces will be painted into walls, onto vases – it will be like turning ash into jewels. These tellers of tales shall remember us for civilisations that have as yet to be conceived and in this way will our lives be forever.

'But they cannot capture this. They cannot capture what I feel for you now because what I feel will not last forever. I will turn to dust; you will turn to dust. Our experiences, our hopes, our dreams will be lost so that even the wind forgets how we railed against the sky. It has only been through loving you that I have held on to this simple truth, Hapi. It is only you that has held me fast where I might have surrendered what we have. And yet… And yet… from one incidental meeting on one incidental night – on a night I might have done anything else – you were brought into existence. Hapi, from all those impossible odds, all that chance and arbitrariness it is you who are here with me now, here now before the walls – the vases – are marked with paint and it is like ash turned to jewels. It is like ash turned to jewels.'

He continues to smile down at his son, wiping the prospect of a tear from his eye. 'And even if it costs me a city, a family and all that I am, I shall not abandon you.'

The sound of laughter somewhere further off in the otherwise silent acropolis brings Hektor back to the present and he fixes his jaw into some semblance of its usual position. He has to get out of here. Tonight. He has to take the children – Hapi and Kaluti both – and get as far away as possible.

'Hapi… Hapi, wake up,' Hektor hisses, shaking his son's shoulder.

Hapi knots his brow, groans through the uninvited disturbance. Eventually his eyes half open and focus in with not a little disgust on his father.

'Wuh?' he murmurs.

'We have to go. Now.'

'Go? Go where? Wan' sleep.'

Hektor glances towards the door, even the prospect of doing 'wrong' bringing out an instinctive alertness in him. 'We have to leave Seha. Now. Come on, out of bed.'

'Wuh? Why d'we have t'go?' The boy is still half-asleep and unreceptive to his father's attempts to drag him from beneath the cosy blankets. Even Kuressar the cloth-cat seems to bear an expression of reproach.

Hektor stops for a moment and considers the best way to win his son's co-operation. 'We are going on a *secret mission*. We are going to *rescue* Kaluti.'

Hapi's eyes grow at once into orbs of delight and he turns to his father with something like compliance chiselled into his face. Then, at once, his expression becomes one of doubt. 'But... she's going to be with that horrible old man now. Everything you said—'

'I was wrong. Yes, it is difficult to comprehend, but I was. You will help me put it right though,' he cuts across, smiling faintly.

A few minutes later, Hektor's head appears from a partially open door and looks both ways up and down the corridor. Finding it empty, he slips out and gestures for Hapi to follow, which he does with excited trepidation.

The *tuhkanti*'s plan is simple, if somewhat crude: he and Hapi will venture down the hallway to where the two guards are accommodated, rouse them, and create a distraction to remove any Sehan guards from outside Masturi's bed chambers. Hektor will then enter – once he is sure Masturi is asleep – and take Kaluti. Together, Hektor, Hapi, Kaluti and the two guards will then steal away to the stables, find their horses and escape Four Forts as fast as their steeds can carry them.

There are a lot of uncertainties to the plan, as well as several assumptions, but Hektor has not the time to consider anything more elaborate or cunning; all he knows is that they have to leave at once.

Hektor and Hapi creep towards the guards' chambers. It seems as though the acropolis is mercifully quiet following the dinner, with the occasional servant easy to evade in the shadows and no one of any social import in sight. Guard activity inside the acropolis is apparently minimal too, though Hektor is fully aware that outside of the building the situation will be very different. *Still, no one will be expecting Masturi's guests to flee, so the advantage is ours so long as we do not draw any attention to ourselves.* Naturally though, there may come a point at which terminal force is required, though the *tuhkanti* prays that it will not come to that.

The guards appear surprised to be woken by their master, fully dressed, in the small hours of the morning, as is their right. Hektor does not doubt that they will acquiesce to his design, despite the fact that they also know the desperation that has commanded their mission. *Guards follow orders just as snails follow rain*, though of course he has more reason than most to consider the possibility that the natural laws of the world are liable to corruption. However, he need not have worried – not that he did anyway – as the guards only raise a few simple queries regarding the *tuhkanti*'s bizarre change of heart and in no uncertain terms make it known that they respect their lord and will follow him without question. It is therefore only a short length of time until the four of them are in the corridors once again, navigating their way in and out of darkness, pressing on towards their goal.

Finding Masturi's bed chambers does not prove too demanding, the Sehan *labarna* keeping a much smaller sphere of wives and lovers than Priam, say – and even then he has not met entirely with success in producing scores of children to use in political negotiations. Consequently, the Sehan acropolis is comparatively small when set in contrast to the great structure that sits above Wilusa on its windy hill. Hektor knows that the *labarna*'s bed chambers sit somewhere in the west wing of the building and so ushers his son and the guards quickly and quietly in that direction. On a couple of occasions, they are almost seen: a rare guard takes a seat, rubbing his head and cursing gently, for near ten minutes before moving off again; soon after, two servant women speed through a discussion in a local dialect that Hektor cannot understand and set off towards the dining hall.

When Hektor and his small company at last reach the *labarna*'s bed chambers they find only one guard on duty at the door. *A rare smile from the gods*, Hektor thinks.

'Right, we will not make this complicated,' the *tuhkanti* explains. 'Here's what we will do: we will knock the guard out and hide him away.' *No need for bloodshed.*

A few minutes later, one of the Wilusan guards runs out towards the Sehan, catching him by surprise. The latter holds his spear out threateningly.

'Please,' the Wilusan pleads, 'you must come!'

'What is it?' the Sehan growls, holding his spear in place.

'My friend! He's stopped breathing. You must help me!'

'What?'

The Wilusan steps backwards, urging the Sehan to follow with desperate gestures. 'Please! You *must* help!'

The Sehan's face suggests an internal struggle, but, with a curse, he lowers his spear and follows his Wilusan counterpart at a trot down the hall. As the guard passes, Hektor slips out from behind a column and whacks the unfortunate over the back of the head with a heavy, decorative goblet that he found nearby. The guard drops, but is caught by the *tuhkanti* before he can clatter to the floor. He drags the downed man into a nearby storeroom and closes the door.

'Good work!' Hektor declares, sounding his appreciation to the Wilusan guard.

The guard grunts by way of response.

Hektor turns back towards Masturi's chambers. It has been a few hours now since the feast drew to a close and he is comfortable in his assumption that the *labarna* will be quite asleep. His eyes narrow and he strides over to the door. Beneath his hands the wood is cold. He presses one ear up against the narrowest of cracks and closes his eyes.

'*Tati*, what can you h—'

'Ssh!' Hektor hisses, waving away his son's question.

'Well, anything?' one of the guards asks, once an apparently sufficient amount of time has elapsed.

Hektor turns to Hapi and the two men. 'All is still. Stay here. If someone comes – hide.'

Before anyone has had time to argue with his dictate, Hektor is inside the *labarna*'s chambers, his back to the closed door. The room is dingy, like the interior of an *arzana*, a handful of flames only tackling the darkness. There is a strong smell of opium about the place and a salty stink all too familiar. On the gargantuan bed, Masturi's naked, chitinous body is sprawled out, the man himself unconscious. Beside him, a far smaller form is entangled in bed sheets; Hektor can just make out little sniffles.

'Kaluti?'

There is no response. He walks around several pieces of furniture and two cups upturned on the floor to get to his sister. There she is, face covered in tears, a cut across her cheek.

'Kaluti!' Hektor says, surprised at the sight. He kneels down, puts a hand on her shoulder, but she flinches at the touch.

'Y-You left me... you left me... you left me... yo—'

'But I'm here now!' Hektor interrupts, fiercely. He takes a firm hold of her shoulder, withstands her struggles. 'Look at me, Kaluti! *Look* at me!... I am so sorry. But I am here now.'

Eventually, Kaluti relaxes, her mouth a little open, her reddened eyes staring, wide and empty into the near distance. Hektor glances over her at Masturi, who stirs but settles just as quickly.

'And we are leaving, yes, we are leaving. You, me and Hapi. We are getting out of here.' He looks behind him, instinctively, keeping hold of his sister's shoulder, and turns back to her, shifting on his knees a little. He keeps his voice as low as he can. 'But we have to leave *now*. Quickly. Quietly.'

Kaluti does not move a muscle. She continues to stare, without seeing. Hektor looks around again. *I don't have time for this.* Putting his hands under the sheets, the *tuhkanti* pulls Kaluti out. She is naked and shivers against the chilliness of the room, not making the attempt to cover herself. Hektor tries not to notice the sweep of blood along her thigh and instead looks about the room, finding the most appropriate costume Kaluti had been made to wear. He picks it up, dresses the girl in a few rough movements. He takes her hand and leads her forcefully towards the door, picking her up once it becomes apparent she will not walk of her own volition.

Outside, Hektor has to calm Hapi; he promises the boy the opportunity to hug Kaluti later. Kaluti, for her part, is quite unmoved by the reunion. Hektor worries at his sister's silence and guiltily acknowledges the fact that perhaps something in her is now permanently damaged, that the spark which so characterised and fuelled her expansive personality before has lost all of its agency now.

Hektor, the two children and the two guards find their way out of the acropolis through a kitchen window, avoiding the occasional Sehan they might otherwise have encountered, finally reaching the stables still a few hours before dawn. Their mounts are present and Kummi, particularly, seems to approve of her master's insurgency. Once the party reaches a postern gate, leading straight out of the upper town, they have to overcome several guards to win safe conduct out into the lower town beyond, but this is the only violence in which Hektor has to engage. Finally, when the sky is flush with dawn, the party are thundering down the Sehan hillscape, away from the main road, back towards the Riven Staircase and Biting Peaks – features that so defined their journey to Four Forts.

With one last look at the capital, Hektor turns his gaze to the prospect of rock, chalk and stealth that will characterise the journey home. He cannot help but wonder if he has done the right thing. What will his father say? What will his father *do*? And what has become of Wilusa in his absence? Despite all these questions and more, a simple glance at his son and at the still-limp Kaluti, delineated by concentrated black in the red light, he knows in his heart that his actions could not have been otherwise, come what may.

Tablet Fifteen

Something is wrong – Hektor can feel it just as surely as he feels the heat of Appaliunas on his neck and on his cheeks. Once more, a headache is coming on, his head angry with more than just the scorch of noon.

The half-moon journey back from Seha has been long and weary. On several occasions, the group had to hide from Sehan soldiers hunting for them – clumps of sparse woodland and boulders the size of ships keeping them from discovery. Hektor has been in shock at his boldness and on the way home he has enjoyed many conversations with Hapi, father and son building on their fractious relationship. Kaluti has been very quiet, flinching whenever anyone touches her. By the time they reached the outermost Sehan villages and the Wilusan border she was at least responding to questions, albeit non-verbally, but her wounds are such that only time, patience and love can hope to bring her back to the person she had once been.

Hektor has been dreading his return home, yet is confident he will be able to stand up to his father this time and assert himself. Still, there is plenty of uncertainty as to what Priam's reaction will be, and this has played increasingly on his mind. Now, as Wilusa itself becomes an indiscriminate shape on the horizon, Hektor's trepidation is such that he has stopped talking with anyone else.

But, the feeling of wrongness is quite tangible, asserting a form of grim prescience in the *tuhkanti*'s mind. The fields – usually so busy with farmers going about their agricultural activities – are empty, the wind catching in the corn with a whisper of warning. Hektor looks towards Mount Parraspeszi: there is a bank of pigeon-blue clouds tottering over the mountainside into this region, threatening all manner of unpleasantness. *Watch over me, Mountain.*

Hektor holds up a hand, calling the children and guards to a halt on their horses. Kummi lifts her head and shivers bodily, the *tuhkanti* soothing her with several scratches of her bell-riddled mane. Ahead is a makeshift shrine, erected, no doubt, by farmers wishing to invoke the benevolence of one of Wilusa's many bucolic deities. Kneeling at the shrine is an old man in the rough dress of a farmer.

'Wait here,' Hektor mutters, slipping off of his saddle, making sure his sword is still attached at his belt. 'I'm going to find out what has happened in our absence.'

As he approaches, Hektor discerns a muttering of prayers above the trample of his feet on dead grass. The old man's hands are held upwards in the traditional posture for prayer. The *tuhkanti* clears his throat noisily, but the old man does not react.

Hektor says, 'Excuse me. I am Hektor, *tuhkanti* of Wilusa, and you are to respond when I address you.'

Finally, the old man lowers his hands, his shoulders slumping too, as though relieved of some great weight. He uses a stone baetyl to help himself stand, turns to Hektor.

'*Tuhkanti?*' the old man breathes, his eyes opening a little wider in surprise. 'Is that really you? My gods, your face... But yes, yes I see it. What hap— No, I must not pry. But... you have returned to us then!'

'Who are you?' Hektor demands, ignoring the man's reference to his appearance.

The old man lowers his eyes. 'My name is Hanma-zitti. I am... I was an army administrator working in the upper town. Attended the acropolis on several occasions.'

The *tuhkanti* glances over the old man's shoulder towards Wilusa, some voice inside his head warning against a return. He shakes the thought away.

'Peculiar to find a man of your age and stature out here alone,' Hektor notes, folding his arms, careful to cover the burned arm against the sunlight; there is nothing he can do about his face though.

'We live in peculiar times, *tuhkanti*. Yes, indeed. Times when our *tuhkanti* can be... can be damaged so. Times when the gods tear down the divide between the deserving and the commoners... Times when the *labarna* can be afflicted by so great a madness. Yes, *tuhkanti*, I mean no disrespect – I see you scowling – but madness it must be for the god has fled him. Truly.'

Hektor is, initially, at a loss for words. To speak as Hanma-zitti has done is enough to warrant banishment at the very least, if not death.

He judges, therefore, that the old man has little to fear on this account, *but for what reason?*

'You speak very easily,' the *tuhkanti* responds, cautiously, curiously.

'And I mean no disrespect to yourself or the *labarna*,' Hanma-zitti adds. 'But since the shaking and since the collapse of the wall and food depot, my Sun has been of an uncompassionate temper, a dangerous will and a violent persuasion. You do not walk back into a Wilusa you recognise, *tuhkanti*; you walk back into a city ravaged by fighting between guards and the general population. My Sun's demands of his people are too severe – the rates of tribute of food to the central storehouses too extreme. We are on the brink of civil war. And with people like that bloody landowner, Xiuri, resisting the *labarna*'s demands at each turn, every commoner takes courage and is of a mind to do the same.'

So Xiuri is resisting. The Bones of the Dead God has always been a strong-willed community. 'And just so, you fly the city,' Hektor snorts.

Hanma-zitti raises an angry eye to the *tuhkanti*. 'I fly because it is the wise thing to do. Do you not understand what I am saying? The deserving are in *danger*. It is no longer safe for our kind, *tuhkanti*. Why do you think I am dressed in this crude farmer's gear?' The old man glances past Hektor towards the children. 'If you want my advice, you would do well to avoid Wilusa. Returning is to risk the lives of those two children, although your appearance may be enough to confound even the keenest-eyed thug. If you do insist on going back, then avoid the main thoroughfare of the lower town and enter via one of the postern gates nearest the upper town – it is there the guard concentration is highest. Now, I have a long way to go before the day is done, so peace and light on your path, *tuhkanti* – may Appaliunas grant you wisdom.'

With not a further word, Hanma-zitti throws a wrap of cloth around his head, makes off south in the direction from which Hektor has come.

Hektor raises a hand above his eyes, gazes back towards Wilusa, a sense of foreboding growing in his chest.

'You are commanded to relinquish your weapons before entering my Sun's presence,' the guard on the door of the throne room says.

Hektor growls. 'But I am the *tuhkanti*, for gods' sake! My Sun would not ask this of me.'

'My Sun *has* asked this of you, with respect, *tuhkanti*,' the guard replies, looking uncomfortable. 'He was informed of your return by sentries watching the plains an hour ago.'

Hektor looks first at the guard who is addressing him, before turning to the guard on the other side of the large doors; both men have crossed their spears provocatively.

'Also, you are not to enter with either of the children,' the other guard notes.

'Why not?' Hektor demands. Ever since the events of Seha, he has found it difficult to let Hapi and Kaluti out of his sight, even momentarily.

'My Sun... did not say why,' the guard mumbles, glances down.

Hektor sighs, runs a hand across the scrape of his bristly hair, looks down at the two children: Hapi, mouth open, perplexed; Kaluti, staring absently up at him.

He turns back to the guard. 'If I am to enter my Sun's presence alone, then have some servants attend to their needs. A wash, water, food. See to it.'

The guards look across at each other. They both nod, withdraw their weapons.

Hektor squats, places one hand on Hapi's shoulder, the other on Kaluti's – Kaluti flinches. 'I will be only a short time,' the *tuhkanti* asserts.

Hapi nods, somewhat reluctantly; Kaluti does nothing.

Hektor claps them both once more on the shoulder, rises, turns, waits for the guards to open the doors for him and enters the throne room.

The doors *dum* shut behind him. The throne room is still a mess of rubble following the shaking, though the four central columns remain intact and the throne is unharmed. Sunshine from the ceiling light is a tribute from the gods to Their own destructive capability, tangled up in the clouds of dust like filth caught in sheep's wool. The wall frescoes are more grey now than they are the brilliant reds, yellows, browns, whites and oranges that once defined them. There is also a smell of something decaying, like putrefied flesh that has been left to ripen in the sun for too long – Hektor grimaces as it burrows into his nostrils.

'*Tuhkanti!*' The *labarna*'s voice is stern, uncomfortable in Hektor's ears, makes him jump as it bounces around the large chamber.

Hektor steps around two of the columns, finds his father on the throne, the *tawananna* beside him and the *mesedi*, his personal retinue of guards, in attendance too. Around the throne room are also various other guards. The *labarna* appears more withered than usual, a trickle of dribble at one side of his mouth, the corners of his kohled eyes yellow with sleep. His white hair looks greasy, the little bells in it *jing-jinging* quite mournfully as though performing a dirge for a greater past now lost. The donkey-headed sceptre in his shaking hand sways from side to side as its bearer struggles with the weight. Hektor's mother seems more tired and worn out than her husband, *which is quite likely, given her commitments to Father.* There is something faded in her eyes, and something akin to, yes, *pleading* when she looks over her son.

'*Tuhkanti!*' the *labarna* repeats in his usual slur. 'Our many eyes have watched you approach. You bring no Sehans. No soldiers. No men to defend Us. Are they still a day's ride away and you come ahead?'

Hektor experiences a plunge of panic. Until now he has tried to put events in Seha out of mind, not caring to consider how he would explain his actions to his father. But now the moment is here, *and my reckless disregard for preparing myself will be my undoing.*

'My Sun,' Hektor begins, clearing a throat that is becoming dryer and dryer as the moment prolongs. *Best be honest and straight to the point.* 'There will be no men from Seha. I have... been unsuccessful in what you asked of me.'

The *labarna*'s one good eye skips across Hektor's face, his mouth juddering.

Parta leans forward. 'You mean to say, Masturi refused the offer?' There is clear panic in her voice. 'Gods, was it the ugliness of your burns? W–Was it the manner in which you approached him? A lack of observed custom? Did you not make it clear that my Sun's very life is in peril?'

Hektor looks down at his hands, wonders momentarily if this is really happening or if some spirit has absconded to a dream with his mind its captive.

'Well, *tuhkanti*?' Priam presses, the anger in his voice apparent.

He presses anger, when it is he *who insulted Masturi to begin with*, the *tuhkanti* seethes.

'Let it be known that Masturi insulted you, my Sun. Let it be known that he did not treat me as a man must treat a guest. Let it be—'

'Excuses are not what was asked of you!' Parta yells, the echo of her voice quickly lost in the room, tears tugging at her eyelashes. 'Explain to my Sun the reason for your failure. Explain why it is you return with that child, Kaluti. Explain why it is you return without a full retinue of guards.'

Hektor tries to slow his breathing. An unruly part of him aches to break with formality and condemn his father for failings that are, at once, entirely his fault but also the unfortunate product of who and what he is. However, to do so would be tantamount to blasphemy, which is not a step to be taken without consequence. With a deep breath, he explains all that has occurred: the attack on the plains and in the woodland near Wida-Harwa... how Masturi insulted both himself and the *labarna*... how the feast devolved into theatre... and how Kaluti was paraded naked and accepted not as an *esertu* wife but seized instead as a *naptartu*.

'So you see, my Sun, I approached Masturi in good faith and was degraded despite my humility. I did all that you asked...' Hektor concludes, looking from the *labarna* to the *tawananna*, relatively pleased that his explanation has not, as yet, evinced any further criticism.

Priam makes a contemplative sound in the depths of his throat. 'And so he did not accept Our bargain? He would not accept you for a joining with his Luha?'

Hektor freezes under the direct question. *I cannot lie – it is cowardly to lie. And Appaliunas looks at me with judgement.* '... He did, my Sun.'

The *labarna*'s one good eye flashes; Parta gasps.

'Then where are the men you were supposed to bring back for our defence?' the *tawananna* moans, almost like a pleading child. 'The violence since you've been gone has escalated. Our guards must repel the commoners at the gap in the wall. The deserving are attacked on sight if there is no one to defend them. Rural communities do all they can not to yield their produce to the central stores – they would see their own *labarna* starve first!'

'Ghastly, ghastly,' Priam mumbles.

'The men must be a day's ride behind you – that's it, isn't it, *tuhkanti*? You wouldn't let us down – not after everything, not in our current situation,' Parta's voice trembles.

Hektor looks down, shakes his head, looks up, meets first his mother's then his father's eyes. 'Forgive me, but there will be no men.'

'Then Masturi offers something else – something better perhaps,' the *labarna* drawls, a note of desperation in his voice too.

Hektor lowers his eyes again. 'He offers nothing. I refused Luha... and I abducted Kaluti. Masturi's men hunted us for days before conceding defeat.'

The wind licks around the top of the ceiling light and, farther off, the tide of activity in the city's lower town can be heard. Parta's hands do not entirely conceal a whimper falling from her mouth. Apart from that, the throne room is silence itself.

'Tell Us this is not so,' the *labarna* whispers. 'Tell Us some demon takes your voice and speaks lies. Tell Us Our *tuhkanti* has not betrayed Us!'

Hektor looks up, alarmed. The *labarna*'s breath is coming rapidly, his one good eye darting about – the panic of prey present. 'My Sun, I—'

'This was the one way to assure Our safety,' the *labarna* hisses. 'Our *one* way... You have condemned us all, boy! You are meant to be *tuhkanti* – your responsibility is to Wilusa, your duty is your life and *all* else is secondary.'

Hektor flushes, momentarily annoyed. His thoughts flicker to his son.

'What reason did you have for betraying Us?' the *labarna* wheezes; Parta rubs his back consolingly.

Hektor presses his hands together, releases them. 'Forgive me, my Sun, but Masturi's terms for the joining were too severe.'

'Terms? What terms?' Parta spits.

'He... He told me I would have to let Hapi go – that a... a bastard could not remain with Luha and me.'

Again, the throne room is silence. But only for a moment.

'You betrayed Us for him!' the *labarna* rasps, his attempt at yelling not entirely successful. 'You betrayed Us for a bastard. The brat of some whore. He is not even a deserving. He will not even reach Heaven when he dies. He is *nothing!*'

Hektor looks deep into his father's eyes, his own blurring, hot. 'Do not speak of him in such a way! He is my son and I love him.'

'You do not know what love is, boy. If you did you would not have betrayed your own *labarna*. That boy has always held you back. He has made you stumble, made you weak. You are Our *tuhkanti* – your life is forfeit to Our needs, the requirements of this city. You look at your mirrored image in the waters of the Katkatenutti, you see the *tuhkanti*. You look into the lines of your hands, you see the *tuhkanti*. You look into your heart, you see the *tuhkanti*. But you choose that bastard over your duty, you rob Masturi of his rightful *naptartu* and gods only know what retribution he plans for Us – and because you have done wrong *We* have done wrong!' The *labarna* pauses, pants, sweat carving his face; Parta holds her husband tightly. 'But no more, boy, no more. We have been lenient. We have trusted you to improve – to prove to Us Our faith in you was always well founded. This though... This is too much.'

'Guards,' Priam growls, addressing the several guards positioned around the throne room. 'You are to seize the *tuhkanti*'s bastard, Hapi—'

'What? No!' Hektor roars, steps forward. Two of Priam's *mesedi* also step forward, in unison, raising their curved swords.

'—and take him to a cell in the prison-house. There he will remain until such a time as We decide what to do with him. You, boy,' the *labarna* continues, addressing his son again, 'will do exactly as We say exactly when We say. You will not eat without Our permission. You will not drink without Our permission. You will not shit unless We decree it. You are nothing but Our property and If you forget it once more then your bastard will die.'

Already the guards have clanged out of the throne room, already Hektor can hear his son's frightened cries. He makes to run out to him.

'Do not turn your back on your *labarna*!' Priam growls. 'If you step away from Us... And guards, while you're about it, take that girl – that Kaluti – to the Temple of Ishtar; she will be a priestess now she is spoiled. You will learn a lesson, *tuhkanti*, you will learn. And your bastard will learn a lesson too – what is that foal of his? Yes, yes, I know it. The day after tomorrow is the Festival of Appaliunas and we need a ritual sacrifice as custom dictates – your bastard's foal will be that sacrifice.'

'Please do not harm my boy. Do not harm his foal,' Hektor pleads, his face red, his eyes watering.

'The foal *will* be the sacrifice and your bastard will learn that this is a hard world – he is soft, childish. And you, *tuhkanti*, you will not see the bastard harmed so long as you do as We command.'

Hektor looks about him, at the *mesedi* with their curved swords, at the frescoes of monsters being tamed by heroes, gods instructing *labarnas*. He looks up at his mother, whose face is drenched both in tears and anguish, eyes pleading with him. Finally, he looks back up at his father, at the madness locked in his eye.

The *tuhkanti* bows his head, in supplication. 'I will do anything. Just... Just please do not hurt Hapi.'

The *labarna* leans back in his throne. 'Good, *tuhkanti*. Good. And your first task must be immediate. The landowner Xiuri and the Bones of the Dead God have stood against Us for too long. But no more, boy, no more.'

Eight harvests have passed since the day Priam returned from Seha after the demon attacked him; Hektor remembers it well. Parta had sent messengers on ahead to the acropolis to explain to relevant officials what had happened. 'Apparently, my Sun was talking with Masturi when the demon took him,' Hektor was told by Hawi, the chief priest of the temple of Appaliunas, after he had spoken with the messengers. 'One of his eyes and one half of his mouth drooped and he complained of difficulty moving one of his arms, but when he spoke he did so with a slur. Then he collapsed. But do not worry, he has not become a god yet, young *tuhkanti*. But… there is more, though your mother is best placed to discuss it with you. Be strong, lad.'

The *labarna* had been hidden on his litter by various goatskins and draperies, the plight of the deserving unfit for common eyes. He was snuck in at a postern gate away from the main thoroughfare running through the lower town and taken into the acropolis. His *mesedi* surrounded him the whole time; closer still were the several spell-widows, herbalists and priests attending his medicinal needs. And closer than all of them was the *tawananna*.

Where Hektor's eyes might have been fixed on the litter, they were instead locked on his mother. Parta had always been cold and demanding, but in her face was something different now: fear, confusion. It unnerved him. It unnerved him further still when Parta brought him aside and actually addressed him as a mother might address her son.

'Hektor,' she had whimpered, 'your father is very ill. I don't know if he is going to pull through. He is speaking, but is very weak. You have to be strong for him… and for me, and for me.'

She took Hektor's hands, squeezed them.

'What is he saying? Does he ask after me?' the *tuhkanti* had queried.

Parta scrunched her mouth, biting back further tears. 'He is… changed, Hektor. He is not the father you knew, nor the husband I knew…' She paused at this, looking towards the ceiling before meeting her son's eyes again. 'You know, when he first opened his eyes, after it… after it happened, he looked up at me, looked me square in the eyes and… and I could see that something was missing. A spark. Gone. He asked me who I was. I said, "Don't you remember? It's me: your Parta. Your wife." But in all his searching, he could not recall. As we've journeyed back from Seha, I've spoken with him, gods, for countless hours. I've told him about our joining day, how handsome I thought he had looked, even though I was scared. I told him about the day you were born, Hektor, how we each took it in turns to hold you, drink your eyes. Adore. But it was all gone. He cannot recite his numbers. He cannot read the simplest tablet. My burden will be to help him learn everything anew, build fresh memories to replace those he has lost. And you must be more than a son – he will rely on you to give body and soul. His loss is ours too; a part of us both will perish now because all that we shared with him, Hektor, all that which made him your father and my husband, all that has *gone*.'

Tablet Sixteen

Hektor gazes long into the cerulean sky, *bo-bobbing* atop Kummi as she *pu-tffts* through the overgrown, yellowing grass. It has been a eaay since Hapi was taken from him and he is journeying out to the Bones of the Dead God with a regiment of twenty cavalry – all that could be spared from guarding the wall – the riders dressed in tough leather, conical bronze helms and green kilts, each armed with a curved sword and a shield emblazoned with a horse's head – the emblem of Wilusa. He is struggling to concentrate on the task ahead. Sleep did not carry him away last night and he has abandoned every plan he has conceived of to rescue his son, all of them, at best, risky or, at worst, suicidal. *Besides, if I mess up a rescue attempt Father will have Hapi killed – and me with him, most likely.* Hektor's conclusion necessarily has been that, no matter how much he hates it, he has no choice but to do as the *labarna* demands. And so, it is two hours past dawn and he is riding out at the head of the cavalry, the Bones of the Dead God in the distance at the foot of the Mountain. But he has to focus, and he cannot do that while images of Hapi suffering sear through his head. *There is no good in handicapping myself with useless worrying; better instead to get this over and done with.*

The Bones of the Dead God is a settlement of quirky appearance, deliberately constructed in the shape of a horseshoe with mud-brick homes, smithies, market stalls and herbalist dens arcing out in a semi-circle. Beyond the horseshoe of properties and businesses, several farms and the homes of landowners and town administrators sit sporadically, erupting out of grass and bush. The local courthouse is set out in the fields too, atop a small hill with a well-trodden path leading out from the main body of the settlement itself. In all these buildings, the town is no different to the several other rural dwellings pocking Wilusa as a region, but what gives the town its region-wide status of wonder – as well as its unorthodox name – is a tremendous skeleton emblazoned across a hillside in the middle of the town.

A skeleton vaster and more obscene in appearance than any known animal.

A skeleton laid out in the image of a monstrous horse outlined in chalk for greater definition – offerings of flowers, food (there is no shortage of apricots and pomegranates) are piled at the foot of the hill.

Hektor has heard various tales of how the skeleton was found and when it was excavated. The prevailing belief – one that has journeyed through the generations – is that horse handlers native to the Mountain settlements, when one day out on a gallop with their stallions, found a partial skull the length of a man bursting forth from the mountain rock. Bringing a group of villagers back with them, the horse handlers managed to dig up the skeleton that is laid out on the hill in the Bones of the Dead God today. The discovery led the local *labarna* of the time to declare that the skeleton was, in fact, the remains of a dead deity and should be worshipped, for to find extinguished divinity here in the very soil of his lands was a clear sign of Heavenly favour for the region as a whole; others thought the complete opposite, but the *labarna* was not to be deterred.

Approaching the Bones of the Dead God now, Hektor looks towards the hill at the impressive skeleton, which would stand easily at three times the height of a tall man if it were ever to be held aloft. Its neck is the length of a spear, its head: horse-like. The *tuhkanti* has heard talk of discoveries like this from all across the Aegean and beyond: the lower jaw of something much akin to a crocodile with teeth the breadth of a hand; birds with beaks the size of a cart; and, from the east, the skull of a man as huge as a boulder. *Such reports give veracity to the myths that Hapi loves me to recite…*

Hapi.

Focus, Hektor, the *tuhkanti* curses inwardly.

The town inhabitants are watching Hektor and his cavalry with fear chalked across their features, a few even diving into the hidden alleys and streets of the settlement. Mothers hold children close. Old men cross their arms, knot their brows. Young men group together, puffing out their chests. *This was always a proud colony*, and Hektor realises that he feels a certain respect for them – for their resistance to his father. Something he has not been able to achieve, *at least not suf-ficiently.*

'I would speak with Xiuri!' Hektor roars, his voice echoing across the town. 'Tell him Hektor, *tuhkanti* of Wilusa, demands he come forward. Tell him... Tell him these people of the Bones of the Dead God will suffer for his cowardice if he does not show his face.'

The *tuhkanti* feels sick for even suggesting the threat of violence against innocent civilians, and feels sicker still as he hears the panicked cries in the crowd. *This is not me. This is not me.*

An old man steps forward from the crowd, holding supplicatory hands up, eyeing the *tuhkanti* nervously. Hektor grips Kummi's reins harder, the animal bobbing its head apprehensively.

'Please! We will send for the master at once. Please do not harm anyone,' the old man begs.

I have no interest in harming any of you, Hektor might have said. Instead: 'Make it quick, old man. Do not measure my patience by the passing of hours or you will not like the result.'

Hektor is an hour waiting in the rising heat, the colossal skeleton in front of him catching the wind in its various delves and holes, issuing forth an unsettling music. The men of the cavalry are ill-disciplined, complaining for having to wait and Hektor has to reprimand them more than once. *Perhaps they itch for blood; perhaps they have seen friends assaulted, killed among the guard population and look for vengeance.* He is intensely aware that the situation could devolve very quickly into something unpleasant. The darker part of his mind imagines a massacre; the more optimistic part suggests an agreement can be reached. What had his father said? '*Tuhkanti*, Xiuri is already banished from Our court for his insubordination. You will go to him in his sty of a village with Our demands. They have already been put to him once and he refused. Not this time. We want thirty-five per cent extra of his corn, ten per cent more meat and as much cheese as you can lay your hands on. Also, he has insulted Us more than once now and We demand an apology in the form of a gift.' 'What gift?' Hektor had replied. 'To demonstrate that the Bones of the Dead God is ready to bend its knee with all humility. We want that skeleton of theirs brought before the acropolis. They call that beast their horse god. But their god is dead and will not protect them.'

Finally, the crowd parts as Xiuri rides forward on his horse, flanked by four administrators and, in a chariot, *yes, the old woman from that night at Ura's house when all those people gathered – they called her Ma. She was the chief priestess of the Dead God, Xiuri's mother.*

Xiuri looks hotly into Hektor's eyes, glances to the left and right: the cavalry. Perhaps he had some clever word for Hektor, some damning indictment of his actions, but he seems to bite his tongue now.

'I have shown my face, *tuhkanti*,' Xiuri says. 'What do you want?'

Hektor nods, a note of respect. 'We will speak in private. There are too many ears here.'

Xiuri looks around him, agrees. 'Ride out with me – just you and I. Into the shadow of the Mountain; let Parraspeszi stand in judgement of what you have come to say… or do.'

A short time later, Hektor and Xiuri come to a stop. The only company to disturb them now is ovine or bovine in origin. Mount Parraspeszi seems to glower over them, as though disapproving of the meeting. Hektor wonders if his men back in town will behave themselves. *Hmm, well, I have ordered them to hold fast.*

Xiuri wheels his horse about, jumps off, lands with a *thtum* in the dirt. 'Come on, *tuhkanti*, let's talk face to face.'

Hektor looks back towards the town, which is near enough to be detailed in its visibility, but far enough away as to be silent. He swings one leg over Kummi's back, *thtums* into the dirt as well. He adjusts the straps on his leather breastplate where they dig into his collarbone, thinks to remove the bronze helmet covering his head and most of his face, but decides against it – the armour protects his burns from the heat.

'So, is this the way of it?' Xiuri demands, raising his voice but not shouting. 'You fucking bastard. You and that damned half-*labarna* you call a father would ride down civilians in their own homes, massacre them. And all for what? For grain. For meat. For pride.' He paces up and down in short bursts. 'You will see this whole region tear itself apart. You are meant to *protect* these people; that is your *duty*. You abuse the gods themselves with your actions. *The gods themselves.*'

Hektor waits patiently, pained by the accusations. *Yes, I am meant to protect these people. But what are these people compared to Hapi?* 'Xiuri, your tongue has never been an ambassador for wisdom. Cool yourself, remember to whom you are talking and, for gods' sake, think about all of those people,' Hektor replies, pointing towards the Bones of the Dead God. 'Those riders wait only on my command to cut down every last man, woman and child should you refuse my terms. I will make a fearful example of what happens to those who oppose my Sun. But I don't want to do that. Only you can stop me though, and you can only stop me by surrendering... For gods' sake, man! Lay down your pride – you accuse me of it, but you reek of it yourself!'

Xiuri meets the *tuhkanti*'s eyes; Hektor returns his gaze. The landowner is the first to look away, curses as he does so.

'What are the *labarna*'s terms, *tuhkanti*?' Xiuri asks, his voice suddenly withered, shoulders drooping.

Hektor breathes deep. *Thank gods for that. At least he'll listen.* 'I believe the original offer involved corn, meat and cheese – yes?'

'Yes,' Xiuri spits.

'The demand is just so.'

Xiuri shakes his head. 'There will be starving for this. I want you to *know* that there will be blood on your hands.' The landowner shakes his head, hands to hips. 'If I agree to this I want you to swear an oath before Appaliunas and Parraspeszi, as our judges, that the Bones of the Dead God will be left alone hereafter.'

Hektor pauses. *Would Father agree to that? Probably not. But if I don't agree to it then there will be blood.* 'Agreed.'

Xiuri narrows his eyes, cautiously. 'Then I will agree to the *labarna*'s terms, cruel as they are. I do not want to give you any cause to spill blood, much as I know you would love to do so.'

Hektor flinches. 'I'm pleased we have come to an agreement so readily. There is, however, one further stipulation, something that was not demanded last time.'

Xiuri's eyes freeze, as does his body. 'What is that then?' His voice is aggressive again. 'What more does your father want? The skin off our backs?'

Hektor regards the landowner coolly, steadying himself for the inevitable reaction. 'As a token of supplication, my Sun demands that you remove your town's skeleton from its hillside and have it transported to Wilusa.' Hektor pauses, decides to add something further. 'It will serve as a gift and be taken as an undeniable display of your allegiance to the *labarna*.'

Xiuri runs a hand through his hair. 'This is a jest, surely?'

'This is no jest,' Hektor says, his voice smaller than he would like.

'Why would your father ask this? Does he mean to insult the Dead God?'

Hektor has no response.

Xiuri's expression is one of pain. 'The town will be stripped of its identity, its religion, its *heart*.'

That is exactly what Father wants, Hektor might have said. Instead: 'Remember your people, Xiuri. Do right by them. The skeleton… It's just bones. The people are real though; alive.'

'No,' Xiuri whispers, eyes suddenly flashing. He rips a knife out of his belt. Hektor instinctively leaps back, one placating hand outstretched. 'This isn't going to stop. The half-*labarna* is mad. Heaven is not with him. Look at what happened to him during the Festival of Parraspeszi. Look at the shaking which collapsed the wall dividing the upper and lower towns. Look at *him*, for gods' sake: broken, feeble – pitiful if he weren't so callous. If the Bones of the Dead God can be a beacon to others of resistance then it will be so!'

'Don't do this. You forget yourself, landowner,' Hektor says, one hand slipping towards his sword.

'No, *tuhkanti*. I *remember* myself. Do your bloody worst!'

Hektor *shwishes* his sword out of his belt. 'I will have them all cut down. I will have every building razed to the ground and that skeleton will be hammered into dust!'

'That's it, *tuhkanti*!' Xiuri yells. 'This is who you are! Let it all out!'

Hektor shakes his head. 'Damn you, Xiuri, this is *not* who I am. Don't force my hand.'

'You love it. You have been itching for this!'

'This is the last thing I want,' Hektor roars, swings his sword in frustration.

Xiuri steps forward, leans towards the *tuhkanti*. 'Then why do it?'

'Because he took my son from me!' Hektor explodes. 'You understand? He took my boy. My father. He took my boy.'

Between the two men: silence. Contemplation of what has been said, the implications. Hektor pants, fingers tingling. The sword in his hand feels heavy, the helmet in front of his eyes seems to melt. Xiuri looks straight at him, mouth slightly agape. Eyes uncertain.

When it becomes apparent that the landowner is not going to say anything, Hektor throws his hands up, puts his sword away.

'I have displeased my father, Xiuri,' he begins. 'And in retribution, he has taken custody of my son and threatened his life should I not carry out his commands exactly... That is why I am here now. That is why you are *not* going to get in my way, the consequence be damned.'

Xiuri seems to listen intently, brow knotting and unknotting at intervals. 'Then I am sorry that a child should be used in such a vile way. But that does not change anything. Do you honestly believe your son's life is more important than the lives of all those men, women and children in the Bones of the Dead God? More important than the lives of all those in Wilusa your father condemns?'

Hektor does not reply.

'The answer is that he is not. And I am sorry for that – truly I am, but my position is unchanged. Gods, if it were me I would kill any man who threatened my child.'

Hektor shakes his head. 'That would be patricide. That would be *deicide*.'

'And if you complete your task here, *tuhkanti*, do you get your boy back? Has the half-*labarna* promised you that?'

Again, Hektor does not reply.

'He's made no guarantee, has he?' Xiuri suggests. 'How long must this go on then? How much is enough for you to get your boy back? There is only one solution to this. And what's more – you know it.'

Hektor pulls his helmet off, runs a hand through sweat-drenched, prickly hair.

'Gods, what happened to your face, *tuhkanti*?' Xiuri splutters.

'Not now,' Hektor sighs, wondering how he is to proceed after his outburst.

Xiuri's eyes flicker: something remembered. 'Gods... that night at Ura's house. That naked man who stumbled down the stairs. The Burned Hero. That was you. You went into that building for the mother and her two children.'

So Ura didn't tell that group who I was. She protected me.

'Indeed. And look what I have become for my trouble,' Hektor whispers, lifting a hand lazily towards his face. 'And I am no hero – burned or otherwise. I was doing what any man would have done.'

'No, I don't think so,' says Xiuri, shaking his head. 'Especially a deserving. Can it be that there is some compassion in you after all? Ura did always have a kind word for you.' The landowner folds his arms; a smirk scrapes at the corner of his mouth.

'I heard you all talking that night,' Hektor continues. 'Your talk of death.'

'Not just that night, *tuhkanti*. Many nights we sat there discussing what was to be done about your father. But... if you heard us, you did nothing about it. You could have returned with a regiment of guards, arrested us all. But you chose not to. Gods, there is doubt in you, isn't there?'

Hektor says nothing, eyes the landowner suspiciously.

Xiuri looks around, as though checking no one is listening. The landowner's horse and Kummi whinny. Cicadas chirrup. Wind *thwoos* through grass.

'Help us, Hektor,' Xiuri pleads; the *tuhkanti* flinches at the landowner's use of his name. 'Help us end this before anyone else is hurt – before something happens to your boy. If we work together we can end this. End the half-*labarna*'s hold on Wilusa. And you can be free of him. You want that, don't you?'

Hektor looks into the noon sky; the sun's whiteness seems to have diffused into the rest of the expanse, diluting the blue. *What am I doing?* He recognises that what is being discussed is treason. The *labarna* is ordained by the gods Themselves: to suggest a problem with his reign is to suggest a problem in Heaven. But the gods are corruptible beings, flawed and fickle in Their whims, desires, hates, loves, needs. It is therefore conceivable that his father's recent failures and the onset of his mad policies are the consequence of some rift in Heaven. *Or perhaps the gods have simply abandoned him altogether, given his performance at the festival.* And what is it that is required of the *tuhkanti*? To serve his *labarna* and to service the region, the interests of the two being one and the same. But there is a discrepancy here. And even without the struggle between the *labarna* and the commoners, *he has my son.*

Hektor looks back at the landowner, swallows hard. 'I will help you. Yes – yes, I will help you. I swear an oath before Appaliunas that I will help you.'

Xiuri tilts his head, almost uncertainly. 'Are you sure? I do not mean to mislead you: our goal has always been, at the very least, to depose your father. More likely kill him.'

Gods, what am I doing? No, if I'm going to commit to this I must do it wholeheartedly. Father took Hapi from me; that is unforgiveable. But to kill a labarna... *To kill my own father.*

'I will help you on the sole condition that you do not kill the *labarna* or the *tawananna*. Depose them, throw them in a cell, but do not kill them. I will not be party to patricide, matricide or deicide.' Hektor finally breathes, controlling his racing heart.

Xiuri puts his knife back in his belt, folds his arms, looks the *tuhkanti* long in the eye. 'Agreed. Neither of them will put up much of a struggle anyway.'

Hektor studies the landowner's face for any hint of a lie, finds none. 'What can I do then?'

'We can do nothing so long as we are kept out of the upper town, Hektor. Quite simply, you must find a way to get us in.'

'That will not be easy. Since my departure for Seha, the *labarna* has conscripted deserv— many men of the upper town to join the guards in patrol duties. The gates to the upper town have three times the concentration of men as usual – even as *tuhkanti* I could not pull guards away from any of these gates without raising the alarm. The hole in the wall is even worse: guards swarm at ground level and patrol the wall too; any disturbance here would also raise the alarm.

There is a postern tunnel underneath the acropolis, but it is booby-trapped, narrow and impossible to open inside without, again, inviting unwanted attention.'

Xiuri runs a hand through his hair. 'Do you mean to tell me there is no way in?'

Hektor scuffs his sandal into the dirt, glances over at Kummi, who is busy chewing her way through what looks a particularly tough weed. 'The only way in without drawing attention is through deception. I dislike deception – it is dishonourable, but it is necessary here.' The *tuhkanti* paces up and down, up and down, stops: a possibility. *Would that work…? Father would never suspect.* 'I have an idea.'

Xiuri's eyebrows rise. 'Yes?'

Hektor looks towards the Bones of the Dead God, allows himself a rare smile. 'It would have to take place on the night of the feast during the Festival of Appaliunas. It would also require you to offer the skeleton as a gift as we previously discussed.'

Xiuri bites at his lip, shifts on his feet. 'Offering the skeleton as a gift… It will be difficult, but if it leads to the half-*labarna*'s downfall then it is a gift worth giving.'

'Good,' Hektor breathes. 'Here is what I propose.'

It was not immediately that Hektor saw his father after his return from Seha all those years ago. His mother had explained that the *labarna* was instead in contact with Appaliunas, Hawi the chief priest helping him reconnect with divinity. 'After all, he does deputise for the gods on Earth,' the *tawananna* had noted. Having lost all recollection of Hektor as a son and Parta as a wife, Priam's most exigent need was not to spend his hours with family, so the *tuhkanti* was informed. Hektor understood so far as a child could understand, and took to spending more time with his infant son, suddenly overwhelmed by a need to display paternal affection. He did not see much of his mother, though in the glimpses he did have of her she could be found on the terraces of the acropolis alone or tearful in her and the *labarna*'s quarters.

When Hektor did finally see his father again he was nervous of what to expect, how to behave. After all, how does one reconnect with a loved one when they have lost all shared memory?

'Hello,' Hektor had begun, taking his father's working hand, careful not to pay too much attention to the other, curled up against his chest. He looked deep into the old man's eyes, searching for some sign of recognition, found nothing. 'I am Hektor, your – your *son*. Do you remember? Hmm?' He had broken off then to look again. The *labarna* had knitted his brow, opened his mouth a little at this, searching. 'Hmm? Perhaps I can help you remember, Father. Perhaps I know how you can remember.'

Hektor had his father brought to the stables that afternoon, the *labarna* carried on the litter he would call his legs ever after. The *tuhkanti*, with all the enthusiasm of a fifteen-year-old, had led Kummi out *tfft, tfft, tfft* through the hay and dirt.

'Look, Father! You remember when we caught her? She was only a foal, chestnut coat catching in sunlight, in the foothills of Parraspeszi. You taught me how to approach without scaring her. You taught me what herbs she might like. I can still smell them – can you? Ah, she was a fine creature. And we broke her together, didn't we? That first time I got the halter over her head – you laughed and clapped me on the back. You said, "That's m'boy!" I'm going to do the same with my boy when he's older. You taught me all of that. Here.'

Hektor clicked, drawing Kummi over to his father, who recoiled for a moment.

'Don't be afraid, Father – it's just Kummi, isn't it? Silly old girl, she is. Here, give me your hand.'

Hektor had reached for the *labarna*'s hand, willed it to stop shaking. Nodded, to encourage his father, borrowed a smile from lies. Slowly, he drew his father's hand out towards Kummi's midriff, pressed it into the animal's soft hair. Father and son, hands entwined, against the horse. Hektor smiled again: real. The pulse of the animal's heart rippling over his fingers, over his father's.

'You see? You feel it?... Do you remember, Father?'

The *tuhkanti* had looked deep into those eyes, as though willing the memory to surface like a priest summoning sunshine after flooding. Then the old hand had pulled away. Those eyes, dulled, had returned to look searchingly into Hektor's face.

'Who did you say you were?' Priam had slurred.

Hektor's smile trickled away, his own eyes dulling. He closed them against a jagged tear, reopened them no longer a boy.

'I am your *tuhkanti*, my Sun. I am your *tuhkanti*.'

Tablet Seventeen

The sun is a scarlet wriggle in the Aegean waves, the sky a calamity of pinks, purples, turquoises. Wilusa's whitewashed walls and cracked buildings are either plum in the shadows or grapefruit flesh in the light. The plains surrounding the city are blackening, cicadas conspiring to liven the evening, and only farmers padding back from the fields or fishermen slugging away from Besik Bay tread the well-worn paths. High above, Mount Parraspeszi stands proud and powerful, watching the region's inhabitants settle in for the night: children urged on to bed; priests lighting sooty little sticks about their temples; prostitutes taking to the streets for another skin shift; guards manning walls, watching in agitation over the lower town as though it is a snake ready to bite.

In the upper town, the main street leading directly up to the square before the acropolis is lined with the deserving: men of stature in dress robes; women joined with the men of stature also in dress robes; children in fineries so elaborate as to suggest a sartorial competition between parents. The atmosphere is solemn, fires lining the way whipped in the wind always present on the bluff. Clunking up the street come precisely 32 large carts, each led by a team of two horses and one driver, containing the remains of the bones of the Dead God. The carts exhale bone dust with every turn of their wheels, giving the impression of life. Hektor watches the carts now as they are driven up the hill. At the head of the procession is Xiuri on horseback, his mother the priestess riding behind him. The *tuhkanti* momentarily catches the landowner's eye, inclines his head ever so gently.

This is the first evening of the Festival of Appaliunas, but it is also an evening of supplication: one man kneeling before his *labarna*, offering a gift by token of apology. A gift of bones. A gift of bones that were thought a horse god. And now the god is shattered, humiliated, brought to the feet of the man who deputises for the sun god. *This is theatre*, Hektor thinks, *but divine cannibalism also*.

'We accept your gift,' the *labarna* informs Xiuri, once the carts are all brought to a stand in the square before the acropolis.

And with these words, Priam is turned around on his litter, taken back into the heart of the acropolis. The *tawananna*, the *mesedi*, Hawi the chief priest and various other guards, deserving and personnel turn to accompany the *labarna*. But Hektor stays to look over each of the carts, loaded with bones, *loaded with my one hope of getting Hapi back safely and ending all of this.* That, however, is for later, when the evening dies and the upper town is at its least vigilant.

The somnolence of the upper town is replaced with the merry of music within the acropolis. Out on the central patio, flutes and syrinxes flutter a tune, drums underlying the airiness with a *dum-dee-dum* rhythm. Rare purple-flowered clematis wind their way up the columns and other flowers and herbs gather along the mosaicked floor, nearly all the rubble of the shaking having been cleared away by now. Sconces are also attached to the columns, their little fires adding much needed luminescence to the proceedings. And the proceedings are of a spirited nature, the worries of the political situation seemingly ignored for this one night, at least by the various people gathered, their conversation a hum.

Hektor ghosts through the crowd, hands behind his back. He recognises many of the people laughing easily, swirling their watered wine and knocking it back, picking at the platters of grapes, cheese, melon, apple, fig, olives, meat, bread, cold boiled fish. *Little do they know what awaits them. Little do they suspect my betrayal.* But he shakes the thought from his head, *as I can ill-afford to lose concentration now.*

The *tuhkanti* avoids his family for what seems a good hour or so, but eventually reaches his father, who, with the assistance of Parta, is attempting to insert a sliver of chicken into his mouth, lips and chin greasy with failure. Behind the *labarna*, tied to a young olive tree is Aras; underneath the foal is a huge bronze bowl and ceremonial dagger. Hektor feels his muscles tauten in anger and frustration that he cannot do anything to rescue the animal from its fate. Every year a foal is sacrificed as a way of commencing the Festival of Appaliunas, the animal an offering to the fiery horse god in a bid to ensure another year of divine protection. It is therefore not a whim that Priam should

choose to kill a foal, though it is – in Hektor's mind – a cruel decision to make Aras the sacrifice. He had been in the stables earlier with
Kummi, the mare snorting, braying, stamping her hooves as though
aware of what her masters had planned. He had not been present
when Aras was taken from his mother, and is both relieved and guilty
about this.

'*Tuhkanti*,' the *labarna* says, through a mouthful of chicken. 'Your
performance has been admirable of late. We were impressed with the
humbling of Xiuri. It is already being said the commoners wept as the
carts were driven through the lower town.'

'I am… gratified by your praise, my Sun,' Hektor replies in as
measured a tone as he can manage.

'*Tawananna* – an olive,' the *labarna* instructs, clicking his fingers
awkwardly at his wife.

Parta's face is a moment of anger before returning to grace, like a
solitary cloud dissipating in a spotless sky. 'Yes, my Sun.'

Hektor is offered a cup of wine by a servant, accepts it. The sky's
competing colours have distilled into a blue the shade of winter seas.
Stars wrench their way through the dark like intruders. *The constellations should avert their eyes tonight.*

'Do you now see, *tuhkanti*,' Priam continues through a spurt of
olive, 'how we are to treat the commoner? The commoner is a herd
animal and We are their shepherd. You, of course,' he emphasises,
pointing at Hektor, 'are Our hound. Yes, boy.'

The *tuhkanti* merely regards his father, not a trace of emotion surfacing in his eyes or mouth. *Masturi did not provoke me and this labarna
will not either.*

'This *alalunza* is excellent,' Parta remarks, taking a bite of some
bread. 'And the grapes must be blessed to make wine as rich as this.
The gods have smiled on—'

'Quiet, woman!' the *labarna* interrupts, with bite.

Hektor's eyes flick to his mother: the pain in her eyes. He looks
back at his father.

'Yes, you are Our hound. And recently you have barked and bitten
as your duties have always demanded of you. Separation from your
bastard has done you good, do you not see?' Hektor sips his wine,

controls his breathing. 'We do not mean to provoke you, boy. We simply mean to demonstrate that you walk again in the light of Appaliunas.' The *labarna* looks up. 'Hawi!' A thin line of sputum trickles down his chin.

'I am here, my Sun,' comes a nearby voice; *clack, cleck, cluck* goes his walking stick.

'Yes, yes, we know. Tell Our *tuhkanti* what you have read. Tell him what communication you have had from Heaven.'

'Certainly, my Sun,' Hawi begins, turns to Hektor. 'Though there has been trouble of late, the entrails clearly show that Wilusa once again enjoys Appaliunas's approval. You see, my Sun's unfortunate speech on the Mountain was in fact due to... due to your failures, *tuhkanti*. But since...' – he pads his foot uncomfortably, looks briefly to the *labarna*, who nods – 'since your separation from Hapi, our fortunes have improved. You have overseen the subjugation of Xiuri and the Bones of the Dead God, the guards have reported fewer incidents with the commoners at the wall and other settlements have grumbled less in giving what was demanded of them in tax.'

Hektor's jaw twists, grinds. His grip on the wine cup is such that his fingers whiten with the pressure. He turns to his father. 'What does this mean for my son? I have done as you requested. I have not seen Hapi since you took him from me. Every night I struggle for sleep, imagining his fear and confusion. So I say: what does this mean for my son?'

Priam sweeps several strands of white hair from his face, the bells around his ears jingling, opens his one good arm. 'Come, *tuhkanti*. Appaliunas smiles once more on Us. The boy' – he makes a gesture as though of refusing an unpalatable meal – 'he can go to the guard barracks, be trained up. We can still match you with Luha – Masturi will forgive all that has happened, We know him.'

The *tuhkanti*'s eyes fog over with anger; he remembers though that it is but a little time until his plan takes effect. And Hektor is spared the ordeal of finding a response to his father anyway. From inside the acropolis: a commotion as though of people shouting, fighting. The *tuhkanti* looks around. *It is too early – this is something else.* Two guards appear from behind a column, hurl a rather dusty man armoured in leathers to the ground. Several women cry out, a small table comes crashing down.

'My Sun!' one of the guards yells. 'My Sun! A plot has been discovered! A plot has been discovered!'

'What?' the *labarna* slurs.

Hektor's blood seems to harden into ice. *Oh gods, no...*

The guards grab at the armoured man, drag him forward as they approach their *labarna*. 'This man was discovered hiding in one of the carts outside, covered over by the bones of the Dead God. Some of the lads were picking through the bones when the man sneezed. We found him armed. We searched the other carts and found a further forty men – all armed, all armoured.'

The patio: an intake of breaths, the grumble of horror.

The *labarna* holds his one good hand up, though it trembles. 'Where is Xiuri? Where is the landowner?' His voice is little more than a whisper.

'Here, my Sun!'

All eyes turn as another guard emerges from behind a column, one hand on Xiuri, who has blood streaming from a cut, already swollen, above his left eye. Hektor meets his frightened gaze, willing him to keep silent.

'Xiuri, what treason is this?' Priam's voice wobbles, some barely suppressed emotion fighting to invade his tongue. 'What is in your head? This was a gift. Supplication.'

Xiuri simply meets the *labarna*'s glare, the fear threatening to overtake his challenge. Hektor stands rigid, discards his wine cup quietly; he can only watch.

'Answer my Sun when he addresses you!' the *tawananna* spits.

Xiuri visibly jumps, lowers his eyes: resignation.

'We have shown our generosity,' the *labarna* sighs. 'We have accepted the apology from the Bones of the Dead God. We have left its people untouched. We have welcomed the gift of the Dead God... But the gift is poisoned. You slur the very gods with this act. What was your plan? What demon was in your mind?'

Xiuri swallows audibly. 'T-They were to... to take you into custody. Your family too. Kill all who defended you.'

Again, the patio: yelps of horror, roars of outrage.

Behind Priam, Hektor notices Aras padding up and down. As subtly as he can, he looks about for all the available exits.

The *labarna* covers his face with his hand, drags a stroke of kohl across his cheek with a stray thumb, shakes his head. 'We don't understand. We don't understand. We are the god on Earth. Why would you defy Us?'

Hektor looks uncomfortably at his father, a shadow of pity. He does not realise. He can never understand the hatred, the suffering, because he is so detached from the pain he has caused. This, Hektor sees.

Priam's face snaps up, his one good eye narrowing as it measures Xiuri. 'Under Wilusan law, you will die for this. Your family will die for this. Your lands will be stripped from you. Your name will be scratched from every tablet in which you are mentioned and no one will remember you even existed. Your plotting will see your shade reach the Under-Spring with the common dead.'

Xiuri breaks forward, is grabbed by a guard. He reaches out with claw-like hands. 'You bastard. You leave my family alone. You leave them alone,' he hisses. 'I may not have succeeded but others will. Your enemies are closer than you think!'

Dammit! Hektor curses inwardly. *Shut your mouth.*

The guard pulls Xiuri away, jabs him in the kidneys as he does so. The patio is a squall of voices, food flying at the landowner.

'Stop! Stop!' the *labarna* manages in a rough voice, hand raised. He waits for the noise to quell. 'What of Our enemies? You speak of them. What of them?'

Hektor steps smartly backwards, mindful of Aras's braying, the foal's shaking head.

'Why should I?' Xiuri cackles, spits blood. 'My fate is sealed anyway.'

'Yours is,' the *labarna* replies, pointing at him. 'Tell Us of Our enemies and your family will be spared. As Appaliunas is Our witness, We swear it.'

Hektor takes another step back; his pulse quickens. Xiuri looks at him, points. 'The *tuhkanti* plotted this.'

Every head turns to face Hektor amidst a fury of gasps, roars and even a few screams. The *tuhkanti* looks at his father: the hideous twist of his face. The *tawananna* is in tears.

'Yes, that day he came to the Bones of the Dead God,' Xiuri continues. 'We devised this plot: that the carts would conceal armed men enough to kill the guards at one of the gates to the lower town, take the royal family hostage. He said that he did not like deception, that it was dishonourable – but that sometimes deception was necessary. You may wonder why he betrayed you. But really you know. He wants his boy back. He wants his bastard. All of this he did for him.'

Hektor realises it is pointless to attempt escape. He has no armour on, no weapon to hand. *And Father still has Hapi.* Instead, he looks coldly into the *labarna's* wreck of a face.

The *labarna's* mouth remains open. He closes it, averts his eyes, tightens them shut as though in pain. '*Tuhkanti...* He knows of things only you could have told him. Have you betrayed Us so?'

Hektor's own gaze is unwavering, though one eyelid swats at a single tear. There is no point in lying. 'It is true, my Sun.'

The patio explodes in a frenzy of people squabbling, screaming at the *tuhkanti*. Aras stamping, neighing. For Hektor, the noise fades away, a wave of nausea. He is vaguely aware of his father yelling instructions at a few guards, then having his arms held tight by unseen adversaries. Time seems to take on no meaning. Minutes disintegrate into nothing.

At some stage later he becomes aware of a child being pushed about, towards the *labarna*: Hapi.

All at once, Hektor is alive to the moment. He bellows his boy's name, tears through the grip of the men holding his arms, but is immediately grabbed hold of again. He continues to roar out to his son, straining against the tight hands about his arms.

Priam smirks, wraps an arm around Hapi. The boy shrinks from the touch, his eyes wide, face filthy. Behind them both, Aras pulls at the rope that holds him to the olive tree, one hoof clanging noisily into the bronze bowl on the ground. 'Boy. What you plotted was patricide. *Deicide.* We did not think you held family in such little regard. The gods.'

'I don't remember when I last thought of you as family,' Hektor snaps. 'You haven't been a father for years. And you are not divine. Divinity is not robbing the common people of the bread they feed their children. Divinity is not holding *my* child in captivity, making threats on his life.'

'We are divinity!' The *labarna*'s voice is a warble. His arm locks around Hapi, whose tears come easily. Aras continues to pad about nervously, rotating a little so more of his rump faces the *labarna*. 'We speak with the voice of Appaliunas.'

'And even if you do, that isn't enough,' Hektor replies. 'What good is Heaven if it ignores the common man? What good is Heaven if it subjects us to lives we do not wish to lead? I have been your *tuhkanti* despite my own aspirations. I have always put your needs ahead of my own, ahead even of my own boy. And that is because I have a duty to you, not as a son to a father but as a subject to his ruler. I am tired of it. I want to be more and I want to be a father to my boy without your interference, your shadow. And without the dictatorship of the gods.'

Priam's face twists again. His arm tightens further around Hapi's neck, the child beginning to flap at it, struggling for breath. Hektor lunges forward again, calls out to the child, damns his father. Aras rolls his head up, down, drags his hind-hooves along the mosaics, *crck, clik, clok*, stepping further around.

'Why should you get that chance, *tuhkanti*? Why should you get the chance to be a father? We warned you what would happen if you betrayed Us again. We warned you!' His voice rises, trembles all the more.

'*Tati!*' Hapi screams, loosening the *labarna*'s arm briefly.

In that moment: the *tawananna* leans over, grabs at Hapi, yells for the *labarna* to stop. But he does not, and shoulders the *tawananna* aside, choking Hapi again. Hektor roars his loudest, breaks free of the guards. Aras whinnies, knocks into the olive tree – its hind legs leap off the ground: hooves, outward, smash into the back of the *labarna*'s neck.

The *labarna*'s arm slides from around Hapi.

His head slumps forward.

He does not move.

The patio is a frieze. Every person is so quiet as to make the distant noises of the lower town audible, punctuated only by the continuing whinnies of Aras. Every head is inclined towards the *labarna*. The *tawananna* shakes at her husband's arm.

'My Sun?' she says. 'My Sun?... Priam?'

Hawi indicates for two of the *labarna*'s *mesedi* to pull Parta back, the woman too stunned to resist. The chief priest presses an ear to the *labarna*'s mouth, feels his neck, his wrist.

'He is dead,' Hawi finally mumbles, his face: shock. 'The *labarna* is a god now.'

Hektor stares, as does everyone else, at his father's body. Priam's eyes are open, sightless. His mouth is open, speechless. Bruising appears around the sides of the neck, sweeping in from behind like a pincer movement. Hapi shuffles across the patio straight into Hektor, who wrenches his arms free from the now forgiving grip of the guards. He wraps them around his boy, kisses his head, breathes tears into his hair.

'I'm so sorry, Hapi,' he whispers. 'I'm so sorry.'

A groan of pain. Eyes fasten on to the first man discovered in the carts as he withdraws a short sword from a guard's belly. He swings it upwards into the other guard's throat. Screams. Xiuri takes advantage of his own guards' distraction, shunts one over into a table, headbutts the other in the teeth. The guards behind Hektor run into the fray, throwing aside the deserving, who shuffle around in a confusion of yells.

'Run, boy, run!' The *tawananna*'s hoarse voice. Hektor looks up at his mother, surprised – her eyes are fearful. 'You must leave here, take your bastard and go while you can.'

Hektor throws wide eyes back at Xiuri and the man who was found in the cart: they are killing indiscriminately and have managed to overcome several guards in the mess of bodies trying to escape. A sconce is knocked to the floor, flames lick at a wooden table, catch. The *tuhkanti* grabs at Hapi's hand, nods as the boy looks up at him, breaks into a run.

'*Tati*, stop!'

'What, Hapi?' Hektor responds, glances about, voice full of urgency.

'We can't leave Aras.'

Hektor looks across at the foal, whinnying still, shuffling around the olive tree. He growls inwardly, lets Hapi go, runs for the foal, shoves past a lost-looking Hawi and the *mesedi* who only now are leaping down into the centre of the patio. He grasps at the ceremonial dagger in the bronze bowl, drags it through the bight of the rope, each individual strand fraying and leaping up. He hauls at the animal once it is free, *tick, ticks* with his tongue, but Aras will not move. Down on the patio, the wooden table is ablaze, the fire reaching out, hungry for other pieces of furniture.

'Damn you, Aras! Move!'

The foal rears up, wild. Hapi steps forward, clicks with his tongue, holds out a hand, smoothes it on the animal's nose. The foal settles, snorts.

Hektor looks at his son, surprised. 'He trusts you.'

Hapi manages a smile back up at his father.

'Now we run, boy.'

The passages through the acropolis: unwinding, terrified deserving, and Hektor knows the guards are coming. But he keeps on running. Hapi trips, keeps his feet, and the walls slip by in images replete with monsters and burning. But he is not turning. Past the throne room he will no longer know as a place where the gods make their home, past the quarters where animals, slaughtered, make their last lowing. But he keeps on going. All this rhythm and tradition – the life he is losing, but the child he has won. So he tells Hapi to run.

Outside, the gathering darkness is enamelled with the bronze glint of guards surrounding the men, pulled from the carts. A number turn at the *tuhkanti*'s hurried steps, the stumble of Hapi, the *clip, tik, clop* of Aras's hooves. From behind him, through the acropolis entrance, Xiuri and the other man from the patio fly in sweat and soot.

'What's going on, lad?' screeches Xiuri's mother, the chief priestess, corralled in with the men.

Xiuri, panting, looks at her, then at Hektor, then at the guards. The man with him does not hesitate in running forward and jamming his sword into a guard's chest, roaring as he does so. In one swift movement, he pulls a couple of blades from the dead man's belt, tosses them to a few of his comrades and throws himself against another two guards. Soon, the guards and the men from the Bones of the Dead God are delirious in combat.

Hektor looks back up at the acropolis as both servants and deserving stream out, panicked faces all.

'The upper town is for the taking,' Xiuri roars at the servants. 'Take up weapons against your masters!'

Some servants keep on running, but others look alive to what is happening: to the men from the Bones of the Dead God slowly overcoming the guards. A chance.

Hektor looks down at Hapi, his frightened eyes. 'We must reach the stables, fetch Kummi and leave the city. We are in great danger. You must be brave for me now. Understand?'

Hapi nods, violently. Aras nods too, as though the foal has understood the instruction.

Together, Hektor and Hapi run off away from the acropolis, eastward and downhill towards the stables nestled in a little hollow near the wall. The courtyard is dim, the shadows of only a few stable-hands apparent. The air is a rolling chorus of horse conversation. The smell of wet hay, dry foods and urine mixes with the floral scents blowing in from the nearby acropolis gardens.

'We'll get Kummi and leave the city at the postern gate to the east,' Hektor whispers, keen not to attract attention.

Aras shakes his head.

'Where will we go, *tati*?'

Hektor looks up at the sky, an indigo blotching. He looks back at Hapi, rests one firm hand on the boy's shoulders. 'What is important is that we get to safety first, then we can decide where to go from there.'

He can make out Hapi's nod in the dark, and imagines a half-smile too.

The creaking wooden stable door unnerves the horses, but above it all is the desperate whinnying of Kummi. Once she sees her foal again, she calms, and Hektor is able to get a halter round her and a saddle on her back.

'You will have to ride in front of me, Hapi. We will keep Aras tied to Kummi as well. He won't be left behind.'

Really, he knows that the foal will slow them down, but Hapi would never permit him to be abandoned. *Besides, his presence seems to make Kummi happy.*

On Kummi's back, Hektor directs the mare down the well-worn path towards the smaller east gate. He ducks his head to avoid the tree branches, tells Hapi to keep clicking to assure Aras that he is safe. Further up the bluff, the acropolis has smoke pouring from it, the sound of screaming and clanging metal not too distant. Momentarily, Hektor wonders if this is what he had wanted, or if he had really considered the consequences of his actions. But he shakes the thought from his head, stubbornly certain that he would have done anything to ensure Hapi's safety, no matter the political or human cost. However, he cannot help but feel that although his actions may make him a good parent, they may also make him a bad person.

The eastern postern gate is not as well manned as it should be, and there appears to be an argument between several guards behind the closed gate. Hektor keeps Kummi in the shadows, hidden behind some trees. He looks at Hapi, breathes a command for quiet. Eventually, the argument escalates into violence and one of the guards is knifed to death. The other guards seem to cow before the murderer, who, along with another guard, hauls open the wooden gate. Behind the gate, a small crowd of commoners rushes by – men armed with pitchforks, lumps of wood and other incidental items. Hektor draws on Kummi's reins, instructing her to step back. He watches for a few minutes as perhaps fifty commoners stream past. *So even some of the guards have sympathy with them. All this killing, all this attack on the deserving – it was inevitable.*

'We are going to break through at that gate, Hapi,' the *tuhkanti* whispers to his son. 'Ride through the few short streets to the palisade and once we're past that we'll be out on the plains.'

'Will we be safe then?' Hapi murmurs. 'Will there be any bad men out there?'

'We should be safe outside of the city, Hapi. And if there are any bad men I will kill them. I'm not letting anything happen to you.'

'Will their lives be shiny now – the common people?'

Hektor looks back up at the acropolis, a silhouette against the fingering orange of fire. It appears, from several other glows, that fires have started elsewhere. The air stings with continued screams, blades-on-blades, blades-on-flesh. And as he watches he feels as though a part of him is burning down, that through the destruction of the world in which he is so interwoven he himself is lessened. *Am I still the tuhkanti?* he asks himself. *If I abandon this city to its fate am I being true to myself? What am I to do when gods and men compete?* He glances down at Hapi. Here at least, in fatherhood, is one responsibility he can view no longer as duty but as instinct, deep within him beyond his political station, beyond even the gods themselves.

With a cry, he heels Kummi into a trot, then a canter, then a gallop, Hapi clinging on to the saddle, Aras powering on in his bid to keep up. The commoners part as he charges towards the gate, and soon he is beyond the palisade, over the bridge spanning the defensive ditch, and hurtling further into the caliginous rough of the Wilusan plains.

Tablet Eighteen

Morning reveals the destruction of the previous night; looking back at Wilusa, even though it is small on the horizon, clearly detailed for Hektor is the writhing of smoke from the upper town. Hapi is asleep, his little head knocking against his father's chest at intervals. Kummi is reduced to a slow trot to allow for Aras, flagged and sneezing, behind her.

Come late morning, Hapi is awake though quiet. Kummi is happier for a drink from a stream, and Aras has a mouth full of parsley torn from a clump of the herb that the boy discovers on a bank when he stretches his legs. Hektor is aware that in his tiredness he has allowed Kummi to wander off a little eastwards where the land clambers up over hills and sharp rock-faces. The view from here is clear, the coast and lower plains and estuary crisp below.

'Can we stop, *tati*?' Hapi asks in a small voice. 'My legs are really sore.'

Hektor looks up towards the mountain range to the east and the forest in the distance. There is still some way to go. He does not know where he is going yet, but he is certain he needs to get as far away from Wilusa as possible.

'*Dek*, Hapi. We can stop – but just for a short while. And I don't want you running off.'

Kummi seems relieved to no longer have so much weight on her back and she circles around to rub her nose into Aras's face. The grass is soft and warm under the *tuhkanti*, and Hektor concedes that he too is grateful for the rest. The pair sit in companionable silence for what seems a very long time, each apparently comfortable in possession of his own thoughts.

Eventually, Hapi knits his brow, looks to his father. '*Tati*, did… Did I kill Broken Granddad?'

Hektor looks sharply down at his son. 'What? Of course you didn't. Why would you think that?'

Hapi turns away, engages his hands in combat with each other.

'It's just that I made the noise that made Aras unhappy and then he kicked out. Sorry…'

Hektor snorts, turns his head away. 'Hapi, it wasn't your fault. My Su—' He pauses, composes himself. '*He* did that to himself. No one else. Him. And I don't want you going and filling your head with nonsense like, "It's my fault".' He sounds more aggressive than he would have wanted, but he is angry that Hapi should feel responsible. *Responsibility is such a burden.*

Father and son keep a private peace once more. Gulls arc and swoop above. Cicadas chirp. Grass wrinkles in a cool breeze.

'*Tati?*' Hapi begins.

'Yes?'

'Are you in charge of Wilusa now?'

Hektor considers his son's question. *I suppose I am the* labarna *now.* He plays with the title on his lips, mouthing it soundlessly, imagining himself with the power his father commanded.

'I am… no longer the *tuhkanti*,' he finally says.

'Does that mean you are like a god on Earth, like you always said Broken Granddad was?'

Hektor looks at his boy, then raises his hands to glance them over as though something undefined but supernatural might be seen playing along his skin. Whether he sees anything or not is his business but as he opens his fingers he can see Wilusa, in between the fore and middle finger of one hand, on the horizon.

'I don't know that I am a god on Earth, Hapi,' Hektor says, dropping his hands. 'I do not feel any different.'

'You don't… You don't want to start calling me "*tuhkanti*" and me call you "my Sun" like with Broken Granddad?' Hapi queries.

Hektor hides a smile. 'I do not think we need be so formal. Besides, what would you be *tuhkanti* of precisely?' He looks around. 'Grass? Horses? Parsley?'

Hapi laughs his weird laugh and Hektor roughs his hair. But Hapi's laughter cuts out, his smile becomes an open-mouthed expression of horror, eyes glazed in terror. He is looking beyond Hektor – behind him down towards the plains.

Hektor turns around.

Skirting the edge of the distant forest to the south: an army. Hektor stands, as does Hapi.

'*Tati*, who are they?' Hapi asks, wrapping an arm around his father.

Hektor watches the army's amble, runs a hand over his hair. From a short distance away, Kummi whinnies: fear. Aras mimics. The sound of chanting and drums from the advancing ranks is like fabric caught on the breeze. *Who are they is a good question*, Hektor reflects. They have banners, yes, but he cannot quite make out... No, it is no use. But wait. What is that beyond the army? Wida-Harwa, the fishing colony, is in flames – fresh flames with only a little smoke. They have attacked innocents. His heart plummets. He suspects. No, *he knows*.

The wind grapples with him. 'Hapi, we have to go back.' Hektor raises his voice to be heard. From out to sea: clouds swallow distance to the shoreline. 'I have to insist.'

'But why, *tati*? You said it wasn't safe.'

Hektor releases himself from his son's arm, jogs over to Kummi, wraps the loose end of her halter about his wrist. 'That army is marching from the south. It can only be Seha. It can only be Masturi. And they have already attacked Wida-Harwa. My father and I have brought this upon Wilusa and whether I am the city's *tuhkanti*, its *labarna* or just another of its sons, I *must* go back. I cannot do otherwise. It is not' – he falters – 'It is not in me to do otherwise.'

He hangs his head, aware that Hapi studies him.

'But I swear,' he continues, finally, 'that I will not allow any harm to come to you. I swear it.' He fixes his eyes sternly. 'Besides, we must go back. Kaluti is still in Wilusa, as is your grandmother.'

'They could be dead already...' Hapi mutters.

Hektor is struck by the uncharacteristically sombre note in his son's voice. 'Hmm, maybe. But we cannot just abandon them.'

'But we were just running away from the city—'

'Plans change!' Hektor snaps. 'Wilusa will not be broken. I will not allow it. And nor will we, Hapi, nor will we. Now, come on – that army will be at Wilusa's gates by nightfall.'

As Hektor and Hapi approach Wilusa, the tide of ingression and egression to and from the city increases exponentially – all of them working people, in laughter, song, celebration. Hektor is reminded of that day he returned to Wilusa all those quarter-moons ago when he had brought medicine for Hapi. *How much the world has changed since then…* He notes that only a smattering of guards patrols the wooden palisade, enclosing the lower town, and even they are alive with conversation, scarcely paying attention to their duties. Consequently, Hektor and Hapi are able to enter Wilusa without so much as a, 'State your business, stranger!'

The lower town itself is wanton in its raucousness, so Hektor decides, with children and dogs careering back and forth across wide streets, hurtling in and out of alleyways. The usual brownness of the mud-brick buildings and wooden stalls has been sculpted, through the process of the uprising, into something altogether more ecstatic and impressive: widows assault the air with yellow streamers; young men chase each other, tossing multi-coloured confetti about; and washing lines are spun with blue, green and silver material – sisters, daughters, mothers and aunts beating the textiles with all manner of kitchen implements that have ceased, for the moment at least, to conjure culinary mediocrities for brothers, sons, fathers and uncles. In short, Hektor would be unsurprised to look up and find Appaliunas driving His searing hooves back in the direction from whence He came.

Finally reaching the collapsed wall, which opens up into an upper town transformed beyond all recognition, Hektor weighs up the situation (fifteen guards and one guard captain relaxed against the rubble) and clears his throat, surprised to find his heart beating uncomfortably fast.

'Stand to attention! I can see that things have changed here this past night but are you all so sloppy in your indolence?'

The guards, instinctively, leap up at the boom of Hektor's voice, the captain stepping forward with spear raised.

'*Tuhkanti*? I did not expect to see you,' the captain says, face forbidding, voice blank.

Hektor steadies Kummi, who is trotting on the spot; he agrees with her apprehension. He pauses, surveying the guards once more. 'I have urgent news, but… I will not be able to make a report to my Sun.'

'The *labarna* is dead, yes.'

The bluntness of the words sends a shock through the very heart of Hektor, despite him having been present at his father's death. He runs a hand through his skull-tight hair. 'And who deputises for the sun god now in Wilusa?'

The guard captain shifts the weight of his spear, loosens it. 'I answer now to a council of common folk. Please, *tuhkanti*, this tension should not exist between us – I and my men mean you no ill will.'

Hektor studies the captain's face: he is fairly confident that the man speaks true.

The captain lowers his spear entirely. 'She told me to bring you straight to her... if you were found.'

Hektor raises an eyebrow. '*She?*'

'Yes, *tuhkanti*. An *arzana* owner: Ura, her name is.'

The Council, such as it is, sits collectively at the top of the steps leading up to the acropolis entrance. The acropolis itself, Hektor finds, still rent with the cracks of the shaking, is scored with graffiti blasts of soot from filthy fires. It is uncanny to find a structure, so intertwined with his own destiny, this way mutilated, and the sight is sad but emancipating.

The *tuhkanti*, off of his horse, shields Hapi with one large arm. He is aware of the guard captain and fifteen guards behind him, as well as an increasing number of commoners trailing along, word of his reappearance no doubt spreading fast.

The guard captain steps up to the foot of the stairs. 'Councillors, you asked for the *tuhkanti* to be brought straight to you, should he be found. This is he...'

'Hektor? Can it be you...? It is good seeing you,' Ura breathes, her voice quite serious, in opposition to her usual jocularity. She is set in the middle of the Council, people around her who Hektor immediately recognises from the night he rescued the children from the fire: they are the faces of the secret group. *Were they planning this even then?* Ura shakes her head, gristly jowls wobbling. 'I imagine this is all shocking to you, eh?'

'Perhaps not so much a shock. However, the stench of death is thick in the air and it does surprise me to find *you* sat above such a grotesquerie,' Hektor responds, continuing to look this Council up and down – he catches Washa's eye briefly; the man is sitting next to Ura.

'Careful, *tuhkanti*,' speaks Xiuri, a sneer on his lips. 'You do not hold sway any longer and you would do well to watch your tongue.'

Ura holds up a hand, looks down. 'The world we wanted to be brought about – no, the world we *needed* to be brought about: not brought about by peace. Still, I am feeling shame that so many died. It… haunts me.'

'Understand that we did not want *this* massacre,' Washa adds to what Ura has said, placing one consoling hand across her enormous shoulders.

'Maybe not,' Hektor concedes, 'but a massacre you have nonetheless.'

'Are we to be judged by *you*, *former tuhkanti*?' Xiuri spits. 'After you turned traitor to your own father. This is as much your work as anyone else's.'

Hektor's eyes narrow. *More hostile than I expected from him. Perhaps he fears a reprisal for his own betrayal.*

Hektor looks at the councillors' faces again, closes his eyes briefly as the wind thrills across his face. He must be careful – the danger is very real. 'I will not pass judgement on you if you do not pass judgement on me. It seems… none of us are clean.' *Perhaps Father was right after all – perhaps there is a sickness in Wilusa.* 'But these are things for Appaliunas to preside over.'

'He *must* be put to death, Ura,' says another man – Basil, if Hektor recalls him correctly.

'Basil – I see you deputise for Appaliunas now,' Hektor notes, lowering his head.

'How do you know his name?' Ma asks, voice full of curiosity.

Hektor raises his eyes. 'Because it was not so long ago I put my ear to the floor in Ura's house to listen in upon your plotting.' He switches his gaze to Ura, who smiles.

'And I was knowing, deep down, that you were different to the others – that you wouldn't bring death to our door.' She claps.

'What?' grunts Basil.

Xiuri grimaces, shakes his head.

'He is the man who rescued that girl!' Basil exclaims.

'*He* is the Burned Hero?' Three-Shekels cries, the prostitute sat beside Basil.

Hektor looks from one shocked face to the next, trying to read his fate.

Ura and Washa both look on, apparently impressed. 'There will be no execution today,' Washa says. 'He spared my life once, where he might have had me killed. And if he is indeed the Burned Hero also, then he has earned his life, despite everything. Besides, none of this would have been possible without him – if Xiuri's account is to be believed.'

Xiuri scowls.

'I also knew that to come before you now was a risk,' Hektor booms, recognising his opportunity.

Ura raises her head, narrows her eyes in curiosity. 'Yes, you could have run. You knew what you were walking into.'

'Yes.'

'Then why reveal yourself at all?' Washa asks. 'We might have executed you before you set foot in the upper town.'

Hektor breathes deeply, looks first to Hapi, who still seems quite fearful. 'I returned to Wilusa because it is still my home and I still have a duty to protect its people.' Hektor turns around to face the crowd behind him, a crowd that has grown thick as his discussion with the Council proceeded. 'Protect it from the army that currently marches on us from the south – an army that has already razed Wida-Harwa,' he roars.

His words have the desired effect, sending the crowd into a fright of hisses, cries, yells.

'What trickery is this?' Basil demands, slamming one fist down on the arm of his chair. 'There is no such army – you are lying to some wicked end. See?' He points, turning to his fellow councillors. 'He is still the man he was – the same weapon wielded by the half-*labarna*. I'll warrant he has concocted some plan to regain Wilusa!'

The crowd of commoners latches on to the Ahhiyawan's suggestion and swear out their approval, pushing forward aggressively.

Hektor looks up at Ura. 'Please, this is no trick. I am not lying. The fishing colony is in flames and this army is coming.'

'Who are they?' Washa asks. 'Do you know?'

Hektor bites his tongue. If he is honest, he could be executed now for, ostensibly, being the cause of Masturi's wrath, though he may argue his father was a greater cause. But something in him urges trust, that while Ura and Washa head this Council he will be safe.

'It is a Sehan force, led by Masturi or one of his generals, if not him.'

Xiuri looks troubled; his words are a plea. 'Surely the sun has warped your mind. Why would Seha attack *us*?'

Hektor squeezes Hapi's shoulder. 'Because it was not so long ago that I insulted Masturi by refusing his daughter and… and *rescuing* my own blood from his bed. I offended him in the eyes of gods and men, and I believe my actions have prompted this aggression. But, truth be told, it has been a long time coming. My father made him continued insult, and Masturi is an ambitious man. What I did… It was simply the justification he has probably been looking for.'

The crowd behind the *tuhkanti* gasps, whispers. The councillors all wear varying degrees of shock on their faces.

'Then we send them Hektor's head!' Basil yells. 'And be done with it.'

Some of the crowd cheer. Ura and Washa give the Ahhiyawan disapproving looks.

Hektor can feel Hapi's hand tightening around his arm.

'Do that,' Hektor calls out, 'and it will count for nothing. Did you not hear me? He has brought an army here – that is not the action of a man seeking only one head.' He does not know that for a fact, but he has to defend himself somehow. 'They are not far away and will likely be here by nightfall. Sending me to them will not be enough. I know Masturi and he is a cruel man. He will take his anger out on all of you.'

'If that is so, I believe him,' Xiuri says, after a silence.

Hektor looks at the landowner with surprise; Xiuri inclines his head to him.

'And I am believing Hektor also,' Ura says with a small smile, biting a finger nervously.

'What do we do then?' Three-Shekels asks, her voice quavering.

'How can we defend ourselves?' Washa adds.

'We will surely be overrun!' Ma wails.

The councillors bicker and talk over each other, their fear transferring to the crowd, which falls about in cries and yells.

Hektor looks about him, breathing in the chaos, trying not to be intoxicated by it. He looks at Hapi again, squeezes his son's hand, mumbles words of encouragement. He lets his boy go, moves up the acropolis steps and turns to the crowd.

'Quiet!' he thunders. The crowd finally responds; the councillors also fall silent. All that is left is the whistle of wind. He looks at all the faces, understands the responsibility he must accept. 'You murder those who live in the upper town and look what happens – chaos! Where are the men who understand the defence of a city? Dead! Where are the men who have spent years commanding soldiers? Dead! Where are–' He cuts himself short. 'The only man left who has a hope of saving you is the son of the man you sought to overthrow!'

'Saving us?' shouts a man from the crowd. 'If some Sehans are coming here why shouldn't we just give them our loyalty? Your father has drained our land in his madness, and we will not see it happen again! Perhaps the Sehans would back down if we became their subjects.' A smattering of the crowd seems to yell in some sense of agreement.

Hektor swallows an angry retort. 'They have already attacked Wida-Harwa, for gods' sake, down to the last child, no doubt. Do you really want people with such disregard for life to hold sway in this region? Maybe you are right. Maybe if you walk out to them as they approach and offer Wilusa over, they will rule over you compassionately and respect every right you care to ask for that my father robbed you of. My gods though, is that likely? Is it worth risking the lives of your children for?' He pauses for dramatic effect. Scanning the crowd, he finds expressions of doubt, mouthings of, 'He's right...' Mutterings, too, mark a growing agreement with him. 'So, you are not confident enough for a gamble like that? I hoped not, because it would mean the death of us all if you were. Now, every moment we debate this, the Sehans get nearer. We are running out of time and we must act.'

'Act how?' calls a guard. 'This city has suffered enough casualties already, and the shaking has left a hole in our walls. We are in no position to defend Wilusa. We have to leave! We have to head elsewhere. The city is lost.'

The bluntness of this statement draws murmurs from the crowd, but Hektor is ready. 'You speak of mobilising the population of an entire city, readying supplies enough for travel, reaching a safe destination before nightfall. Out on the plains we would be cut to pieces. Despite the damage to our walls, the city offers us our only hope of survival.'

Hektor senses the people are beginning to accept his authority, accept the truth of their predicament. *Good, I must use that.*

'But how do we defend a wall that is already breached?' comes Washa's voice from behind him.

Hektor turns, faces Washa. 'I have been considering that and I have a plan. And you and every guard will hear it. Soon. But...' Hektor turns to the crowd again. 'I have only a small number of soldiers against what is to come. So I ask: are there any men among you willing to help me defend our home? There were those among you, only a short time ago, willing to be violent when you felt it was warranted. Gods know, I aided your cause at the end – for better or worse. And now, if you want your actions to mean anything at all, you will have to be violent again... Anyone?'

The air is soundless for what seems a prolonged period. But as Hektor asks again, individual responses come, offers of support. The voices increase, and soon a large number of men have declared themselves, including the men of the Council.

'Hmm, well, we got there eventually,' Hektor harrumphs. 'The lower town cannot be defended. It has only its palisade and moat, and there are not enough men to man the walls. We will make our stand here in the upper town, where the walls are high and made of stone. Now, the women and children will have to take refuge. The acropolis is ide—'

'Wait a moment, Hektor.' Ura raises her hands, shakes her head. 'There are thousands and thousands of us living here; we won't *all* be fitting up here on this hill. Besides, it is not just you men that can help; we women are not helpless, eh?' A number of women shout in agreement, some more fervently than others. 'I may be no fighter, but even I am seeing that all you men will be needed up on those big walls surrounding us. You're going to be wanting supplies carted about, no? And I'm sure there'll be plenty of fires to be put out too.' The crowd does not appreciate the mention of fire. 'So how about you let all us women who are wanting to help, help?' Again, women in the crowd yell approval, matched by the disapproving grumble of elderly men.

Hektor stares long at Ura. 'All right. Any women who wish to help with supplies, or who wish to put out any fires, may do so. Your help would be… welcome. As for the rest of the women, and the children, you know what to do so get to it! Soldiers, and everyone else joining in with the defence, gather at the stables, we still have everything to discuss.'

Tablet Nineteen

Hektor is keenly aware that the breach in the perimeter wall surrounding the upper town is a problem. The city has been taken in centuries before but where it has been successfully defended, it has never – to his knowledge – had to contend with quite as overt a problem. But what to do? The standing soldiers, performing guard duties, are depleted in number, so he learns, and the men from the lower town who have volunteered to fight for their home are not trained in combat.

'Numbers of their forces, any guess?' Washa asks Hektor, directly, half an hour later.

Hektor looks up towards the sky, his face a frieze of concentration. His eyebrows suddenly rise, as though a realisation has struck him for the first time. 'Hard to tell. But they have arrived here quickly. It was not so long ago I was in Seha. And that means… Masturi has acted in anger, not coolly.'

Anger, thinks Hektor. *Anger is good.* Anger, despite its ability to drive a man does not lend itself to the finer art of warfare. He anticipates that Masturi's attack will be reckless, fuelled by the ill-formed conclusion that Wilusa is wholly unaware and unprepared for what is to come and will thus be taken by surprise. The attack on Wida-Harwa suggests ill-discipline and in this regard a night assault on the lower town will sow chaos in the initial stages of the attack. In their arrogance and fury they will swarm about the walls to the upper town, Hektor decides, employing ladders to scale the stone and tree trunks to break the wooden gates. *Yes, Masturi does not look for a prolonged siege – he wants this done quickly and completely.*

Hektor turns to face Ura, who, quite simply, nods – as do the other councillors, all of them looking fearful. He does not relinquish his hold on Hapi, his preference being to keep the boy safely in his presence. Together, they walk towards the stables.

As Hektor surveys the men he has to work with, a plan begins to form in his mind. He will have to move quickly though – Appaliunas is advancing through the sky at what seems a pace far in excess of His usual leisurely arc.

Over the following two hours, Hektor explains his plan to the men. Masturi, he declares, will advance on Wilusa from the south under cover of darkness, his army teeming into the lower town. Before this advance, his scouts will no doubt take stock of Wilusa and in this, they must not be allowed to suspect that anything is out of the ordinary. Hektor therefore instructs that some men will have to patrol the palisade surrounding the lower town to maintain the appearance of normality. He is candid in that he admits this task will likely mean death, but notes that Appaliunas will welcome such heroes into Heaven. There is no shortage of volunteers.

With the Sehan advance into the lower town it will quickly become clear to the enemy that, indeed, not all *is* as it should be. This is when the attack from the rear will take place. Hektor instructs that cavalry be stationed, hidden, inside the many farmers' stables outside of the lower town, on the lip of the plains. Once the Sehans have entered the city and approached the upper town, the cavalry will explode from their concealment into the rear of the enemy troops, causing mass panic and, hopefully, dealing many casualties. The cavalry will use their knowledge of Wilusa's streets to carve through the enemy in their most aggressive fashion.

As this attack happens, archers stationed on the upper town walls will rain flaming projectiles on the Sehans, magnifying the panic with the addition of fire. Of course, the enemy will recover, but will have suffered greatly for their troubles and be at a disadvantage, morale crippled. Naturally, the break in the wall will be an attractive target for penetrating the upper town, but Hektor will fortify it with a large force of men. *If Masturi's troops are funnelled there then it will be all the easier to kill them in their masses*, Hektor decides.

'I am counting on you all to remember your duties,' he yells out to the men. 'Discipline is key and we cannot afford any mistakes. Give them no quarter. Give them hell.'

Meanwhile, it will be the women's job to carry fresh arrows, replacement armour and more to the walls, extinguish fires in the upper town, if necessary, and tend to the inevitable casualties. Hektor is impressed with how staunchly Ura assumes leadership, and how ferociously she presses her voice over the women beneath her.

While Hektor delivers his commands to the men, and Ura to the women, the councillors direct civilians who are not performing a role in the upcoming battle towards the acropolis, royal gardens and the mansions that have survived the shaking, where they are settled into shelter. It takes several hours, but eventually all civilians are transferred into comfortable accommodation, even if some of that accommodation consists of lying across rubble and broken pottery.

Soon, Appaliunas declines, His searing colours bleeding into the magenta of an early evening Aegean.

Hektor settles down outside the blacksmith's workshop, the area busy with men dressing for battle. Only a minority can boast bronze armour, most having to make do with leather or simple wool. The cavalry races by at intervals, heading out of the upper town towards the farmers' stables beyond the city itself.

Pulling on his scale vest, Hektor becomes aware of a man sitting beside him. It is Washa.

'Do you think your plan will work?' Washa asks, his face betraying no certain emotion.

Hektor tightens a leather belt about his waist, wrenching the material into place. 'You should never ask a tactician whether he think his plan will succeed. And you should definitely not be asking *me* that.'

Washa pauses. 'Why?'

Hektor sighs. 'Because I'm not even a tactician. You think I've fought wars? I haven't. I have led defence patrols and fought off bandits and that's about it. I'm a… a politician more than I am a fighter.'

'Then…' Washa searches, perhaps, for the right words, 'how can you stand now and be so decisive?'

'Because if not I then who?' Hektor snaps. 'That is what a good leader does – that is what a good *labarna* does. This is my home and these are my people and I lead them now because I cannot do otherwise. I am scared, Washa – scared of what the night will bring, but that will not stop me from fulfilling my duty. Whether the gods have ordained our survival or extinction, we can do nothing but fulfil the role that has been set before us. And if we die, and if anyone remembers who we are, then I would have them remember that there is nothing special about us' – he thinks of Hapi – 'save for how we embrace each other as special. And that, Washa, is enough for me to stand and take up a weapon.'

Did I refer to myself as the labarna?

Washa falls silent, bobs his head, presses his fingertips together. After several moments, he changes the topic of conversation. 'Do you know what it is that I wanted as a result of this… this revolution, this uprising – whatever it is?'

'No,' Hektor sighs, bending down to set greaves to shins.

'Well, I told you once before that I used to be a physician. That I experimented in ways that would make your *hasawas* and spell-widows recoil. But my work was successful. And you have seen that success – it was how I saved your son.' He pauses. 'All I want is to do that again. To set up my surgery, train others in the techniques I have discovered. We may only be "common" to people like you, but we are not ignorant and should not be kept in ignorance. And *that* is enough for me to stand and take up a weapon.'

'And what will your weapon be? Pomegranates? Apricots?' Hektor snorts.

'No… A sword, most likely. A sword I do not know how to use.'

Hektor turns to face Washa. 'You will likely die then.'

'Better to die striving for something more, than living for something less.'

Hektor inclines his head. 'And perhaps in this defence I have found something more for myself.'

A heavy shuffle announces the arrival of Ura. She says something quietly to Washa, who nods, leaves. Ura settles down next to Hektor with a groan.

The pair maintain an awkward silence.

'Looks like everything is ready,' Ura says, after a while.

Hektor grunts his approval.

'I notice you haven't been asking about… about your family.'

Hektor adjusts the buckle on each of his sandals for perhaps the eighth time. 'I am not sure I will like what I hear. Besides, I betrayed them.'

'Hapi has asked after a girl called Kaluti.'

'Tell me this,' Hektor interrupts, turning to face his old friend. 'Where is my father's body?'

Ura's face decays into something painful; she tries for words but fails.

'I... understand.'

'Kaluti lives though – that is what I told Hapi. And your mother, Parta – she lives too.'

Hektor's brow creases. 'Are you sure?'

Ura nods.

Hektor stands, abruptly. 'Where are they?'

'They are in the prison, in a cell together... Hektor, maybe don't.'

But Hektor is already striding off.

The prison is a grey ruin set above the rubble. *It is a miracle it can still hold anyone*, Hektor thinks. He orders the guards to take him to his mother and Kaluti – he is appalled at what he finds, so much so that he roars at the guards to leave.

Parta is huddled in a corner, hair shorn, face bloody, clothes torn. In her arms is the limp body of Kaluti, the girl covered in a thin sheet of filthy linen. The smell is overpowering: a seemingly physical force of faeces, urine, other sickly smells.

Hektor steps quickly forward, but Parta holds up one trembling hand as though to ward him off. Hektor stops, covers his mouth, close to tears for a woman he has never truly loved, but for whom now he cannot hide his pity.

'You did not run, boy,' Parta manages in a weak voice.

Hektor grips a hand across his neck, as though to choke himself. 'I have no need to run. This is where I belong. This is where I have always belonged.'

Hektor continues to look over his mother's broken body, aware of the wind trying to burrow through the fissured walls like some half-starved predator seeking its prey.

'What happened to Kaluti?' he whispers, lowers himself into a squatting position.

Parta's arms visibly tighten around the girl. 'She died half an hour ago. I was already here in this cell when they brought her to me. The inside of her thigh was bloody and she could not walk. She'd been beaten mercilessly. It was too much for a child. What is it in men that women must be broken so when all the world goes to hell?'

Hektor hangs his head, vows that Hapi will learn the truth of Kaluti's death. *The horror of it must be a lesson for him never to repeat such evil. But later – he has enough to fear for the moment.* He holds out a hand to his mother, pushes past her flinch, takes hold of her cold hand. Squeezes it.

'I will arrange for you to be taken back to the acropolis,' Hektor finally says.

'No,' Parta struggles through a cough. 'Please, I am comfortable just here. I never wish to set foot in the acropolis again. My life has been defined by that building, but now I think I should like to be forgotten. When the eyes of gods and deserving are no longer upon you, you do not have to be a specific person, act a certain way. Here it is dark and I think not even the gods remember me. I like it this way. It is a relief and a weight has gone. I think I would like to just hold Kaluti now. And I think, yes, I think you do not yet belong here in such a place. That world out there belongs to you and I think it is good for you to return to it now. I love you, son. I always did, despite what you may have thought of me, despite what I had to be.'

Parta gently, but firmly, removes her hand from Hektor's, leaving Hektor to look down at his empty fingers. He looks once more into his mother's eyes, finds he is envious of the peace he sees there, and picks himself up, leaving the cell and the prison behind.

On his way back from the prison, Hektor is approached by Hapi.

'Why are you not inside yet?' Hektor demands.

Hapi scuffs one sandalled foot in the dirt. 'I–I wanted to see you again, before you went up onto the walls... Also, Aras is asleep now so I thought I would leave him alone. Sorry, *tati.*'

Hektor grunts, folds his arms. 'Why did you decide to go in the stable? You could have chosen to stay somewhere much better.'

'I wanted to be with Aras. He might get scared when all the fighting starts.'

'Aras? Do you think Aras is missing his mother?'

'Yes. He doesn't want anything to happen to her.'

Hektor scrutinises his son's expression. 'Well, you have seen me now. And it is time I went up onto the walls.'

Yellow sconce-light from the nearby smithy flickers in Hapi's eyes.

Hektor sighs. 'There is something else?'

'What's going on, *tati*? Why's everyone so quiet? Why's everyone looking so scared?'

Hektor has not even considered Hapi might not precisely appreciate the importance of the situation. 'You are only a child,' Hektor says, more as a personal revelation. 'This must all be very peculiar to you... Well... Do you remember not so long ago, when you had that little demon inside your belly?'

'Uh-huh.' Hapi stealthily wipes his eyes. 'Sometimes it's still sore.'

'Yes, I suppose it must be. Well, I was very worried about you. I did not know if your body could hold out against the demon's influence.'

Hapi screws up his eyes. 'What's the demon got to do with what's happening now?'

'I was going to use it as an analogy.'

'What's an analogy?' Hapi queries.

'Never mind. Many people are scared right now. They are looking out of the city, and they are imagining terrible, terrible things. They are trying to peer through the dark, but they can see nothing. All they can do is wait, which is not good, because when you wait, you anticipate all the horrors of your imagination, and your imagination is always far scarier than reality.'

'Are you scared?'

Hektor looks at the nearby walls, the darkness settling in like some undesirable guest. 'No, I am not scared,' he lies. 'Do you know why? I am not scared because I am not looking out at the dark and picturing terrible things. I am looking inside this city at the people... at you. Because of that, I do not have time to worry about worrying.'

'You're not scared... because you're staring at people?' Hapi looks confused.

Hektor shakes his head. 'Not exactly that, no. I am not scared because I have a duty to people here; to make sure everyone is safe. And that is something I can understand. A task I can perform. If you do not want to be scared, then I think you should give yourself a responsibility.'

'Like what?'

'Like Aras. Aras is only a foal – only a child. He does not understand what is happening at all. He is even more scared than you.'

'So... I should worry about Aras instead?'

'Sort of. If we have someone who needs us, then we have to put our own interests, and our own feelings, second. That is what responsibility is. Tonight will be something you should experience together; it will bind you. This will break him in. This will join you forever.' He pauses, sighs. 'You will hear a lot of noises later and I'm afraid they will be frightening. But if you ever feel like fear is taking over, just remember that you have to put it out of the way for Aras's sake. Do you understand?'

Hapi swallows noisily. 'Y–Yes, *tati*.'

Hektor sighs, then kneels. Placing a hand on each of the boy's shoulders, he looks Hapi straight in the eye, and is upset to see his tears.

'Hapi? Look at me. Look at me. While you are looking after Aras, I will be looking after *you*. You see?'

'Some people are saying we're all going to die.'

'Well, the people saying that are frightened. And they have nothing more important to take their fear away. You do. Now, we are not all going to die, because I will not let that happen.'

'Can I have a cuddle, please?'

Hektor sighs again, pulls the boy to his chest. He feels a little awkward, as people are watching. He is more uncomfortable with just how tightly Hapi hugs him back though.

Hektor mentally counts to ten, then carefully prises Hapi away.

'Now, it is time you went back to the stable... Are the other horses behaving well down there?'

'They're okay. They're really quiet, but sometimes they make these little rolling noises in their mouth.'

'Probably excited by all the commotion. Foolish old animals.'

Hapi laughs uncertainly.

'I really do have to go now.'

Hapi nods. Hektor squeezes Hapi's arm once more, disengages, turns his back, strides off towards the wall.

After the animation of evening, the town settles into a hush of apprehension. There are no owls tonight, though the occasional bat appears as an intermittent slip across starlight.

Along the upper town wall, the Wilusans are flattened behind the merlon-styled parapet, which has always looked to Hektor like a line of goat's teeth. Around each gate, the men are particularly cramped, with the largest force stationed where the wall has collapsed. Several fortified towers beside the gates are also filled with men – civilians-turned-fighters primarily – as they can be guaranteed the most protection in these positions. Everyone maintains a disciplined silence, much to Hektor's satisfaction, shuffling bodies only when wall patrols look for space in which they can move about.

Hektor leans his head against an individual merlon, watches his breath wash over the bronze relief of other men's armour. He occasionally leans an eye past the merlon to look out into the night. For hours, the scene does not change: black taverns, empty roads, dewy grass and a mist that has slid off Mount Parraspeszi, disrupting line of sight. Arma, obscured in cloud, rolls across the sky. Every now and then, the Wilusans take in sharp slices of breath, when they imagine distant sound. Whenever this happens, the men remain especially still for a while after, trying to find slivers of noise in the night. But nothing comes. Hektor occasionally peers out from behind a merlon towards the lower town palisade where he can still see the little roving orbs of torchlight where men patrol. Inwardly, he prays to Appaliunas for their souls, knowing that they will most likely be killed.

Hektor is incredibly tired, and knows he would gladly fall asleep if in bed. To his right, Washa – who has decided to fight alongside him – is perfectly still.

'It must be three hours after midnight, Hektor. I think they would have attacked by now. Perhaps it won't be tonight after all.'

'Why would you say that?'

'Perhaps they know that we know about them. Maybe they have spies.'

Hektor grunts.

'Maybe they decided Wilusa isn't worth the trouble,' Washa continues.

'Would you be quiet?'

Washa is still again. Then: 'My, what if they've started attacking other settlements? Think of Wida-Harwa...'

'That does not make any sense. Now please, just be quiet; I am trying to concentrate.'

Washa looks up, exhales heavily. '... Maybe they got close to the town without us knowing and saw everyone's breath rising above the wall. There are hundreds of us up here, after all.'

Hektor turns in irritation, but notices Washa's long trail of breath moving upward. He considers Washa's idea for a moment and looks around at the men, half-reclined, many looking up at the clouds and stars. Their breaths are long and drawn out, and as they fill the air, they dance in the moonlight before disappearing.

Hektor leans around the merlon to look back out again. 'No. It is misty out there, no one could see well enough from any distance...'

'Well, I hope you're right. It would only take one of their men to have keen eyesight, and they'd know— Hektor, what is it?'

Hektor's eyes are wide.

A loud whipping noise followed by several shouts and a collective scream wrenches the silence. Hektor looks towards the eastern gate, and sees the remnants of a volley of arrows hailing upon the 200-man force lying upon the wall. In the immediate confusion, Hektor yells above the panicked cries, ordering a quarter of the force beside the hole in the wall – where he is stationed – to move along and reinforce the eastern gate. Hektor pulls Washa up, and together they run the wall's lengthy perimeter.

Approaching, they watch the remaining guards at the eastern gate move into position behind the parapet, firing arrows out at, as yet, unseen targets... Now they see out into the lower town streets leading up to the eastern gate... A small force of Sehans moves huge ladders into position, body-length figure-of-eight shields deflecting Wilusan arrows... A short distance behind the ladders, several thick lines of Sehan archers fire at the Wilusans, standing in front of several damaged buildings. Where guards hold firm, a number of civilian men flee down the steps leading into the upper town... A number more are in foetal positions, murmuring to themselves... Hektor is disappointed that so many men should break so easily. However, he is pleased the women, down in the upper town, are busy tending to the men injured by arrows.

'They're picking us off too easily. See, even the men in the east tower are struggling to get shots away!' Washa yells to Hektor, as they continue to run.

'We will not be enough to reinforce the eastern gate – look, the Sehans have plenty more men out there... You! Yes, you!' Hektor grabs a guard. 'I want you to run across town to the west gate and tell your captain, who is positioned there, that I want him to send half of his men over here. Go. Now!'

How the hell did they get past the men patrolling the palisade?

More cries reach them from somewhere above the eastern gate. A second bevy of arrows looms over the walls – burning. They drop, like tired fireflies, among the wooden buildings of the upper town. Hektor and Washa watch separate fires pollinate the darkness: orange fungi over decaying tree stumps. To Hektor's relief, small groups of women are already dragging over buckets of water to each fire, systematically tackling them.

Soon, Hektor, Washa and the men from the south-eastern gate reach their destination, diving behind the merlons. Arrows migrate into the upper town, catch numerous guards and civilian men who interfere with their trajectory. Hektor glances above the parapet, archives to memory a passable imprint of the Sehan positions.

'They have four ladders, each carried in teams of sixteen or more – those ladders are just about at the walls. They have a number of archers in front of some buildings, though we have managed to kill some of them. Behind the buildings are more archers: they are the ones lighting their arrows,' Hektor yells to Washa. Hektor looks back down at the upper town – most enemy arrows have failed to start any fires, and the ones that have are almost all contained. 'These ladders we can deal with. The archers nearest the walls need to be targeted though.'

Hektor looks at his men – casualties increasing.

'Everyone, down! Get down!' Hektor orders. The men obey this command. 'None of you are directing your fire properly. Each of you: have you measured the distance to the archers? Yes? Good. Now, ready arrows in bows…' The order is followed; Hektor does likewise. '*Dek*, on the count of three, we jump up and fire a volley into their archers. We then fall behind the parapet, and repeat with two more volleys with delays of ten seconds each time. Understood?… On the count of three. One. Two. Three!'

The Wilusans are up in unison, bows fire a volley, take the Sehans by surprise, kill perhaps a quarter of the archer unit. They drop down, repeat. By the third volley, the Sehan archer unit is devastated; the remnants retreat back among the mud-brick buildings of the lower town.

No time for cheers. Sehan ladders are in place, soldiers sidling up the rungs. Hektor and several other men try to dislodge them, but they are being held securely at the foot. Soon: Sehans atop the walls engage in close-quarter combat. Only guards armed with swords and spears meet them, civilian men fall back.

As chaos unfolds, a new unit of Sehan archers appears, and behind them fire-archers continue to launch volley after volley over the walls. In what little time Hektor has to glance down the stairs behind him, he is proud to see Ura and the other women continuing to extinguish fires, though one or two have petalled out into larger blazes.

With ladders secure, more Sehans leak past lower town buildings, ready to move up onto the walls. The Wilusan guards are able to kill most of the ladder-mounting enemy, but slowly even their numbers dilute. The Sehans keep coming.

Hektor glances towards the palisade surrounding the lower town.

The torchlight of the guards that had been patrolling are extinguished. There is no sign of the cavalry, though the mist that has come off the Mountain is obscuring his view. He turns his attention to a tower near the east gate itself. Civilian men continue to fire arrows from its windows, but aim haphazardly into the mass of enemy troops below.

'Washa! We cannot hold with these ladders here. I need you to take a torch into the gate-tower, every archer to light his arrows. Then, have them aim at the foot of each ladder. Chances are, at least one of them will catch. Understand?'

'Right!' Washa ducks from combat, grabs a torch from its sconce, runs to the tower.

Following Hektor's example, the guards hold the Sehans at bay for the time it takes Washa to have the men in the tower light their arrows and fire down upon the base of the ladders. Eventually, three of four ladders catch, disintegrate upon all Sehans immediately below the walls. Shortly afterwards, reinforcements arrive from the west gate, help Hektor and the guards cauterise the Sehan flow appearing at the last remaining ladder. Soon, the ladder is abandoned entirely; a cheer goes up from the Wilusan men.

Is this all Masturi can muster?

The moon is audience to the battlers for what seems an age...

As night progresses, the mist retreats into sea and woodland, and the plains' blackness scabs into a rusty blue in discomfort at approaching sunlight. Panicked screeches reach Hektor from the west wall. He turns abruptly, sees many men driven through with arrows. Someone seems to be yelling something across the width of the town, but Hektor, frustratingly, cannot make out what is being said. He can, however, make out another, familiar voice, screaming frantically from the street.

'More of them outside the west wall, they've set the gate on fire! That's bad, no? They have a siege engine too, a siege engine! You've got to get over there now, eh?' Ura's face billeted with soot.

Instinctively, Hektor commands a guard to run down to the south-west gate and have them send reinforcements to the west gate. Next, he turns to Washa, who has long since returned from the tower.

'I am leaving you to watch over the situation here. Maintain the defence, and if anything changes for the worse, send for me. Do you understand?'

'Yes, but don't you want me over th—'

'I do not have time to argue. You have done... passably well in your duties so far tonight. Do not let me down now.'

'Your warmth touches me.'

Hektor grunts, leaps down the staircase, grabs Kummi's reins from a lad, is soon hurtling across the upper town towards the newest point of battle.

Wilusa is a disorientation of men wailing as their lives end on top of walls, and women screaming for water as fire-arrows plummet into timber. In front of Hektor, a small warehouse that he knows to contain precious textiles for trade is engulfed in flames. The heat is astounding; the light clots shadow across nearby houses. On the ground, two women lay dead, charred arrows extending from crumpled chests. The older woman's eyes are still open, pursed with an expression of shock that even she could die. The younger woman appears more peaceful, one hand falling over a tiny mound on her belly. Hektor looks away.

Galloping on atop his horse, the image in his head of these women is replaced with a vision of Hapi, arrows growing from the boy's stomach, his wobbling lips opening around a cough. But Hapi is with Aras, safe – he knows this. Still, he hopes Hapi remembers all he said earlier. As he passes the hole in the wall, he notes that only a few Sehans have detached from their fellow men-at-arms and are trying to penetrate the upper town.

Strange. This would be the sole point I'd attack...

Hektor finally reaches the west gate; Kummi rears up in alarm at the noise. On top of the wall, the guards hold firm, though they are unable to return fire, as a consistent current of arrows locks their backs to the merlons. Many are dead or dying.

Dom – the siege engine speaks as it strikes the gate.

'Well?'

The guard captain finishes yelling orders. '*Tuhkanti*, they caught us unawares; they came out of the dark – hundreds of the bastards. They pinned us down and ignited the gate. Their siege engine will break through very shortly – but how do we stop it? We've tried fire-arrows but the fucking thing won't light!'

'Probably dampened with water or vinegar,' Hektor yells above the noise. He hangs his head, strokes Kummi's mane. *Easy, girl.* 'Let me look at it.'

Hektor leaps off his horse, follows the guard captain up to the top of the wall. Poking his head out from behind a merlon, he sees how the Sehans arrange their forces. In front of a row of market stalls, two lines of archers fire continuous – though anarchic – volleys of arrows up at the walls. Reversing... preparing for another ram... the siege engine is large and, unfortunately, impressive. It sits on three sets of wheels, driven, supposedly, by men inside its bulky structure. At its front, a sharpened pine trunk protrudes the length of a man. Around the engine, various soldiers keep a loose semicircle; some carry heavy torches, waiting for their chance to infest the upper town.

'*Dek.* Firstly, we need to barricade the gate.'

'Already given the order!'

Dom – the siege engine speaks again.

'Good. But barricading will not keep them out forever. If they maintain this tempo, they will be inside the town by dawn. There is no other choice – we have to take that siege engine down. And if fire will not work from the outside, then we only have one option.'

'There must be something else we can do. Whoever goes—'

'There is nothing else we can do. If we cannot take it down with fire-arrows from the wall, then there is nothing else in the town that will do any better... It has to be burned from the inside out. And yes, I am fully aware what that means.'

The guard captain glances down. 'I will go. This is my gate – it should be my responsibility.'

'I appreciate your nerve. And I know you would go if I told you to. But this is something I have to do. It is my idea, and I will not send others to do it while I sit here. I *will* need a number of soldiers though.'

'... I will give you the ones that are better geared for close-quarter fighting.'

'*Dek*,' Hektor sighs. 'And... be honest about what it is they are doing.'

'If that's what you want.' The guard captain crawls away to where guard numbers are thickest.

Dom.

Hektor knocks his head against the stone palisade, looks into the sky. Stars recede against the growing dimness of Appaliunas's light. He looks at the upper town walls, smiling as he pictures his son with Aras. He wonders how Washa and Ura are doing further across town. South: all is quiet, except for the long stream of men running to reinforce the west gate. Nearer him, the west postern gate seems to be quiet too; the ideal place to sneak out onto the plains. Over the misshapen triangles of the mountains surrounding Parraspeszi, the magma red of dawn infiltrates the sky at a growing speed. Hektor wonders if Appaliunas will see anything of the next half hour.

The guard captain returns, bringing thirty men, all with bronze armour, shields and close-quarter weapons. Their faces: fear, fortitude.

Dom.

'You know what we are doing?'

The men nod.

'We have to succeed. We will succeed. If we fail... then Wilusa is gone. Gone. Do you understand? Everything you see will burn. All our people will... Do your duty. Make sure Appaliunas does not look down on our failure, but our success.'

The men, again, nod.

'Now, we will leave the town via the postern gate further down the wall. Your guard captain' – Hektor looks at the guard captain – 'will hold here for the reinforcements coming from the south-west gate. We will move along the outside of the wall until we reach the clump of trees near the west gate. As the siege engine attacks the gate, we will charge the Sehans, and cut our way to the back of the engine where we will move inside and set it alight; we will use the torches being held by the Sehans down there for that. As we rush them, your guard captain will order every man on this wall to fire a single volley of arrows at the Sehan archers – they will be the ones most likely to kill us.' Hektor looks at the guards' faces. 'May Appaliunas protect us.'

Dom.

The men accompanying Hektor sidle towards him. Other guards and civilians bless themselves. The mutter of 'Appaliunas walk with you' and 'Peace and light on your path' reach Hektor's ears. Down the steps they move swiftly into the upper town.

Hektor leads them south until they reach the west postern gate, manned by more guards and civilians.

'It is quiet outside here, yes?' Hektor asks the postern gate's captain.

'Yes, it is. We've had few enemies here so far, but—'

'Good,' Hektor interrupts. 'My men and I must get out though.'

'Yes, sir...'

Hektor slips down the steps to the door, waiting while it is unbolted. Stepping outside, Hektor keeps his head down and looks around. The Sehans at the west gate, further up past a number of shacks and trees, are not intruding upon any ground near the postern gate. Hektor moves his head back inside the door, nods to his men.

Hektor scurries, bending low, staying within the shadow of various trees, shrubs and crowds of dead grass. The men follow in single file, mimicking their leader's movement. Mist still clings about the lower town, the shapes of houses leering eerily out of the gloom. Again, Hektor looks behind him, can see that there is little activity by the hole in the wall. Looking back in the direction he is headed, he can see the Sehan force on this side of town is far larger than that in the east. Enemy archers are numbers-thick, and an even greater body of men surrounds the siege engine, like dogs hopping about a butcher who chucks them meat-gristle. Hektor signals to his men. They move forward again, finding cover behind trees and outhouses when necessary, shifting bodies towards the ground.

Reinforcements from the south-west gate will have arrived by now, and the guard captain should have explained the situation and set the men up in anticipation of firing at the Sehan archers. Further up, next to a small horse shelter and stall, a large clump of trees stands perhaps fifteen paces from the west gate. Hektor decides that if he can bring his men into those trees, and jump the siege engine as it nears the gate again, he will have a greater chance of success. The siege engine itself continues to roll ravenously into the gate, emitting the same heavy *dom*. Hektor indicates his plan to the men with more hand signals and, together, they creep forward again, before falling flat into the grass as they near the preoccupied Sehan archers. Hektor prays no light will glance off the bronze armour his men wear, but darkness digests them.

They reach the trees, and Hektor orders the men into formation. A few retch. Hektor is surprised to find his own hands tremble sympathetically. Above: arrows *shing* over walls, and further down the path leading up to the burning gate, the siege engine reverses impatiently, preparing for another run.

Hektor looks out at the Sehans, many singing some faint chant. He finds his shield-hand still trembling, so clenches it. He breathes deep. But his heart beats faster. All thought of duty fails to cut away his anxiety. The siege engine finishes reversing. Hektor pictures Hapi, keeps the image lodged in his mind.

'This is it. I know you are scared. And I know there is no comfort I can give you. All I shall say is: do this. Do this because it must be done.'

Hektor turns back, watches as the siege engine rolls forward. The Sehans seem to count, before lifting their voices in a roar. Hektor stands, raises his sword, screams as well. His men mimic. Together, they jump from among the trees, fall straight into the side of the Sehans, taking them by surprise, killing many.

On the wall, the guard captain gives the order to fire. Every guard and civilian releases a volley of arrows into the Sehan archers.

The Sehans recover as the siege engine slams into the gate. Wilusan and Sehan alike find themselves impaled on spears, gutted with swords, knocked unconscious by shields.

Hektor tries to ignore the men dying around him, focuses instead on a torch gripped in the hand of a dead soldier. He cuts through several men, moves towards the torch and falls to his knees as an arrow rips into his shoulder. He grunts against the pain and immediate coldness in his chest, shields himself from several more arrows. *Get up.*

He lurches towards the torch and grabs it in his shield-hand as a second arrow glances his thigh. A Sehan moves towards him – aims his sword for Hektor's neck, but Hektor ducks the attack and pulls his own sword up into the soldier's stomach. Dragging himself on again, he watches men from inside the siege engine pour out, looking for weapons to vulture. Hektor defends against two more attacks while, all around him, men continue to fight and die. Finally, he reaches the back of the siege engine, pants, blinks away a crackle-black in his eyes, tries to ignore the pain. He holds the torch up inside the dry, wooden innards of the siege engine and watches the flames devour it.

Behind him, angry, panicked yells indicate the approach of more Sehans, who quickly realise what has happened. On the walls, the guard captain and his men yell in celebration as the siege engine dissolves in upon itself, bright-blooming. Some of Hektor's men have survived, are busily cutting down enemy troop after enemy troop. He tugs the arrow out of his shoulder, growling against the quick-leaping pain, ducks in time to avoid a sword-stroke, swings his own weapon around to slash open a man's chest.

For the first time, Hektor dares to imagine victory.

'*Tuhkanti! Tuhkanti!*' It is the guard captain on the wall; Hektor looks up at him, heart skipping momentarily at the familiar sound of his old title. 'Over there! Over there!' He jabs one furious finger away to the east – towards the middle of the wall, towards the gaping hole.

Hektor spins around and, to his horror, witnesses a flood of Sehan troops breaking upon the wall, clambering over rubble in their attempts to invade the upper town. Wilusan troops up on the walls unload volley after volley of arrows into the aggressors, and ground troops throw themselves out of the upper town to combat this new threat. *So, this was your plan, Masturi… Part our defences and throw the weight of your forces at our weak spot.* He feels idiotic for not having guessed it sooner.

Taking one more look behind him, and finding the siege engine completely destroyed, Hektor takes a deep breath, as though before plunging into the sea, and flies forward, the only thought in his head to protect the upper town – to protect Hapi.

Hektor is breathless. His body is a rock battered by a stormy sea. His head is a persuasion of coldness, sleep. Part of him says, 'Rest. You have done enough. Rest,' but it is a voice to which he gives no heed. All the time, he keeps the image of Hapi in his mind's eye, holding it securely. For all his courage, he fears that without his determination to fight for his son, he might otherwise break. For once, he is not ashamed to admit such a weakness but finds it instead a relief to accept himself as purely human.

Hektor roars into the flank of the Sehan troops, sweeps his sword through one man and then another, drives onwards with a ferocity he never knew he possessed. Clearing a space in which to fight, he raises his sword to rally the men of Wilusa, who, in turn, surge forward into the lower town, countering the Sehan advance. In between clatters of weapons and increasingly sluggish feints from killing blades and driving spears, Hektor looks out at the mass of enemy troops driving on, swarming through the city streets. He realises that he and his men cannot hold the hole in the wall, not while also having to defend the east and west gates. Archers on top of the wall persist with their flurries of arrows into the Sehans, but their numbers are finite and enemy archers pick them off man by man. Civilian and soldier alike fight to the death in close quarters, Wilusans teeming over the rubble and debris of the once-was-wall, but Hektor can see where their numbers end, and it pales in comparison to the depth of the enemy.

But Hektor seldom stops for a pause, hardly even for breath. The pain in his shoulder is numbed with adrenaline, and when his sword eventually shatters against an enemy shield, he disarms his opponent of their spear and wields that instead. He is only dimly aware, some time later, that another arrow is lodged in him, protruding from his belly. He falls, briefly, to one knee, sucks in a flash of breath, pushes himself up, jabbing his spear first into one man's chest before striking it across the face of another.

Ghostly movement suggests other Wilusan men about him, dying and fighting and dying and fighting. He is inspired by their sacrifice, throws himself full into yet more advancing Sehans. When the spear point enters the small of his back, he feels it as a spike of heat tearing up his spine, quenched at last by a freezing in his head. He gasps, coughs, turns in time to punch his attacker away, snatch a knife from the ground and jab it under the man's ribs. In the grey light, he stares at one trembling hand, a peculiar sensation in his fingers as though of tiny fish nibbling at his flesh.

The ground rumbles. Away in the guts of the lower town there is screaming. Hektor looks up to find a sight he had dared not imagine: cavalry charging down Sehan troops from the rear. In this moment he forgives them all their lateness, marvels only at the catastrophic impact they have on the enemy troops.

Again, in his mind comes the image of Hapi: his one success, his one good contribution to this world.

Hektor smiles, turns himself around and pants. As he does so, a spear rips open his bronze armour, buries itself deep inside his chest, supplanting his heart with chill metal. He weeps with the pain, falls backward, head slamming into the earth, coughs, coughs, coughs, decides movement no longer seems important.

He looks up. A nearby fire worships the sky, which itself is riven with a paler shade of blue. He has not seen Appaliunas rise again above the watchful eye of Mount Parraspeszi, but it does not matter. Hapi stands firmly in his mind. He smiles again and decides life, this surprising event in between two forevers of darkness, is actually rather amusing... For perhaps the first time, Hektor abandons himself to laughter.

His laughter never ceases.

Four Moons Later...

A breeze, fresh off the Aegean, dissipates within the long grasses of the Wilusan plains, tangles itself around the legs of Aras, Hapi's horse, whom he leads along by rope. Hapi brings Aras to a halt, pulls out a skin of water from his belt, takes a slug. Holding a hand up to shield his eyes from the sun, Hapi looks back at Wilusa. About the city's wooden palisade, infant orchards of pomegranate and apricot trees are being attended to by farmers. Shrines to Appaliunas and the Dead God sit sentry about the orchards, with conscientious priests arranging the many floral offerings. Hapi looks at the hill, upon which Wilusa's upper town sits. Where the acropolis once sprawled, scrappy housing developments now flourish in a garden of brown and white. Near the west gate of the town, the black scorch of the destroyed Sehan siege engine lies among the twisting of weeds and flowers. Hapi smiles sadly to himself.

'He'd be proud of you, if he could see you today. And maybe, just maybe, he'd be proud of Wilusa if he could see it today.'

Hapi shakes his head back to attention, nods stalwartly. 'I hope so, Washa. He told me that he wasn't frightened that night, because he had his responsibilities. I didn't understand what he meant then. But...'

'But maybe there was something to what he was saying, after all,' Washa replies, smiling a little.

'Do you think he felt alone at the end?'

Washa pauses. 'No. No, I don't think he did.'

Hapi also pauses, smiles back. Then he looks off into the distance; his shoulders drop.

'What is it?' Washa asks.

'Will... Will *tati* be remembered? Broken Granddad is dead, Grandma died after the battle and... and Kaluti is dead. No one remembers them anymore. What if it's the same for *tati*?'

Washa draws in a sharp breath through his nose, moustache hairs wriggling. 'You know, when I'm dead I'm not going to worry whether I'm remembered or not.'

'Why?'

'Because I'll be dead!' Washa smiles widely.

'Oh...' Hapi's head drops.

Washa clears his throat. 'But what I mean is that I'm alive now and what matters to me now is what I can do for the people I love while I still have strength in me. Oh yes, I'm sure your father was quite pre-occupied with how he and Wilusa will be remembered in centuries to come, but I don't think that's what is important. What *is* important is how you impact people now because all we have is to be alive and the happiness, the sadness, the joy, the hopes, the fears and the aspirations that come with that. So, maybe your father won't be remembered, but he has changed you and your memories of him are all that matter – not what people do or do not think ten, one hundred, one thousand years from now.'

Hapi listens intently, bites his lip. 'And... do you think the bad men will come back?'

'Hmm, this has been playing on your mind, hasn't it?' Washa says, crosses his arms. 'Well, I could never promise that the "bad men" won't come back, but if they do then we will have to be ready for them. What your father did that night... He saved us all. The Sehans would have broken through the wall if it was not for him. I think his death has taught us all something very important.'

'What?' Hapi asks, looks up, squints as the sunlight hits his eyes.

'That we do need to be mindful of our responsibilities. There is no point in keeping this world we have built if we cannot take respon-sibility for it. Perhaps your father, in some strange way, would have been at home in this Wilusa...'

Hapi and Washa stare off up at the city, content in each other's silent company. Aras snorts, brings their attention back to the present.

'Right.' Washa claps his hands. 'You going to try then?' He indi-cates the small saddle swinging at the flank of his own horse, Kummi. 'I've just about gotten used to Kummi not trying to bite me. I think you're having more luck with Aras.'

Hapi takes the saddle from Washa, holds it out towards Aras, clicks his tongue. Aras nods, as though inviting the boy to continue. Hapi nods back, eases the saddle gently onto the animal's back, buckling it firmly but gently under the belly.

'That's it! You did it! You've broken him to saddle!' Washa applauds, stops as Kummi headbutts his shoulder disapprovingly.

Hapi chuckles his strange chuckle.

'Now, you just need to hop up on his back – here, let me give you a hand.'

Washa boosts Hapi up and, despite Aras's sways, the boy manages to settle into the saddle. He is only light and the foal accepts the weight without complaint, though Hapi does look somewhat large on Aras's back.

'Hmm, better not spend too much time in the saddle just yet,' Washa says, sagely. He leaps up onto Kummi's back. 'But... seeing as we're out here, let's have a ride.'

Hapi's face lights up. 'You mean it?'

Washa winks. 'Why not? Kummi might throw me off, but you've clearly got the trust of Aras.'

Together with Washa, Hapi rides off into the Wilusan plains, orange light and mauve clouds constructing his path ahead.

Acknowledgements

Breaking the Foals has been a big part of my life for many years now and we have had many ups and downs together. I must principally thank my wife, Johanna, for always being supportive of me, while tempering some of my excitement with common sense; all of this is infinitely more wonderful because I share it with you. I also thank my two daughters, Freya and Eleanor, for being such incredible human beings and the reason I wanted to be published in the first place: anything is possible if you're pigheaded enough, girls. Keeping with family, I must acknowledge the generous support from my parents at the crowdfunding stage – not to mention their unfailing belief in me in everything I do. On top of that, my mother and father-in-law have been vital figures in my life and without their presence I seriously doubt I would be where I am today. Thank you also to my sister, Evie, for being there for me through it all. Grandma, I'm delighted you've hung on long enough to see your grandson in print! Bokka, I wish you could have seen this. Lotte, I wish you were able to understand.

And then there's my *second* family. Thank you to everyone in Croydon Council's Leaving Care Service: your support has been constant, warm and exceptional. I hope none of you will feel the novel to be inadequate.

I cannot leave one man in particular unacknowledged: Mr Peter Cook, my English teacher at GCSE and A-Level at St. Joseph's College, Lambeth. My love for reading and, indeed, writing, only exists because you were so extraordinary in inspiring me. Plus, you introduced me to *Captain Corelli's Mandolin*, where my career began! I also owe thanks to Dr Sara Upstone and Dr Jane Jordan at Kingston University; you were both such influential figures in my education.

I owe a particular debt of gratitude to Fiona Sampson of The Writers' Workshop, whose advice proved crucial to the development of my novel. Then there is the team at Unbound. Thank you to Kwaku, Annabel, Xander, Leonora and everyone else who was involved in making all of this a reality. But a special thanks to my editor, Gill, whose help and advice was gratefully received.

This book would not exist without the efforts of many noted researchers and academics whose work has inspired me over the years. It would be difficult to list absolutely everyone who has been an influence, but I am particularly indebted to: Trevor R Bryce, Michael Wood, Caroline Alexander, Barry Strauss, Bettany Hughes and Rodney Castleden.

I am much obliged to John, Ed and James for being beta readers; you have seen different iterations of this novel and I hope you like the end result. I have cut down on the harrumphing.

Finally, a *major* thank you to each and every individual who pledged to my book despite a questionable video on the Unbound site and the name of some unknown author attached to the project. However, refunds will not be given.

Patrons

Tina Ayeni
Debby Bentley-Ross
Hermin Billy
Cecilia Blanche
Chris Chantrey
Martin Connelly
Peter Cook
Robert Cox
Michelle Dike
Sheila Dobbs
Okailey Dua
Michael Evans
Martin Fernandes
James Gill
Daniel Goldsmith
Syed Habibullah
Anna Hammond
Evie Hawker
Johanna Hawker
Fiona Hawker
Lotte Hawker
Daniel Head
Jacqueline Jackson
Imran Khan
Dan Kieran
Mit Lahiri
Sean Lawrence
Elizabeth Li
Keiron Liston
John Martin
Edward McGurran
Adam Mitchell

John Mitchinson
Maxwell Owusu-Brempong
Mark Phillips
Justin Pollard
Zachary Pyne
Reni Ravi
Theodore Robson
Liz Rowland
Peter Salter
Peter Toner
Janet Toner
Peter Tucker
Alexandra Turney
James Vella-Bardon
Serge Vincent
Kay Wallis
John Warren